THE PERFECT SHOT

THE PERFECT SHOT

Elaine Marie Alphin

CAROLRHODA BOOKS MINNEAPOLIS • NEW YORK

Carolrhoda Books
A division of Lerner Publishing Group, Inc.
241 First Avenue North
Minneapolis, MN 55401 U.S.A.

Website address: www.lernerbooks.com

Library of Congress Cataloging-in-Publication Data

Alphin, Elaine Marie.
      The perfect shot / by Elaine Marie Alphin.
         p.   cm.
      Summary: Brian uses basketball to block out memories of his girlfriend and
   her family, who were gunned down a year ago, but the upcoming murder trial
   and a high school history assignment force him to face the past and decide
   how far he should go to see justice served. Includes facts about miscarriages of
   justice in American history.
      ISBN-13: 978-1-57505-862-7 (lib. bdg. : alk. paper)
      ISBN-10: 1-57505-862-6 (lib. bdg. : alk. paper)
      [1. Murder—Fiction. 2. Basketball—Fiction. 3. Justice—Fiction. 4. High
   schools—Fiction. 5. Schools—Fiction.] I. Title.
   PZ7.A4625Pe 2005
   [Fic]—dc22   2005003159

Manufactured in the United States of America
8 – BP – 1/1/10

For David and Leo,
and all the other innocent citizens
who find themselves behind bars, unfairly convicted

and for Art
and the other experts and lawyers
who struggle to uphold justice and the law
and set the innocent free

The smallest injustice anywhere
Threatens justice everywhere

—Shahriar Shahriari, "The Sweater"

The time is out of joint; O cursed spite,
That ever I was born to set it right!

—William Shakespeare, *Hamlet* (act I, scene v)

AUGUST

BEFORE

Amanda stared straight ahead, refusing to look through the SUV's tinted windows at Brian as her mother drove home from the swimming pool. Just the sight of him, still shooting hoops, made her anger flare up again. But anger couldn't drown out the thump of his basketball, its dull bounce off the backboard, its clang off the rim, and the thuds as it bounced away from him, out of control down the concrete driveway, forcing him to chase it. *Good,* she thought as Brian missed his next impossibly long-range shot, and his next. *It serves him right. He should have made time for me and Cory, instead of insisting on playing with Julius and the other guys so we didn't have any choice but to go to the pool with Mom. I told him I didn't want to.*

There was no sign of Julius in the cul-de-sac now. He'd probably sunk his trademark long jump shot and won the game, then gone off and left Brian practicing on his own, trying to make the ball soar for himself the way it did for Julius.

Beside her, Cory twisted in his booster seat, waving madly at Brian. "Roll down the window," he ordered.

"Not now," Mom said, turning into their curving driveway. They didn't park and go through the front door, where Amanda might have relented and glanced back for a quick peek at Brian. Instead her mother turned out of sight behind the cluster of pines that masked their garage, and clicked the automatic door opener. Amanda watched the heavy garage door rise on its pulley in front of the SUV.

She started singing softly, not quite under her breath, but too faintly for anyone else to be sure what melody she had in mind. There weren't even any words to her singing, just an exhalation of air in a sequence of la's and hmm's that sang to her, if not to anyone else. Amanda didn't have to see her mother's mouth tighten in the rearview mirror to know that her singing was driving her crazy. It did that to some people, especially parents. But it had also inspired Julius to christen her Songbird in his private lexicon of friends-only nicknames — his names for enemies were far less kind. Amanda liked the idea of herself as a songbird, rare and lovely.

She changed melody, promising herself that one day she'd go far away from Indiana and make her own special music. She wasn't sure where she'd go, or what song she'd sing, but she knew she'd do it somehow, and when she did her music would change the world.

The SUV slid to a smooth stop in their shadowed garage. "Let me out," Cory begged. "I want to play with Brian."

Amanda wasn't ready to forgive Brian, even if Cory was.

"You can play ball with Brian later," Mom said, sliding out of the front seat and coming around to help him get unbuckled.

Amanda reached for her own seat belt release, then stopped, her thumb poised over the button. "What's that?"

"What?" Mom asked, one hand resting on the door handle. The shadow Amanda thought she'd seen move in the back, innermost corner of the garage was somewhere behind her mother. Cory still looked out the rear window toward the trees, as if he could see Brian through the leaves.

Before Mom could open his door, a figure stepped out of the darkness. Amanda felt a moment's vindication. She *had* seen movement in the corner. Then the man touched her mother's shoulder, his hand sliding down her arm, turning her around, propelling her through the door that connected the garage to the kitchen.

He must have said something to her mother, because she paused, then abruptly told Amanda and Cory, her voice low, "Stay there." With a grating groan, the garage door slid closed behind the SUV.

"What happened?" asked Cory. "Where's Mom?"

"In the kitchen," Amanda said slowly. She didn't want to alarm him. She wasn't even sure she should be alarmed herself, since it wasn't any sort of a stranger. At the same time, the way he'd been waiting in the shadows disturbed her.

Cory fidgeted in his seat, not nearly as much of a baby as their mother thought. "Don't be mad at Brian," he told Amanda earnestly. "He likes us. You know that. He's just scared sometimes that he can't play ball as good as Joyous. But Brian really is good."

Amanda couldn't help smiling at the kid's faith in her boyfriend, and at the way Cory still used the nickname he'd given Julius years earlier, when he was just a toddler and his three-year-old tongue couldn't quite pronounce the older boy's name. "Anybody tell you lately that you're a pretty smart kid?" she asked, popping the release on her seat belt and reaching over to hug him.

"Yuck," Cory complained, giggling as her long hair, still damp from the pool, dripped down his neck. "You're getting me all wet."

"You're already wet, you dolphin," she teased him. When she was stuck babysitting too long, he drove her crazy. But at times like this, she was glad she had someone who understood her — and Brian — so well.

Then her mother reappeared in the kitchen doorway. Cory looked over, squinting at the way the bright fluorescent lights from the kitchen silhouetted the two figures, his giggles from the unexpected hug dissipating. "What's he doing?"

Amanda wasn't sure whether she answered him. She heard a noise that sounded strangely like a sharp hand clap, almost like the single bounce of Brian's basketball, heard from a long way off. *Cory's right, Brian,* she thought, *you can do more than you give yourself credit for.* But the thought was cut off by the sight of her mother collapsing beside the SUV's front tire like a marionette whose strings had been sliced.

"Mommy!" Cory cried, his voice high and panicky for the first time.

I don't know what to do, Amanda thought, stunned into helpless immobility. Then, as if a switch flipped and cleared her brain, she remembered what she'd just been thinking. *Brian — he'll help.*

With a lithe twist she climbed over the back of her seat into the rear storage area. *I can pop the back open, raise the garage door, and shout for Brian to come. I know he can be there in a heartbeat. And I know he'll drop the basketball and come, this time. I know it.*

Amanda stretched her hand out toward the back door handle, but her wraparound skirt tangled around her legs, trapping her as Cory's door opened.

I'm sorry I didn't look up at you, Brian. Please help us.

There was another sharp hand clap, and then a third. But Amanda couldn't hear either one.

THE FOLLOWING SPRING

CHAPTER

1

The gunshot is much louder than I expect, and the muzzle flash is brighter. Then, strangely, my chest burns, and I double over, hugging myself. How did the front hallway get so hot? My hand feels wet as it comes away from my side and I look at it, wondering why it's covered with dark blotches. I've got to sit down, and suddenly the wooden floor rushes up beneath me. The gun has grown too heavy to hold. I know I can't lose it, but if I'm on the floor I guess it's okay to let it slip out of my hand, as long as it stays right beside me.

My eyes burn in the brilliant light, so bright I can hardly see the scene around me any longer. There are too many people in the room. Why are they shoving at me, banging on my chest? I need to sleep—just let me sleep. I can work out what's going on later, if they'll only let me alone. But I can't sleep—the gunshot goes on echoing inside my head, a double *thud*-thud, *thud*-thud, *Bri*-an!

I'm falling. Not the kind of falling you do in dreams, sliding down and suddenly waking up safe before you fall too far. I feel impossibly heavy, yet I'm falling up, toward the ceiling. Except I never actually pass through the ceiling—it just seems to rise with me as I fall higher and higher.

I hear faraway voices.

"Sucking chest wound. The bullet's taken at least two lobes in the right lung."

That's a woman's voice.

"Pupils dilated. He's going into shock."

That's a man, with a high, almost hysterical edge to his voice.

"Get me some Ringer's and a tube set, NOW." That's the woman again.

When I look down, trying to work out what's happening, I see only the white light, brightening until it becomes impenetrable. I try to reach through it, and suddenly golden light blazes around me—not the electric light I remember from the living room, but the sunlight that fills the upstairs domed room of my father's wood shop. It's as if I've flown there somehow, out of the house and into the shop building—flown out of time, too, because I'm not alone. Amanda sits cross-legged in front of me, strumming her guitar. Amanda—who I haven't seen since that horrible day in August, seven long months ago. And in spite of the burning in my chest and my confusion, joy surges up inside of me at the sight of her.

She hasn't changed one bit. She's wearing that full crepe skirt that drapes across her legs like rippling water, and her long blonde hair drifts down over her face as she fingers the guitar strings. Beside her rests the conch shell that calls to her from unseen oceans.

She looks up as if no time has passed at all, and smiles as she says, "So it's true, Brian, isn't it?" Her voice hasn't changed. It still has that lilt to it that makes her words almost sing, even when she's only speaking.

"What?" I ask. I realize my own guitar rests across my knees. Without lifting it to actually finger a chord I stroke the strings, just letting them hum softly underneath her stronger melody.

"Remember? We wondered once whether our whole life really could pass before us, just as we're about to die," Amanda says.

I shiver, remembering the day last summer when we talked about death. Her father had stopped a suspicious driver who turned out to be a mule carrying drugs to be sold in another state. Amanda's father could have been killed, because the courier was armed and dangerous. It was just luck that the mule didn't think the police could make his plates—he figured he could just take the speeding ticket and go on down the road instead of getting arrested. In the end, it was a big bust for her father, but it scared Amanda. She might complain when he was working long hours or out with the guys, and she might be furious with him when he fought with her mother, but she'd light up like sunrise when he made time for her. And she was so proud of him for being a good cop who caught real bad guys. She'd just never realized that being a hero could mean you ran the risk of being killed.

"Yeah," I say. "I remember."

"Well, it does," she says. "But do you think we get the chance to change anything?"

My hand flattens the guitar strings, silencing them. "Change anything?" I repeat stupidly. "What do you mean?"

But time is tilting, and Amanda can't hear my words because I'm falling again, falling up, leaving her bent over her guitar, going on in the memory without me. A different scene unfolds before my eyes, and I slide into it, letting cold January sunlight fill my mind. My teammates crowd my driveway, the six of us playing half-court ball like we do year-round, unless snow and ice force us into the gym. The lane opens up and Julius breaks free of Ricky for a second, long enough for my pass to hit his waiting fingers. Then Julius goes up for a sweeping jump shot and puts the ball in the hole for three.

Stu's cheers drown out the chorused groans from Ricky, Irv, and Ray, but I find myself looking over my shoulder, down my driveway, across the cul-de-sac to the empty house. I'm willing Amanda to be seated on the sun-bleached deck chair on the front porch where she can see us, smiling and clapping for my pass, with Cory beside her, playing with his plastic basketball. It must be part of a pattern too hard to break, because I know she won't be there ever again. There's nothing left except the shell of a house, cut off from the living world by locked doors and darkened windows. The police took down the barrier of yellow crime-scene tape last fall, but it's as if some ghost of it remains, warning us that it protects spirits that once lived, watching eyes that are still too strong to resist.

Then Julius is high-fiving me, and Highrise Irv, the tallest guy on the team, tosses the ball to Ray. The half-court game is under way again. Ray passes to Ricky, who goes up for a shot that lands on the edge of the hoop, then spins out. But Ricky tends to play an inside game that inspired Julius to nickname him Ricochet, and he's already in place to tip it in. His fingers nudge it perfectly—over the rim and into the net. Stu snatches the ball before it can bounce, steps off of the court, and tosses it toward me, but Shooter's better at distance shots than passes. Take-away Ray spins around to intercept the lazy pass, dribbles around Julius and flicks his wrist, sending the ball soaring high into the cold blue sky and then down into the hoop for three points to tie the game. Their team cheers, and Shooter takes the ball out again, slapping it like a kid who's misbehaved.

This time he doesn't rush it. He makes his pass with two hands, and the ball lands securely in my grasp. Ray bangs his chest against my back, his long arms straining for the ball, but I take my time, too, watching the shifting patterns of the bodies on the court. There—the opening appears as if by magic. Julius flashes into the clear. I fake left and Ray follows, grabbing air as I spin back to the right and slam a pass off the concrete to Julius. Highrise dodges in for the steal, but my pass spins around him and curls neatly into Julius's waiting palms. He goes up for a perfect shot. The ball seems to freeze above us for a moment as if asking us to admire it before dropping with that soothing swish through the hoop to win the game.

The guys erupt into cheers, even the other team, because we're only mock opponents here in my driveway. When we're facing a rival school we're all one team, and it doesn't matter which side wins these practice games. The better we play here, the better we play together when it counts on the court.

Mrs. Malik's horn sounds as her car curves into the cul-de-sac. She's barely shifted into park before the door opens and Julius's little brother, Leon, bursts out.

"Man—I saw that move! Nothing but net!"

The guys laugh, and Julius catches the kid up and swings him onto his shoulders. "Give me the ball," Leon screeches.

Ricochet flips it up with one foot as it rolls down the driveway, and bounces it to Julius, who holds it above his head, fingers lightly balancing its weight while Leon grips it unsteadily in his small hands, tongue caught between his teeth in concentration. As Julius maneuvers his brother under the hoop so he can sink the basket, time warps again, and I see Cory perched on Julius's shoulders—not Cory of last summer, right before the murders, but Cory of about three years ago.

"Shoot basket!" Cory orders. He's toddled across the cul-de-sac again, with a stern frown on his round face and Amanda at his heels. Julius laughs—that open, bright sound that makes Cory's accidental nickname "Joyous" fit perfectly.

Cory is the only one who calls me "Bro." Julius tries to explain to him that that's what the black players call each other—if there were another black guy on the team, he and Julius could call each other Bro, but I don't qualify. Cory just frowns, not understanding. Then he shakes his head, and stubbornly goes on calling me Bro instead of Brian, and I answer, because he's a cute little kid. And Julius shakes his head and laughs. We take turns scooping the little guy up on our shoulders, high enough to toss the ball into the basket.

"That's my scoring man!" Julius tells him. "Way to go, Scory!"

Cory shrieks in delight, "We did it, Joyous! We did it, Bro!"

Then time warps, letting Cory fade out of the picture, and I see Amanda—not the Amanda of three years ago, babysitting her toddler brother. It's the Amanda of last summer, her eyes laughing with a special joy she means only for me.

But I only have a momentary glimpse of her. The sight dissolves along with the summer warmth, and I'm alone in the January chill again, watching the guys head home from our pick-up game.

Without Amanda, I keep shooting hoops, going through my regular practice until I lose myself in the driving, rhythmic beat of the basketball's bounces that drown out the sounds that can distract you during a real game— the squeaking of rubber soles on the polished court, the shouts of the players or cheers of the crowd, the zebra's whistle, the trash-talking in a one-on-one street game. One long step, bounce, then it slaps my hand, two quick steps, no traveling, bounce, slapping my hand again, leap, the pebbled texture urging my hands to angle the ball, shoot, then the rattle off the backboard for a sweet layup.

Each bounce makes a hollow, empty, echoing sound like the isolated thump of a heart that has lost its reason for beating. Once on the concrete driveway, a second time on the concrete, the third bounce off the backboard, loud enough to drown out one, two, three gunshots. And the whisper of the ball swishing through the hoop covers the sighs of the dying. If I pause to listen for those other sounds, the ball comes back to me, each bounce smaller and softer, until it rolls reluctantly over the uneven concrete, as if apologizing for those hollow bangs, hiding its guilt by begging me to pick it up again and forget everything in a perfect shot.

Except I can't make that shot, not like Julius's soaring hook. Layups, yes. An occasional three-pointer from the sideline. Most of my free throws, and nearly all my passes. But not the perfect pressure distance shot that makes fans freeze in awe and makes reporters and college scouts check your jersey for a name. Not the shot I know Dad wants to see swish through the net, the one that makes everyone point to me and say *He's the best.* Dad says it anyway, and wants it to be true. But I know it's not. And the basketball knows it too. Its driving rhythm takes on words:

Good—*but not*
good—*enough.*
Good—*but just*
se—*cond best.*

The ball sounds regretful, but final.

"Pulse is fading, blood pressure is falling."

"His arteries are collapsing, I can't intubate him."

"Here, let me try."

CHAPTER

2

I'm disappointed in your work this year, Brian," Mr. Fortner comments, as the crisp winter sunlight of our basketball practice dissolves into the stuffy, overheated fluorescence of our history classroom. He tosses the essay onto my desk with the circled C– glaring up in red ink. "I'm sure you're counting on basketball to get you into college, but you need some semblance of grades too. You used to be aware of that."

When I don't react, he continues, "I really am concerned about the dismal way you've let your grades slide. Have you considered what you might do with your life after you run up and down the court for a few years and burn out your knees? After all, a little education can make life in the slow lanes much more bearable, wouldn't you say?"

I shrug, not bothering to banter even though I have no clue yet how fast knees can burn out. But I saw how quickly life burned out for Amanda. I somehow doubt a little education made her death much more bearable.

Mr. Fortner stares at me, frowning. His sharp gray eyes see into most students in core history and English, but he can't understand the first thing about me because of the inflated orange-brown sphere perpetually bouncing between the two of us. I can't figure out how the man can talk to me almost every day and come to every game and fail to see that I'm not the guy I was last year, before Amanda was killed. Then I cared about lots of different things—saving the world with Amanda, making music, playing ball, even studying, because discussing things with her made them real and important. But mostly I cared about Amanda. Now I'm just marking time in school, trying not to think about anything except basketball. Mr. Fortner has no clue what I'm going through.

Finally he shakes his head and moves on. "They may not award basketball scholarships for brains, but they do require a minimum degree of academic accomplishment," he says, tossing Julius's essay at him. "And even if your fancy shots on the court make the scouts turn a blind eye to get you into the college of their choice, what are you going to do if you don't have the moves to get into the NBA, and don't have the smarts to make it in life?"

Julius's grade must be worse than mine. He waits until Mr. Fortner's back is turned and quickly flips him the finger. The rest of the team muffles their laughter.

"Be careful, Mr. Malik," he says without turning around, and the guys stop smiling. "I don't think you'll be able to palm the ball so easily if you wear out that digit." He glances over his shoulder at Julius, one eyebrow cocked. "Not to mention the fact you'll have even more difficulty writing your next project with a . . . stiff finger."

While the class snickers, I rewind to a year ago, as juniors—both of us racking up better grades with Amanda's help, in spite of Julius's carefree attitude toward every subject except math. Amanda never treats us like a couple of dumb jocks, and around her we're not. She actually likes hanging with us—especially with me, because I think even then she likes me as much as I like her. But she likes Julius, too. Maybe she thinks she can be a good influence on him, exposing him to her "save the world" projects, or maybe it's just loneliness, between her dad busy at work and her mom busy with fifty community projects going at once plus cooking and cleaning and only stopping to carpool when it's her turn to grab the kids. A lot of the time Amanda's on her own, or babysitting Cory. Maybe she likes the way Julius distracts the little guy, so Cory stops whining or crying or bugging her for attention. And maybe she likes bouncing her ideas off of me as we sit in the wood shop together and talk. But without her, I'm incomplete when it comes to grades, as well as incomplete at heart.

I stare down at the red C–. Somewhere in the background, Mr. Fortner praises Todd, who slides his paper into his black backpack without looking at it. Then Fortner disses Darla, who giggles and simpers as if getting a low grade is cool. But all I'm really listening to is the steady bounce, bounce, bounce, swish of the basketball in my brain that blanks out everything else.

"'Those who fail to learn from history are doomed to repeat it,'" Mr. Fortner announces. His tone fairly drips quotation marks. "Source?"

There's a profound lack of response from the class. I imagine Amanda's hand shooting up last year, but without her there's no star student to make the rest of the class look inadequate. Finally Todd's hand rises to half-mast. "George Santayana," he mutters, refusing to meet Mr. Fortner's eyes.

The teacher nods, clearly pleased that someone knows the source, but I wonder who Santayana is and how Todd recognizes the quote. Ashley rolls her eyes and Ricochet and Highrise make rude noises too softly for Mr. Fortner to catch them.

Amanda's eagerness to show off her knowledge in class used to get her teased, but most of the kids didn't seem to mind too much. Unless you dress like everyone else and talk like everyone else, you always get some strange looks, and Amanda's long multicolored skirts stood out in school as much as her hand stood out in a classroom full of downcast heads. But the kids put up with her.

Okay—when she'd snatch a soda can or plastic bottle somebody just pitched into the trash so she could move it to the recycling bins, they might have groaned or sighed, but they didn't call her rude names behind her back. The cheerleaders tolerated her at our game celebrations because I hung out with her, even if we weren't exactly going together yet, and they didn't make snide fashion digs at her, at least, not that I ever heard. In fact they all showed up at her memorial service, even though it was still summer, even though it wasn't a proper funeral because of the police investigation. Most of the kids we knew came to the service, not just the team and the cheerleaders, everybody looking hot wearing black in August, carrying bouquets of her favorite wildflowers. They didn't know her, but they accepted her. I can't understand why they refuse to accept Todd.

Somehow, his reluctance to answer anything always gets him ragged on when a teacher pulls the answer out of him, and most of the kids, especially my teammates, bump into him in the halls, knocking down his books, kicking his boots, talking about him loud enough for him to hear the names they call him. Maybe it's because he never fights back. Maybe it has something to do with the way the guy looks like a Goth, in his unvarying black jeans, boots, and T-shirts or sweatshirts. But he doesn't hang with the Goths, so it makes no sense to dress like them. Or maybe it's because he seems to have built a black wall, thick as obsidian, around himself that warns everyone to keep out, so they all feel dared to break in.

"Correct," Mr. Fortner says. "And what does the profound philosopher mean?" Todd cocks his head to one side, his expression faintly amused, but Mr. Fortner is scanning the rest of the class. "Brian?"

Jock isn't synonymous with stupid, despite what some teachers think. "Just what it says," I tell him. "If you don't understand what happened in history and learn how not to make the same mistakes, the same things go wrong again and again."

"Surprisingly accurate, Brian," Mr. Fortner says. Julius rolls his eyes at the backhanded compliment and I wait for the inevitable "but." Instead, Mr. Fortner launches into the assignment.

"Your next grade will be based on what you can learn from history that's relevant to today's problems. I hardly expect you personally to find a way of preventing history from repeating itself, but I want you to show how people have either learned from history to prevent such events, or failed to do so."

Most of us, including me and Julius, groan. Todd looks faintly interested. "This is a big assignment," Mr. Fortner continues, ignoring all reactions. "Big enough to include a written report and an oral presentation. Big enough to incorporate half of your semester grade."

And that rocks the team. If we're going to make it to the playoffs and all the way to State Championship this season, we don't have time for something like this. Todd's expression doesn't change—he just goes on doodling notes in a spiral pad.

"Big enough," Mr. Fortner continues, "that I don't expect you to do it alone. Therefore I have assigned teams— no, I have not put you with your best friend, next-door neighbor, sports teammate, true love, or even with someone you like. History makes 'strange bedfellows,' so to speak."

"Shakespeare," I mutter, not caring if Mr. Fortner hears.

The teacher raises one eyebrow in mock amazement. "I'm impressed, Brian."

I almost stand up to take a bow, so Amanda can scold me, like last year. But there's no point without her. I just shrug, and Mr. Fortner goes on. "I have made unlikely assignments, in the hopes that working with someone you don't know well, and might not otherwise choose to ever get to know well, will stimulate your thinking. For your presentation to the class, you may draft other students to help if you choose, for example performing or doing busy-work like painting posters you design. But you and your partner must do the research and plan, which includes write, the presentation on your own." He opens a desk drawer and pulls out a wrinkled paper bag. "And I have a grab bag here of historical events, which I will assign randomly to each pair.

"Julius Malik—you and Leslie Johnston will work together. Your topic will be—" Julius's expression matches the hotshot student's glare as Mr. Fortner draws out the drama, reaching into the bag, fishing around, and finally withdrawing a piece of paper. He unfolds it with a flourish and reads, "George Washington's farewell to his troops." He smiles thoughtfully. "What have we learned from that moment in both military and presidential history, I wonder?"

Before I have a chance to shoot Julius a sympathetic look, Mr. Fortner moves on. "Ashley Howe, you will work with Ellen Garfield." He stirs the papers in his bag, then pulls one out. "You two get *Gideon v. Wainwright* in 1963. What have we learned from that about the right to have a lawyer?"

He leaves Ashley looking blank. "Stuart Anderson, your partner will be Isabel Pearson. Your topic will be—" He fishes around in his bag and comes up with, "The Posse Comitatus Act of 1878 in conjunction with the assault on the Branch Davidian compound in Waco. What does that tell us about military participation in law enforcement?" Shooter looks as if Fortner's speaking some foreign language that tells him absolutely nothing.

Then Mr. Fortner drops his bombshell. "Brian Hammett—you will work with Todd Pollian." If possible, Todd looks even more horrified than I feel. "Your topic will be—"

Mr. Fortner digs through his grab bag of human disasters until he draws one out. His face lights up at first, then he hesitates. He almost looks like he's going to drop the paper back in the bag, but I can see him thinking he told us he'll assign the topics randomly, and he can't back out now. "All right, you two will work on the 1913 Atlanta Leo Frank case. What have we learned from that? And what has our justice system learned from it, for that matter?"

"Who was Leo Frank?" Todd asks, frowning. That's another mystery about Todd—he hates looking smart in class, but doesn't mind admitting he doesn't know something.

"Leo Frank," Mr. Fortner says, almost reluctantly, "was a Jew from New York who moved to Georgia and was tried for the murder of a young teenager named Mary Phagan."

He continues matching up unwilling pairs of students and assigning unlikely topics, but I can't hear any of the others. All I'm thinking is: another teenage girl murdered. Like Amanda.

CHAPTER

3

Man, what are we going to do?" Shooter complains at practice that afternoon, his dribbling echoing weakly in the gym.

I understand why he's ticked off. As sixth man, Shooter has just as much practice time as the team starters, without as much glory. And this project of Mr. Fortner's is going to end up taking a lot of time and work. But it's all too easy for a team to defeat itself, thinking that way.

I dart in, like I'm Take-away Ray, steal the ball with a quick slap, and dribble fast to midcourt. As always, Julius anticipates my moves. I flip him a smooth, arcing pass and watch him go up for a perfect jump shot. Three points.

"Nothing but net, Brainman," Julius announces, grinning and pointing me out as he dances backward like a fighter.

I grin back, then turn to Shooter. "Ease up, man," I advise. "You get through this by thinking basketball on the court, and nothing else." That's how I get through things since Amanda's murder—thinking basketball and nothing else. Sometimes I see an unexpected bird feeder hanging on a park tree's branch, or some earnest little kid picking up soda cans and plastic bottles for recycling, and, just for a second, wish I could still be part of Amanda's pet projects to change the world. Once there was a Brian who could think about those as well as basketball. The memory slices into me as if I've picked up one of Dad's carving tools by the blade and watch my fingers fall, severed, to the floor. I tell myself Amanda is severed from my life, but if I let her go, what do I have left? I can't see any answer, except basketball. If I concentrate on that, I can shut out all the rest.

"Save the history stress for class and homework, Shooter," I finish, looking down at the court's polished wooden floor.

Shooter objects, "But I think basketball at home and on the court and—"

"And if you want to stay on the team, you'll think history in Mr. Fortner's class, and for as long as it takes to do that project." Coach Guilford claps Shooter on one shoulder and scoops up the ball as it rolls back from the goal.

"Well, at least he could have let teammates be partners," Ricochet complains. I privately agree.

"No kidding," a voice coolly concurs from the bleachers. I snap my head around to see Leslie perching on the hard seat, elbows propped on knees, a bulging book bag beside her. Julius rolls his eyes at his project partner, and turns back to Coach. But my eyes travel on up the bleachers to see Todd sprawling near the top. The black shrouded figure meets my gaze evenly.

"But since that's not the way Mr. Fortner chose to do things," Leslie goes on, "when does this ball-bouncing, time-wasting sweat session of yours end?"

"Practice," Julius tells her, biting the word off hard,

"ends when we're finished."

He turns on his heel, but before he can take the ball, Coach Guilford calls up into the bleachers, his tone mild, "Practice ends at 4:30. You're welcome to stay and watch your team, or return to collect your project partners then."

"Thank you," Leslie says crisply. She hefts her book bag, climbs down from her seat, and strides out of the gym. Trailing her on their way through the gym to their own practice room, Keesha leads the rest of the cheerleading squad in a silent version of the cheer they save for saluting the visiting team after we demolish them. The players crack up, and even Coach suppresses a smile as Leslie glances over her shoulder at the other girls, not sure what they're doing to cause the hilarity.

The cheerleaders jump up and down, clapping like they do after a routine during the game. Ashley's tight little ponytail bounces *(her dark hair so different from Amanda's long blonde hair falling straight and loose)*, and she flashes a dazzling smile that I know she means especially for me. I automatically smile back, then swallow it, not wanting to encourage her. But she throws me a little wink as the squad heads off to their own practice.

Out of the corner of one eye, I see Todd watch Leslie's retreat, then turn back to the players on the court, sighing and shaking his head in dismissal. It hasn't been all that long since Julius and the other guys would cram Todd into his locker most afternoons. I tell myself I'd stop them if I actually saw them doing it, but a sixth sense kept me out of their way most days. When did their victim shoot up to over six feet? And when did he stop looking scared all the time?

Coach's whistle brings my head back to the court. "Okay, guys. We've got to stay focused these next weeks. We have some major games coming up if the Warriors are going to make it to the playoffs, and you need to plan study time for this project as well as your other classes if you're going to keep your grades up and stay on the team."

Julius snorts softly as Coach Guilford looks down at his clipboard. I know Coach is torn between his original job and the coaching position. He's the school's guidance counselor and used to be the assistant basketball coach. But then a Class 1 private school asks Coach Ritter to come on board as their head coach, and he takes the job without a backward glance. So Assistant Coach Guilford gets an unexpected promotion. Most of the time he keeps his mind on the game, but every now and then he remembers his guidance counselor persona and starts worrying more about our grades than our win-loss record.

Ignoring Julius's snort and the grins on the faces of the rest of his team, Coach flips open his dog-eared copy of the *High School Coaching Bible* and calls out, "Okay, guys, let's get your heads into the game. The Raiders have a wicked full-court press we need to beat. You too, Eddie."

Eddie jumps up and jogs over to join the rest of us at the top of the key. He's a junior who's still learning the ropes, even though he spends most of his time riding the bench as the team backup man. He warms up with us, doing easy passes and shooting from the top of the key, while Coach Guilford studies the training drill his book recommends.

Julius mutters as he runs by me, "Coach ought to get his nose out of a book and get out here on the court with us— nobody ever learned how to play hoops by reading !"

The other guys chuckle. "Give him a break," I say, keeping my voice low. "He's doing his best to fill in for Ritter."

"Well, we're better off without Coach Quitter," Julius answers. "But Coach-in-training should just let us get on with it. We know how to put the ball down the hole, and that's what wins games, not fancy drills out of a book."

Julius has some great moves, no question there, but you can always play better. Maybe Coach Guilford isn't the best, but he loves the game, and he wants to win. And he's right about the Raiders crushing other teams with their full-court press.

He gets all tangled up in explaining the drill, though. I get the idea after a while, and use my captain status to get the team in place.

"That's it, Brian," he calls, approving. I just hope he doesn't see Julius rolling his eyes.

By the time we've run defensive drills and Take-away Ray has stolen the ball from each of us in turn, it's nearly time to quit. We take turns at the free-throw line to cool down until Coach blows the whistle. Eddie's still struggling to put the ball in the hole. The guy's a whiz at wrestling the ball from someone on another team who thinks he's broken into the open for an easy bucket, but he's got to practice his shooting if he expects to be a starter on a winning team next year. I just hope Coach sees some sophomores and freshmen with great potential for when we graduate.

"So, you up for pizza, Brian?" Julius asks as we sluice off sweat in the showers. "Ashley's sure hoping you are."

I doubt it's going to make a big difference to Ashley, but I've got a clear image of Todd stretched out at the top of the bleachers, waiting for me. It matters to Todd. "What about meeting Leslie about your project?"

Julius snickers. "Leave Lesbo to figure out I could care less about anything except hoops." He towels off, studying my face. "Don't tell me you're actually worried about the steaming Turd waiting out there for you?"

It would be easy to go out the back of the locker room with the other guys and leave Todd sitting on the bleachers until the janitor shuts off the lights and chases him out. I doubt Todd would even be surprised. But something stops me. Maybe it's knowing Todd expects me to do just that. Maybe it's the nagging thought that Amanda would be disappointed in me if I just blow off the project. It could be simple curiosity about Leo Frank and what history is supposed to have learned from him and the murdered girl. I end up shaking my head. "No, but I am worried that I'd better do something to pump up my grades so Coach doesn't bench me. You have a slice of extra pepperoni for me, okay?"

Julius laughs. "Whatever, Brainman. But Ashley's going to be majorly disappointed."

I shrug and smile a little. "Like she cares."

Julius shakes his head. "Man, All-the-way Ashley is doing everything to get your attention except flashing the red neon 'Come in here, baby' sign!"

I laugh, embarrassed. "She is not!" I've never been clear if Julius's nickname for her means she actually went all the way with him, or just that she acts like she would.

"Brainman, you can't stay hung up on the Songbird forever," Julius says flatly. "Amanda is gone. You've got to get back into life, you hear me? Go out with Ashley—or

Darlin' Darla, if you'd rather. And hang with your team for a while."

I look up, startled. I hang with the team. He goes on, "So what if you used to go off with Songbird after practice last year? She's not here anymore, but the rest of us still are."

"I know that," I tell him. "I just don't want to talk about her, okay?"

"Either you got to talk about her or you got to do something about getting her out of your head," he retorts, "because she's like a ghost, choking the life out of you."

Since last August, everybody wants me to talk about Amanda. But I can't. There's this dark hole in my life that nothing can fill except basketball. Other people can't begin to fill it, certainly not Ashley with her pert little ponytail and her teasing eyes. That just makes me miss Amanda more, not less. But I can't tell Julius that. I can't tell anyone how I can't let go of her memory. It's not choking me—it's the only thing reminding me of who I am.

"I'm alive, man. Just watch me on the court against those Raiders, and you'll see some life." I punch him lightly on the shoulder. "Don't worry about me so much, okay? You just keep your mind on giving Keesha some joy."

Julius rolls his eyes. "Man, there's no reason that girl's after me except because I'm black! So what? We got zip in common except color. Me, I'm not prejudiced. I like Bright Eyes, even if she is white."

Maybe Julius doesn't know himself as well as he thinks. He and Keesha have a lot more in common than their color. They're both hard chargers who leap first and look later, and do what they want even if it gets them in trouble. And then they both laugh it off. Bright Eyes Brittney may be a cheerleader, but she's more serious about grades and schoolwork, like Amanda. Or maybe Julius just hopes that Brittney can help him bring up his grades by drilling some history and English into his short-term memory.

But it's not my place to tell my main man who to take out. "Well, you and Brittney share a slice of pepperoni pizza in my honor, okay?"

Julius flashes me a broad, white-toothed grin. "And you squash the Turd for me, okay?"

I shake my head as I pull on my clothes. Sometimes I wonder about Julius.

CHAPTER

4

Todd raises one eyebrow as my footsteps echo across the otherwise empty gym. He drawls, "I didn't think you cared."

Before I can make a sharp retort, I see one corner of his mouth quirk upward in a faint smile, and my own frown relaxes into the start of a grin. "Okay—you got me. I care about keeping my grades up enough to stay on the team." When Todd simply cocks his head to one side and waits, I add, "And I'm kind of curious about the Leo Frank guy and . . ." I swallow. ". . . and the girl who got murdered."

Todd nods. "Fair enough. I was curious, too—maybe a bit more than you, because I stopped by the library on my way here." He stands up, slings his backpack over one shoulder, and climbs down the bleachers. When he reaches the gym floor, I find myself surprised all over again by how tall the guy's gotten. We're eye to eye now.

Either Todd doesn't feel my gaze or he completely ignores it. He sets his backpack down on the bleacher seat and extracts two books. One jacket shows a black-and-white photo of an austere man wearing old-fashioned spectacles and an expression of incomprehension—with a second photo in the lower corner of a man hanging from a tree, surrounded by an orderly crowd of men in an assortment of suits and work clothes, looking proud of themselves. The book's title reads: *The Leo Frank Case*. The other volume shows a retouched photo of a pretty teenager with ringlets, wearing a ribboned hat and a frilly dress. She looks sweet and innocent and soulful. The title blares: *The Murder of Little Mary Phagan*.

"Which do you want?" Todd asks.

"Huh?"

Time and space fold around me, sweeping me out of the gym and back to last summer. I'm lost in a memory of Amanda looking disturbingly like the pretty teenager as she smiles up at me on the Fourth of July. Time accordions to a summer-soft night, with crickets chirping and stars too faint to shine through the brilliance of the fireworks. I'm sitting on a blanket with her so close to me our arms are touching, the heat in mine way beyond the summer night's record high. Amanda oohs as fireworks canopy the deep blue sky above us. Part of me wants nothing more than to kiss her. But even then, part of me still aches to make the perfect shot.

I'm beat after playing HORSE with Julius, then spending the afternoon trying to make the beautiful long shots that Julius hits so consistently, so effortlessly. I didn't plan to lose the whole afternoon trying to make that big-play shot. In fact, I lay awake last night, imagining what it would be like to lean closer to Amanda under a burst of golden sparks, and press my lips against hers.

But then I watch the ball soar out of Julius's hands like it's an extension of his body, with me stumbling along, always a step behind, making the easy shots, but falling short on the long jump shots, the beautiful sweeping hook shots that Julius owns. Mine only clang off the rim, or teeter on the edge while my heart catches, then roll out before I can reach the hoop to tap the ball in. So all afternoon I'm just thinking about making that pro shot, not about kissing Amanda. And now it's night and we're under a shower of red-gold sparks blinding me with their glare until I see basketballs swishing through nets instead of Amanda's face lit by the fiery celebration.

Amanda turns to me, smiling, her long hair falling back from her radiant face, and I forget I'm second best on the court. I lean toward her and she meets me halfway and the fireworks explode inside my chest, electricity fizzing through me from lips to belly. We're so close we're almost one person. I want the moment to never end. I want to pause so I can tell her I love her, but I can't shape the words and, anyway, there isn't any time because we don't pause. We go on kissing forever.

Then time folds back on itself and Todd is asking, "Which book?" He weighs one in each hand. "You know— research? Read first, plan project after?"

"Oh. Yeah." I reorient myself—it's a January afternoon and I'm in the school gym. There's never been a day when I make the perfect shot, or a day when I tell Amanda I love her. I reach out for the book titled *The Leo Frank Case*. "This one, I guess." I don't want to look at the picture of the dead girl.

Todd nods, zipping the other back inside his backpack. "That would have been my guess as to your choice. Take care of it—it's checked out on my card."

"Right." I shove it into my own stack of books.

"There are more—plus online sources," Todd volunteers. "But I figure these two will get us started. Then we can figure out what point Fortner is getting at."

"What history has learned from Leo Frank being tried for the murder of Mary Phagan," I interrupt, wanting to make sure Todd knows I'm not just a dumb jock. It suddenly occurs to me that Todd Pollian might not turn out to be such a bad partner for this project after all.

"Or what history has failed to learn, and is doomed to repeat," Todd caps me. He shoulders his backpack and grins unexpectedly. "You know," he adds, "you might not turn out to be such a bad partner for this project after all."

With that he turns and strides out of the gym, leaving me feeling totally faked out by the moves of a man I expect to breeze past.

"More Ringer's and another tube set."

"Punch him."

"It's not there for me."

"Give me the needle. I'll find a vein."

CHAPTER

5

I wait on the corner to hook a ride with one of the men coming off work. Willisford's a small enough town that everybody knows the team. Everybody also knows that the town's too small for the players to find jobs that fit around practice and games so we can earn enough to buy our own cars. Not even Julius is brash enough to accept the gift of a car, or cash, from the college scouts. He wrangles the use of the family car sometimes, and a couple of the cheerleaders drive loaners or hand-me-down cars from older brothers in college, but if we go our separate ways after practice we're stuck with our feet or a thumb.

I fill in the half hour until what passes for rush hour in Willisford by reading about Leo Frank, the collar of my team jacket turned up against the cold so that I lose myself in the summer heat of Georgia. They were celebrating Confederate Memorial Day that Saturday in 1913, everybody except Leo Frank, who was a Yankee. Folks in town saw him as an outsider, a carpetbagger come down to make a fortune off the South's defeat, even though more than a generation had passed since the original carpetbaggers descended on the South after the Civil War.

Leo Frank came to Atlanta to help his uncle by taking a temporary job managing the teenage girls who worked in the pencil factory. He stayed because he fell in love with a young woman named Lucille and married her. There was a good-sized Jewish society in Atlanta, but Leo Frank didn't exactly fit in there even though he was Jewish. Lucille and the rest of their family and friends seemed more Southern than Jewish, and they honored the Confederate dead with heartfelt respect, leaving Leo Frank with the guilty feeling that they somehow saw him as a symbol of all the evil forces responsible for the war and its aftermath.

So he was in the factory going over the books, instead of out celebrating that Saturday. One of the girls who worked for him was Mary Phagan, only thirteen years old! She stopped by the factory to collect her week's pay so she could enjoy the day. He paid her, but she never made it to the Memorial Day parade. Instead, her murdered body was found in the factory basement, and Leo Frank—the Yankee—wound up on trial for her murder.

Mr. Garrett rolls down the window of his elderly pickup. "Need a ride, Brian?"

I'm so caught up in the story that I miss the increase in traffic entirely.

"Thanks, Mr. Garrett." I climb into the cab, grateful he's keeping an eye out for players while he drives.

"Wouldn't want you to freeze before tomorrow night's game," he says, shifting into first and pulling away from the curb. "Hitting the books?"

I nod, shoving the Leo Frank book back into the stack. "I don't want my grades to slip and keep me out of the starting lineup."

He shifts again and shoots me a sidelong glance. "Well, you burn that midnight oil, Brian. We're all counting on you boys taking us all the way to state this season. Not to mention creaming Jackson while you're at it."

I grin. Before Indiana basketball got divided into four classes, based on the size of the school, Andrew Jackson High was always our biggest rival at regionals. They're only one town north, a little closer to Indianapolis, but that distance makes all the difference in terms of size and money. Jackson has a varsity team of eighteen, with backups for every position and role players for special situations, not to mention a junior varsity squad ready to step up if one of the varsity guys gets hurt. We're lucky to bring seven players to the court, and there's no junior varsity in reserve, just freshman and sophomore wannabes who need another year's seasoning before they can even try out.

Back then the road to the championship always lay through Jackson, with their bigger gym and their bigger cheerleading squads and their bigger crowds. We might win sometimes, but they usually laugh us off. Now they're in Class 2 (not, I remind myself with smug satisfaction, Class 1) ball, and we're in Class 4, but there's always a non-league game with them on our schedule. It's got nothing to do with our going to the championship, but it has everything to do with our feeling like winners.

"Don't worry, Mr. Garrett," I assure him, "we'll beat them this year."

He lets me off on my corner, and I wave my thanks, then walk the long block down into our cul-de-sac, glad to open my door on the smells of home. Most places it's the sounds I hear, some places it's the sights that bring the scene to life. Here it's the smells more than anything else. Sweetly pungent onions browned with mushrooms and herbs in butter, mingling with the faint scent of wood dust from Dad's work clothes and traces of printer ink from the work Mom does for him on the computer upstairs. But the onions are strongest, and I follow their scent to the kitchen, to see Mom tossing a salad and Dad turning tender pork chops in his special onion and mushroom sauce.

"Ummmm. If you'd asked me what I was hungry for, this would have been top of the list," I announce, my stomach growling in a loud assist.

Mom laughs and Dad puts the lid back on the pork chops and looks up with a smile. "Late practice today? I didn't hear the Bomb." Ashley has a car that runs, but it needs a new muffler.

I shake my head. "The guys went out for pizza after Coach ran us through the drills, but I had some work to do for Mr. Fortner's class. Mr. Garrett gave me a lift."

"I'll make sure to thank him," Dad says. "What's Fortner giving you now?"

As we carry things to the dinner table, I tell them what Mr. Fortner said about those who fail to learn from history being doomed to repeat it, and how our term projects are supposed to make the point.

Mom looks interested, but Dad frowns. "That should make for a good research project all right," he says doubtfully, "but it sounds like it's going to take a lot of time to do the job right. I can't help wishing your teacher had come up with this assignment last semester, before the season got into full swing."

Mom raises her eyebrows at him. "Maybe Mr. Fortner

figured winter was a better time for sitting inside doing research than autumn."

Dad sighs and I know what he's thinking: winters are a tough time all round, especially in the contracting business. In hard winters when we get lots of snow, he can't schedule much building. Sometimes he even has to lay off a few of his guys temporarily, not knowing if they'll come back when the weather improves. Even in easy winters he worries all the time.

"Sure," Dad says, "winter sounds like a great time to stay indoors. But you can't always do that. Remember—this season Brian's going to lead the team to the championship game. The scouts are going to be recruiting our boy, and they're going to be looking at his performance on the court, not his grade on a history project. Grades matter, sure, but he's got to have enough time to work on his game, to stay the best."

"Dad . . ." I'm not the best. I know I'm good, but I'm not the best. I wish Dad wouldn't keep saying that.

Mom pokes him in the left side of his belly, hard enough that he yelps and rubs it, even though he's smiling as he tells her, "Quit that!"

"Well, you quit talking like that, Danny," she retorts, poking him again for emphasis. "For one thing, it just puts more pressure on Brian. It's a game! He should be enjoying it, not thinking he has to be the best all the time." Dad grins at me across the table and rolls his eyes, totally disagreeing but not arguing. Mom goes on, "And for another thing—remember, Brian doesn't go to school so he can play ball. He goes to school *and* plays ball to prepare himself for real life."

Mom's been saying that as far back as I can remember: education, fitness, sportsmanship—all these things work together to prepare me for real life.

"But Laura," Dad says, half teasing Mom and half meaning it, "basketball is real life!" After she laughs a little, shaking her head at the same time, he adds, "And a basketball scholarship is going to be his ticket to college, so he's got to make sure he stays the best player on the team."

Time slip-slides again. The fragrance of sweet onions fades and the scents of cedar and rosewood surround me. I'm up in Dad's wood shop, the special room he's built like a dome to catch the sunlight, no matter what season or what time of day it is. He's got a round worktable in the center of the room, with a stool on wheels that he can swing around the table so the sunlight always shines on the piece of wood he's working on. This is where he does his special carving—he calls it engraving—every afternoon after he gets home from work and on most weekends too.

Dad's face is unlined, and he's got more hair, so I must only be five or six, just a little kid like Cory. "You're the best, Daddy, right?"

He makes gorgeous patterns on guitars—rosette inlays around the sound hole, delicate engraving along the neck, and beautiful inlays in contrasting wood in the guitar's body. Then he and Mom and I travel to craft fairs almost every weekend in the summer, down in Kentucky and Tennessee, and up across Indiana and Ohio. Mom plays the guitar Dad gave her the day he married her, and sings. People stop and smile. They look at Dad's guitars and strum the strings, and run their hands up and down the polished wood that seems to glow from inside. They tell me, "Kid, do you know you've got a real artist for a father?" And some of them give Mom what looks like lots of money to the little kid I am then, and take away Dad's guitars, even though not everybody who praises them buys one.

"You're the best guitar maker there is!" I tell him, watching his hands deftly moving the tools across the smooth wood.

He laughs, a big round chuckle that enfolds us like a bear hug. "I don't know about the best, Brian, but I'm pretty good."

Only not good enough, I guess, because those laughing, sunlit days in the wood shop don't last. Instead of smelling wood dust, I hear voices talking about money and bills. Dad says, "But wood is all I know." He carves little animals dancing and playing miniature guitars, and sells them at the craft fairs because they cost less than the real guitars he loves to make. And he carves tables and chests and children's rocking horses, hoping that people will buy those.

But in the end Dad brings big boxes into the house, and sets up a computer in the tiny room upstairs that was supposed to be a nursery, and Mom learns how to use it. There are fewer craft fairs, and at one of them somebody swipes a bunch of Dad's small carvings. None of his buddy crafters admit to seeing anything suspicious, and the police think maybe Dad is lying about it in order to make a false insurance claim. Dad quits going to the fairs entirely, and sinks everything into his own construction company, and the work carves lines in his face the way engraving guitars never did.

"No, Brian, I'm not the best guitar maker," he says one day, his voice heavy. "And even if I were, you can't make a living making fancy guitars for people who don't even know how to make music, or carving furniture or toys for peanuts. Not when half the people at these craft fairs are crooked—shoplifters in the crowds, liars behind the booths, and police who don't bother to find out the truth and treat innocent people like suspects. But you—" his voice lightens with hope. "Now, you're going to be the best basketball player Willisford has seen in a long time, and all the scouts will be fighting over you. You'll make a living playing ball fair and clean, and set your old dad up so he can whistle and carve and only build houses for people he likes, right?"

Right, Dad. Just follow the bouncing ball:

Per—fect shot!

He's—the best.

That's the plan. And projects about learning from history, or failing to, don't have any place in it.

CHAPTER

6

I don't watch much TV alone. Sitting there staring at a screen makes me itch to get out and start moving. I can see myself watching movies with Amanda and talking about them with her after, or watching cartoons with her when she's stuck babysitting Cory, throwing popcorn at each other and laughing. I call us the ABC Club—Amanda, Brian, and Cory, to make the little kid not feel left out. But it's really me and Amanda who make up the team, a team for talking, or thinking, or just hanging out and growing closer, because we fit together.

On my own, though, I usually only watch ball games. And sometimes the news. Not always. But I switch on the set after finishing my homework, thinking I'll read some more about Leo Frank and keep my ear tuned for the sports news. Tonight I'm in time to catch the lead story, and it jolts me so that I don't get around to opening the book. I just pick up my basketball and hold it for comfort.

                ANCHORMAN (voice-over)
Former Willisford police officer Michael
Daine will go on trial next week—

(Camera pans the courtroom, comes to rest on two men wearing suits, standing behind a table littered with papers, one man's expression disbelieving under haunted eyes, the other man's expression resigned.)

—on three counts of first-degree murder in the summer shootings of Daine's wife, Caroline, and children: Amanda, sixteen, and Cory, six. Daine pled not guilty and claimed he was in a local gym, playing basketball with friends, when the shootings occurred. But prosecutors insist that forensic analysis of the crime scene, along with evidence proving motive and opportunity, point strongly to his guilt.

(New picture: camera panning a house with yellow crime-scene tape cutting it off from curious neighbors in the cul-de-sac; an identifying caption below reading "File Footage.")

Our cul-de-sac. My hand clenches around the remote control, but I can't bring myself to turn the news off. I roll the basketball back and forth along the couch cushion, barely feeling the nubbly surface under my fingertips.

ANCHORMAN (voice-over continues)
Mr. Daine claims he discovered the bodies of

his wife and children in the family garage several hours after Caroline Daine drove the children home from the local swimming pool last August seventh. Each victim had been killed with a single shot from a .380. Daine owned a handgun in that caliber, but claimed he had sold it some time before the shootings. No weapon has been discovered in his possession, but the prosecution believes he disposed of the firearm before reporting the deaths. Natalie Hart is on the scene.

(New picture: the man with the haunted expression, Michael Daine, being led out of the courthouse in handcuffs, his lawyer looking worried beside him as reporters shout questions.)

I really don't know Amanda's father all that well. He was always busy with work or with the other officers, and when he was home he and her mom used to argue a lot. I guess I didn't like him all that much, because when I did see him he was kind of arrogant and bossy. And Amanda said he sometimes told her not to spend so much time with me. But she always lit up when he had time to take her to a movie, or play ball with her and Cory. I don't want to believe he could hurt her or Cory or her mom. I don't want to believe he could kill them.

(Camera comes to rest on an attractive red-haired woman holding a microphone;

an identifying caption below reading "Natalie Hart, Live at County Courthouse.")

                    NATALIE HART
Thank you, Peter. Despite the evidence that the prosecution presented to a grand jury in order to get the indictment against Michael Daine, former Officer Daine insists that he is innocent. He claims to be concerned that misguided police focus on proving his guilt has resulted in the real murderer's trail growing cold. If the preliminary motions before the court can be settled this week, on Monday the prosecution and defense will begin choosing the jury that will determine whether Daine is right—or is guilty.

                ANCHORMAN (voice-over)
In other news—

I fumble for the remote and switch off the voice, not caring anymore about the sports news. I sit there, the ball on my knees, arms wrapped around it, rocking blindly, the day playing over and over in cut scenes in my mind, like the news report.

        CORY (running across the cul-de-sac)
Play ball, Bro!

            (HIGHRISE and RAY chuckling)

CORY (frowning)
Pick me up, Joyous! Let's shoot baskets!

BRIAN
Not now, Cory. We've got a game going, man.

Can that be me in the summer sunlight? That kid looks so much—younger. Almost as young as Cory.

Me, a lifetime ago, I guess.

JULIUS
(straight-arming sweat off his forehead)
Later, Scory—Brainman and me, we got to beat these guys.

CORY
Let me play, Joyous! Let me be on your team. Then we'll beat them—I can score.

JULIUS (laughing)
That you can, my man. But that wouldn't be fair—three against two.

CORY
(scratches his head, then lights up)
Let Amanda be on the other team. Then it's even!

AMANDA
(following Cory across the cul-de-sac more slowly)

That sounds like a good idea. What do you
say, Brian? Can we play?

Her expression looks almost pleading, in spite of the
other guys' presence, and I'm surprised. Usually she just
watches from her own lawn when the rest of the team's
here, though she comes on over if it's just me and Julius.
She's been coming over a lot more often this summer, between things getting better between us and worse between
her folks. But the game with Highrise and Take-away Ray
is running hot and heavy, and I can tell Julius doesn't want
to kill the momentum any more than I do.

                BRIAN (dribbling ball)
Maybe later, okay? Why don't you watch and
cheer us on?
    (pointing   to   her   long   wraparound
    skirt, grinning)
Besides, you can hardly play in that!

                    AMANDA
I can change.

                AMANDA'S MOTHER
    (voice-over from the Daine garage)
Come on, kids!

                    AMANDA
    (glances over   shoulder,   then   turns
    back to Brian)
Mom wants to spend the afternoon gossiping

at the pool.

                    BRIAN (impatient)
Sounds cool to me. You can play with us when
you get back.

                    AMANDA (lowers voice)
Please, Brian. (Pause.) I don't want to go.
(Pause.) Things aren't so good at home right
now.

                    BRIAN (holds ball, looks at her)
What's happened?

                    HIGHRISE
Oohh—true love wins out over basketball!

                    (AMANDA looks hurt)

                    JULIUS
      (shaking his head while BRIAN blushes)
Don't believe it, Highrise! Brian's a team
man all the way—loving's for after the game,
not on the court.

                    AMANDA'S MOTHER (voice-over)
Amanda? Bring your brother back and let's
get going.

                    CORY
I don't want to go swimming. Can't we stay

with you, Brian?

    AMANDA (not looking at BRIAN)
Forget it, Cory. Brian doesn't want to waste
his time on us when he could be playing basketball with his *friends*.

And that is so unfair of her.

I'm kind of worried because I've heard arguments over at her house while I've been practicing—not the words, just the tone of voice—enough to know that things are getting worse between her folks. But I'm mad too, because she's looking at me like she thinks now that we're kissing in the tower wood shop instead of just making music and talking, I'm going to start treating her the way some of the guys treat their cheerleader girlfriends—like trophies, instead of people. But Amanda and me—we've been friends since practically as far back as I can remember. We've only just started going together instead of hanging out together. Why should she think it would change everything, just because the guys are clowning around?

She should trust me.

And she should understand that I can't drop everything for her—sometimes I have to hang with the team.

(New picture: the Daine SUV cruising
up to the garage in the late afternoon
sun; the impossibly younger BRIAN
shooting hoops all alone, trying to
make the perfect distance shot and
failing time after time; soft whisper

        of a garage door closing; time lapse,
        masked by close-ups of BRIAN's hands
        releasing the ball from the farthest
        points of his driveway, of the ball
        clanging off the rim, bouncing off the
        backstop, rolling down the driveway.)

How much time elapses? I still have no idea, because I'm not counting time. One part of my mind knows that Amanda's home and remembers she was worried about her parents and upset with me, but most of my attention stays with the ball. Close, but not quite—how does Julius play so big? He hangs in the air, like he's weightless, and releases these impossibly long shots that go straight down the hole. I go up, but gravity drags me back to the concrete and the ball clangs off the rim. The next time, for sure—no, then the next time. As soon as I sink that perfect long-range shot that will earn me an NBA career, I promise myself, I'll go over and see how she's doing, say I'm sorry if she's still mad. Just as soon as I sink that shot.

The cul-de-sac is quiet in the late August afternoon— too hot for most people to be outside. Mrs. Graidey walks past, getting her exercise in spite of the heat, listening to her headphones and raising one hand in my direction. I wave back absently, still thinking about my setup and re- lease. How does Julius make it look so easy? Why can't I do it, too? I'm fast, I can see the shifting patterns on the court, I can distribute passes right where they need to go, and I can make layups and foul shots all day, even under pressure. *But I can't be the best, Dad, if I can't make this shot.* If you ask me five minutes later, I can't tell you what Mrs. Graidey is wearing. Maybe she doesn't even have headphones on, but since I never see her walking without them, I'm assuming she has them jammed onto her ears.

I miss again, and the ball bumps down the sloping driveway, almost hitting a jogger—someone else so determined to get his exercise he's braving the heat, sweatsuit on with hood pulled up, his only concession to summer weather being sunglasses to cut the glare. I scoop up the ball, apologizing in winded gasps, but he barely waves an arm indicating he's okay before he's past the driveway, past the lawn, abreast of the next driveway, and I'm turning back to the hoop, shooting again, missing again, shooting.

I can't bear to remember the rest. I can only stand to see it as faded memories distanced by a news camera, like the one on television.

(New picture: Officer Daine's truck
pulls into the cul-de-sac, turns in at
his driveway; sound of garage door
opening.)

OFFICER DAINE
No! NO! (more hysterical cries, becoming in-
coherent)

I slam the Leo Frank book and my basketball together and practically run down the hall to my room as the scene in my head disintegrates into chaos. Doors banging open, people coming out. Willisford isn't like a big city, where people act like they don't notice trouble. Folks here might pretend they don't hear neighbors shouting at each other in a family argument, but they won't ignore real trouble, and Amanda's father sounds like he's in pain. So why do I just stand there, holding the ball, watching them?

At first, I'm thinking I really screwed up not letting Amanda play, and I'm hating myself for not telling the guys to take an afternoon off. But that turns into fear pretty soon. I try telling myself it's just a movie about somebody else, not me, not Amanda, not her family—I'm just watching and I can't do anything. And then he comes running down his driveway, and there's red spatters on his T-shirt, and red on his hands, and he's crying, real tears that scare me more than anything, because men—especially policemen—don't cry. And through his sobs I can make out the words "They're dead! They're dead!"

CHAPTER

7

I prop myself up in bed, the Leo Frank book open against my knees. Frank said that Mary just came into his office to pick up her pay and went away again. His office boy had already gone to the parade, but Frank kept working, ignoring the Confederate War Heroes celebrations that made no sense to a Yankee like him. Then he went home, and he said he knew nothing about the girl's murder until the police came to ask him about it. The night watchman had found her body in the factory basement.

Leo Frank insisted he didn't do anything, but after the prosecutor talked to the girls who worked in the pencil factory, he told the press they were all scared of their boss because he'd come on to them. The prosecutor, Hugh Dorsey, implied that Frank had tried to "have his way" with Mary and killed her when she resisted. They made him sound like some kind of rapist, even though medical reports revealed later that she'd never had sex with anyone. At the inquest, most of the girls (but not all of them—I wondered about those others) got up on the witness stand and gave, almost word for word, the same evidence about feeling threatened by Leo Frank.

At the trial, Dorsey presented his star witness: the factory odd-jobs man, a black guy named Jim Conley. Conley testified that Frank had young girls and women up in his office all the time. Apparently the prosecution had bought Conley a suit, so he looked clean and trustworthy in court, and they'd coached him on how to tell his story. He even claimed that Frank had paid him a little extra cash on the side to keep an eye out so he wouldn't get caught with any of the girls. But the prosecution couldn't produce any witness that was willing to say she'd been one of those women who'd gone up to his office. That didn't matter in the end—Conley testified that Frank had called him up to his office that Saturday, told him that he'd killed Mary Phagan, and promised to pay him two hundred dollars to help him cover up the murder. Conley said the two of them carried the body into the elevator and hid it in the basement. It was his word against Frank's.

Leo Frank's defense attorney tried hard, but he was careful, too. He was in a lose-lose situation. Most people in town thought Frank was guilty—they blamed him not only for the murder, but for being a Yankee and a Jew. His lawyer was Jewish, too, and he wanted to be fair, but he didn't want the town going after him if the jury found Frank innocent.

I shake my head, letting the book fall flat on my stomach. Atlanta in 1913 sounded more like a mob than a city. They weren't after justice so much as they wanted revenge. It was a sad murder, but still. . . . The trial seemed like a staged play, with everyone except Leo Frank knowing their lines. Everyone except Leo Frank and his wife, that is.

The community tried to be sympathetic to her. She

might be Jewish, but she came from an old Southern family—she was all right. Unlike Leo Frank, she belonged. But Mrs. Frank wasn't having any of it. She insisted her husband was innocent. And when the jury convicted him and sentenced him to death by hanging, she appealed all the way up to the Georgia Supreme Court. When they ruled that not even the fact that witnesses admitted they'd lied under oath should change the verdict, Mrs. Frank demanded the governor look into the travesty of a trial. If they couldn't get a new trial to set her husband free, at least his sentence should be commuted from hanging to life imprisonment.

From then on it was politics versus justice. Governor John Slaton was in line to run for senator. The guys high up in his political party suggested, strongly, that he not look at the case too carefully or they'd find another candidate—maybe that bright young prosecutor. But the speedy trial and the fact that witnesses lied in court bothered the governor. He ordered the Prison Commission to hold formal hearings, but when their vote was divided he had to make the decision on commuting Leo Frank's sentence. The governor held the final hearings in his office and even asked hard questions about the evidence himself.

Governor Slaton found such overwhelming problems that he decided there was reasonable doubt as to Leo Frank's guilt—and more than enough justification for him to commute Frank's sentence from hanging to life imprisonment. He said it was a matter of conscience—as governor, he had to do what he thought was right. But a lot of people in Georgia didn't think his decision was right at all. They rioted in outrage, burning Jewish homes and stores and even attacking the governor's mansion.

That governor never became a senator. He and his wife left Georgia and never came back. And he got hate mail until he died.

I swallow, feeling sick. Governor Slaton was still better off than Leo Frank. After Frank went to this prison farm to spend the rest of his life at hard labor, one inmate was paid to try to kill him. He failed, but then a group of good citizens broke into the prison farm at night and took Frank out and lynched him. They said they were just carrying out the original sentence of the court: death by hanging. But it was a lynch mob, pure and simple.

Right before they strung him up, they asked him again to confess to killing Mary Phagan. One last time, Leo Frank told them, "No." He just asked if someone would take his wedding ring and give it to his wife. The next day a boy showed up at the newspaper office with the ring wrapped in a piece of paper. Mrs. Frank kept it—and despite Atlanta's hatred for her husband, she signed her name as Mrs. Leo Frank until her death.

I close my eyes, just for a minute, trying to think what it would be like to have so many people hate you so much for something you said you hadn't done. Do people around here hate Mr. Daine that much? I wish I could concentrate on Mary Phagan and Leo Frank, but Amanda's death keeps replaying, whether I want to watch the aftermath or not. Mr. Daine crying. Mr. Francis, from across the street, running out to ask what's wrong, then calling 911 on his cell phone. The police finally coming, stringing yellow crime-scene tape everywhere as if our cul-de-sac had turned into some TV cop show.

"No," I whisper as time warps and I'm transported back to that evening in August, when I realize the sirens and yellow tape and sobs mean I'm not going to ever see Amanda again. "No—it can't be true!" The words are tiny, squeezed out because I have no air to speak.

Mom's arms circle around me, like I'm a little kid, then Dad's around us both, and I fight them. "Maybe she's just hurt! I need to help her."

"Oh, Brian," Mom cries.

"No, son," Dad says gently. "It's a police matter now. They'll do everything they can to help her." After a moment he adds, softly, almost as if he's not talking to me at all, "That poor man."

At the pain in his voice I stop fighting and lean against them, wanting to cry like Mr. Daine but having no breath to spare for sobs, scarcely feeling helpless tears trickling down my cheeks.

Then Mr. Francis comes across to our driveway and Dad lets go of me. I stay in the circle of Mom's arms, only taking in snatches of the conversation.

"Daine . . . murder . . . definitely, all dead . . . suspect . . ."

His wife calls to him, and I see the Francis twins, Paul and Matt, standing on their front walkway, their faces wide-eyed, innocent, curious. Tears blur my eyes again. "Dad," I say.

"Shh," he says, coming back and holding me again, as if I were younger than the twins (*just Cory's age*) and could still sit on his knee and cry my heart out over a scooter fall. I'm so tall, but not too big to feel safer in Dad's bear hug than standing unsteadily on my own feet.

"She wanted to play ball with me—not go to the pool," I whisper into the crumpled cotton of his T-shirt. "It's my fault. If I'd let her play with me, she'd be alive now. . . ."

"No, honey," Mom says, her voice soothing.

"But I told her to go away." I can hardly bear the weight of my guilt at sending Amanda to her death. "She'd have been safe with me, but I wanted to play ball with Julius and the guys. . . ."

Dad's quiet for a little while, long enough for my shuddering breathing to pick up the steady rise and fall of his chest and fall into its rhythm. "Brian," he says finally, and I can hear how much he cares in his voice. "There's nothing you could have done, son."

He breaks off as a uniformed police officer comes up, light glinting off the badge on his chest. "I'm Officer Recks," he says in a flat, dispassionate voice. "I've got a couple of questions for you about this afternoon."

Mom hugs me tighter, and I see him notice. "You seem pretty upset. . . ." He lets his voice trail off into a question, and I finally realize that's his way of asking my name.

Dad answers for me. "I'm Danny Hammett. This is my wife, Laura, and my son, Brian. The Daines have been good neighbors ever since we bought this land—well, you must know they're good people if you're on the force with Mike Daine. It's got to be hard for you, too. But this is especially hard on my son—he's been best friends with Amanda Daine for years—they practically grew up together."

Officer Recks nods. "I understand. This must be very painful for you, Brian." Somehow, the words don't sound very sympathetic. But I guess a policeman can't let emotions get in the way of finding out the facts. "Mrs. Francis said she believes you were out playing ball all afternoon." He lets the statement hang there, until I figure out he's waiting for me to say something.

"Yes." I straighten a little but don't pull away from Mom completely. "Most of it, anyway."

"Most of it?" he echoes, a gold pen poised over his leather notebook.

"Well, I went in a few times for Gatorade, then for supper," I explain.

"Did you see Mrs. Daine drive the family SUV home?"

I nod, thinking that I'd expected Amanda to roll down the tinted windows and wave at me—I'd been hoping that she'd forgiven me. Now Amanda would never be able to wave at me again. . . .

"Did you see Officer Daine drive his pickup truck home?" His voice is so flat and even it almost sounds monotonous.

I nod again.

"And when was that?"

"You mean, when Officer Daine got home?" I ask, confused. He nods, and I shrug a little. "I don't know what time—not very long ago. It was right before he came running down his driveway, calling for help." I remember Dad saying "poor man," and I try not to think about his screams and sobs, and the blood on his white T-shirt. "Right before Mr. Francis called 911—he could probably be more sure about the time."

Officer Recks stops writing and looks up at me. "No," he says patiently, "before that. Did you see Officer Daine drive home earlier, and then leave again?"

I shake my head, confused.

"But you might have been inside, getting something to drink, or having supper?" he suggests.

"I guess," I say, wondering why he's asking so many questions about Amanda's father at a time like this.

"Did you notice anything else?"

I start to shake my head, thinking I didn't notice anything—not anything that mattered, anyway, like how much Amanda needed my help. Then I remember Mrs. Graidey and the jogger. "Nothing really," I tell him. "Just a couple of people out exercising."

Officer Recks's gold pen pauses on the page. "Could you describe them for me?"

"Not really," I stammer. "I mean, I was paying more attention to the ball. There was Mrs. Graidey, out walking. And there was a jogger. That's all."

"When was that?" His voice still sounds flat, but he's writing it all down.

"I don't remember—sometime after Mrs. Daine got home." I swallow hard. "I wasn't really paying attention to the time. I'm sorry."

"I understand," Officer Recks says. "Where does this Mrs. Graidey live?"

My mind goes blank. From behind me Dad tells him, "Just down the block, at number 683, on the right side."

"Thank you, sir. Now, about this jogger..."

I struggle to see the figure again, but it's just a gray sweatsuit jogging past me. "I don't know—I didn't see his face because of the hood. Actually, I don't even know if it was a man or a woman. It was just a jogger in a sweatsuit."

"Are you sure you can't give me any better description, Brian?" the officer presses. "Any little detail could help us work out what happened to your friend."

I wince, feeling guilty for not remembering anything clearly, except the thudding of the basketball. If I think hard enough, could I bring the jogger into sharper focus in my mind? Or is it even important?

Dad rests one hand on my shoulder and says, "Look, Officer, a lot of our neighbors walk or jog around here. Sometimes people from town even come here to run, because it's such a quiet street." He pauses involuntarily, as if struck by how unquiet our cul-de-sac is right now. Then he goes on, "Brian's used to tuning everything out when he's playing ball—you know how it is. If he says he doesn't know what he saw, he doesn't know. Maybe one of the other neighbors can tell you who the jogger was."

Officer Recks continues writing for a few moments, then looks up. "Maybe they can, sir," he agrees. He turns briefly back to me. "Thank you for doing your best to help, Brian. If you remember anything else, please get in touch with me." And he hands me a business card, like he's some sort of door-to-door salesman hoping for a follow-up order or something.

Then he asks Mom and Dad if they saw Mr. Daine come home earlier and turns to leave. Dad watches Officer Recks cross the cul-de-sac and start talking to the twins, and looks relieved. Then he turns back to me, standing there holding the business card helplessly. Concern floods his face and he takes the card out of my limp hand and hugs me again. "Oh, Brian, son, I'm so sorry about Amanda. But you can't blame yourself. Nothing you could have done would have changed what happened."

Time warps and tears well up in my eyes, now as then.

I know Dad is trying to make me feel better, but I can't let myself off so easily. If only I'd let her and Cory play ball with us that day . . . I just can't imagine never seeing her again.

I stare at the book, trying to make out the letters and words through the tears, so tired of remembering, tired of reading, wanting only to feel the basketball in my hands, hear it pounding on the court, drowning out everything else, see it soaring through the air and swishing into the hoop. I close my eyes, trying to forget everything except the sweet sensation of putting the ball in the hole, but as I sink into sleep I see Amanda's face, her smiles turning into the bitterness of betrayal. . . .

In the dream, blood-red light drenches the street, even though August sunsets fall much later by the clock. But the screams of the sirens, the buzzing of the police radios, the squad cars' flashing lights and, cutting across everything else, the wrenching sobs of the huddled man can't blot out the whisper that drowns the unending moment in blood-soaked haze.

Help us.

Eventually there are smells: the choking exhaust of the emergency vehicles, the acrid tang of cigarette smoke punctuated by uncrushed stubs that smolder on, the rich bitter fragrance of coffee in wave after wave of styrofoam cups, half drunk and then abandoned.

I swear to myself I will never smoke or drink coffee. Never.

Blue velvet night falls. More investigators come with new chemical smells, their portable lights bleaching the crime scene. So why is everything still burned red and reeking of blood? And why is the whisper still calling me?

Help us.

I walk through the yellow police tape as if I'm a ghost. I weave my way between men wearing uniforms and men wearing suits, past photographers snapping perfect shots and officers wearing plastic gloves. I try not to look at them carefully placing shop tools and cleaning tools and bits of metal and pieces of clothing into plastic bags of different sizes and labeling them neatly. In the center of the maelstrom, seemingly unnoticed by the crowd of strangers, lies the source of the blood that smears my sight, which makes no sense, because the bodies look as if they're hardly bleeding at all. But their presence leaves a red film over the whole scene.

Cory, sagging in his car seat. His mother, collapsed on the hard concrete floor of the garage. It must be so cold, lying there. Why doesn't anyone wrap her in something warm? But I don't stop to worry about her too long. I can't. The whisper keeps calling.

Help us.

I turn to the SUV, to the body draped over the back of the rear seat as if trying to climb over it to freedom, to Amanda. Her long blonde hair hangs down, hiding her face, and dark red streaks mat its silky softness. I can no longer smell the sweet flowery fragrance of her clean hair through the coppery scent of blood that makes me gag. One hand dangles into the back, reaching for the rear door. The side windows are tinted so I can't see her clearly, and I move around to the rear of the vehicle through the squad of investigators, an unnoticed ghost like the ones she and her family have become.

As my eyes fill with bloody tears, I seem to see two figures in the SUV—not just Amanda lying over the seat, reaching toward me, but a girl with tight blonde ringlets, lying awkwardly in the rear storage area as if dropped there, her head tilted at an impossible angle. I blink hard, trying to see clearly through the red film, and then Amanda's dangling fingers twitch. Her hand reaches up toward me. Her head lifts itself so the matted hair falls back, and I can see her eyes, open and staring at me. I realize the other head has moved, too, crumpling the perfect ringlets as it turns to me, still twisted on its broken neck, blue eyes open and looking into my own.

Help us.

Both girls are reaching out to me, begging me to do something. I can't just leave them alone and defenseless. I have to do something, but I don't know what. The whisper that only I seem to hear pounds in my head:

Bri-an,
your fault!
Why not
let us
play ball
with you?

And then the two whispers in chorus:

Help us.

Please!

I sit up to the first hint of dawn, sweat plastering my T-shirt to my chest, my arms running with it.

It's just a dream, I tell myself, a mixture of memory and imagination, tangled up in the book I couldn't put down until I finished, the book that now lies on the bedspread beside me, pages spilled open to admit the horror of poor Mary Phagan's murder, and the lynching of her killer when justice got confused. Only the writer wasn't sure exactly when justice had gotten mixed up. Was it when the jury convicted Leo Frank and condemned him to be hanged for murdering Mary? Or when the governor changed his sentence to life imprisonment? Or when the lynching party dragged Frank out of the prison farm and lynched him? What was the real justice of the murder?

Is that what Mr. Fortner wants us to figure out? Is that why Mary was there with Amanda, both asking me for help? But Amanda was also blaming me for not letting her play ball that day, for not keeping her safe. I shove the book aside. Everything's too mixed up.

I read once that you don't dream in color. Not true. The colors may differ from reality, but they're vivid all the same. I can't let them stay so clear in my mind. I have a game today. I have to think about that, only that, only winning the game. I have to make the pounding of the basketball drown out the girls' pleading whisper.

*"Roll him a little. Keep the left
lung above the wound."*

"I don't have the power."

"You, give him a hand. You, keep the IV lines clear."

CHAPTER

8

I can hardly concentrate on classes, but it doesn't matter. Mr. Fortner drones on about the checks and balances built into the American government, so no branch can become all powerful, and I let it all go right over my head. I've got to stay focused on the game, on getting the ball to Julius past the roughneck Raiders. Coach's voice echoes in my head: "They play hard, really pushing the definition of foul to the breaking point." But I already know that, just the way I know the checks and balances on the court come from the refs' eyes and whistles, and the fact that Warriors play clean, hard, unbeatable ball.

Near the end of the class, Mr. Fortner has us break out into discussion groups with our project partners.

"So—did you get any reading done after practice?" Todd asks, flicking a piece of lint off one black sleeve as if he doesn't care about my answer. "Or do you just veg out in front of the box at night?"

He's never heard of the ABC Club, of course. He doesn't know anything about me except that I play ball. "I don't watch much TV, unless there's a game on," I say, refusing to think about the news story, or my dream.

"Good," he says, after a fractional pause. "Then you had time to look at the book."

I see Julius leaning back in his chair to talk to Shooter, while Leslie shuffles papers on her desk and Shooter's partner, Isabel, looks exasperated. "Or would you rather BS with your teammates than discuss the project?" Todd asks.

"It's game day," I say, turning back to face him. "Everybody's pumped. And yeah, I read the book."

Todd studies me for a minute. "I know there's a game tonight," he informs me. "I always go to the home games, sometimes the away games too, if they're not too far." My surprise must show on my face, because he adds, "No reason you should have seen me."

True enough, although he sort of stands out in a crowd. Out of the corner of my eye I see Mr. Fortner say something to Julius and Shooter, and I concentrate on the project again. "Anyway, I finished the book before I fell asleep last night."

His eyebrows shoot up, and he grins unexpectedly. "I got hooked too. In fact, I went online and found out that the newspaper accounts are archived—you can read the way the investigation and the case unfolded, day by day."

"Really?" I'm surprised, but I have to force enthusiasm into my voice, because news coverage reminds me of the news report last night about Amanda's father.

"Anyway, I was thinking maybe we could do something like the daily unfolding of the case for our presentation," Todd is saying, but his voice is flat now, and his face is closed—back to the guy who doesn't like to stand out in class for knowing anything. "Something visual—if we focus on news reports of the trial, maybe we can hold people's attention better."

"Can you shoot video?" I ask absently. I'm trying to shut out the distractions of the news and Julius and the rest of the team, but my mind keeps sliding away from the project. I think about the game. The students like watching hoops, but it's more than just because it's visual. It's action. It's a lot of guys on the move all the time, shooting baskets, twisting, turning, even running into each other. It's whistles blowing and free shots and near misses and the mind-blowing thrill of not knowing what's coming next. Then I realize I actually am thinking about Todd's suggestion for the project. News is just about what's happened and speculation about what might happen next. It's a cool gimmick that will grab the class's attention for about three minutes. Then they'll see it's just me and Todd on the screen reporting century-old news, and they'll get bored.

"Sure," Todd's saying, enthused again. "I saved and bought a digital video camera, and I make digital movies on my computer."

"Hold it!"

He breaks off, looking wary again.

"That's it," I tell him. "Not just newscasts—why don't we make a movie? a mystery?"

Todd's looking skeptical, but I barrel on, seeing the way to do this and hold everybody's interest, just the way I see a passing lane open up on the court. "We cast the class as the witnesses. Remember, Fortner said we could use other students to help with the presentation itself. And the witnesses from the pencil factory were teenagers, like us. If we make a movie we can keep the action hopping as the mystery unfolds. That'll hold their attention even better than a newscast—both the mystery and seeing themselves on screen!"

Todd's eyes light up at first, but now he's shaking his head. "It's a great idea." His voice has gone flat. "But nobody's going to be willing to make a movie for me."

I look at him again and wonder for the hundredth time what it is about him that rubs us all the wrong way. It's more than the all-black look and the closed-in expression that brand him everybody's target of choice. "Well, maybe you're right about that," I tell him. "But I'm your partner, remember?" I pause a second. "I'm betting they'll do it for me."

He still looks uncertain. "But they'll have to learn lines, and rehearse, and put up with me as well as you. . . ."

I'm shaking my head, the idea getting clearer and clearer. "Picture the guys on the team, and the cheerleaders," I tell him, figuring that's not so hard, since they're all around us. "They're used to working at practice, and then repeating the moves when it counts. Forget dialogue—think action."

Todd shrugs. "Sure, you're right about that. They'd be great at action. But how can you just forget the dialogue?"

"Easy," I say, grinning. "It's 1913, and silent movies are king. We film the action without any dialogue, and add in music over it all plus written screens: 'Oh, sir, unhand me!'"

He's grinning back now. "That's a great idea!" Then a small square of folded paper lands on the notebook in front of me. I glance over to see Julius holding up three fingers.

"No way was that a three-pointer," Todd says dryly.

I almost chuckle, but manage to unfold the paper straight-faced. "What do you say you dump the Turd and cut the rest of the period with us in the can?" it reads.

Oh, really smart, Julius—it's game day, and you want to risk getting benched by cutting class? I slide the paper into my notebook and shake my head slightly. I hear a pained sigh, but ignore it.

"Go on," Todd says, his voice curt. "I don't care."

He's obviously pissed off—why go to the trouble of lying about it? "Look, I'm not kissing off my grade in this class just because Julius wants to blow off some steam before the game," I tell him bluntly. "You've got to stop getting insulted by everything and climbing into that shell of yours."

He looks surprised.

I sigh, exasperated. "We're working together on this thing whether we like it or not, and we're both actually interested in the subject, which is a plus. But I've got a life outside of schoolwork, with the team and all, and—well, you've got a life outside of school too. So we've each got other stuff on our mind. But I'm still going to get this project done." I smile a little at him. "You don't know me well enough to get ticked off at me if some of the other stuff distracts me, okay?"

After a moment, Todd nods. "You're right. I don't know you that well at all."

I'm not sure if that's the answer I want, but I'll take it. "Okay. And I won't take it personally when other stuff distracts you. So what's our next move?"

He hesitates, then says, "What about getting together over the weekend? In addition to the newspaper accounts there's also a bunch of magazine articles about the trial on-line, and a lot more sources I didn't have time to get into. We could work together to read them?"

I hate giving up practice time, but he's right. If we're going to do this movie right, we need to work together on it. I can't expect him to read all the material for me. "Sure. What time?"

"How about Saturday—10:00 at my house?" He proba-bly guesses I was expecting to meet at the library, because he adds quickly, "We can just stay online there without anybody telling us it's somebody else's turn for the com-puter, like they do in the Internet research room at the li-brary."

I nod. "Yeah, it sounds like a plan. 10:00 at your place, which is where?"

He gives me directions and tells me to be sure to come to the door with the lion, which I write off as saving face by being cryptic. Then, after a minute, he asks, "Do you re-ally think your friends will be willing to do this silent movie thing?"

He still sounds a little distant, but I don't see what more I can do about that. I tell him simply, "Keep your fingers crossed for a victory tonight. If we win big, they'll say yes to anything."

Todd smiles, almost reluctantly, as the bell rings.

"Just be glad it's game day," I tell him, as I grab my books and head off to link up with Julius and the other guys. "The timing couldn't be better."

"Well then—Go, team," Todd says.

I grin. I'm sure we've got a winning team, and a win-ning project.

CHAPTER

9

Game day slip-slides into game night. The Raiders come out in a stifling man-to-man pressure defense to shut down Julius, but we're ready for them, dominating the point to rebound. We trade baskets, and after the first quarter we're tied, 22 all. But then Take-away Ray cuts in to steal the ball from the Raiders point guard. He drives down the center of the court only to be picked up by their fast-moving center. But the damage is done. He bounce passes to me on the left, I feed the ball to Julius in the corner, and he pulls up and hits a three-pointer. Keesha and Brittney look at each other, nod, and signal the girls for the cheer:

"We shoot it,

We pass it,

We got a basket!

Warriors, all the way!"

The Raiders take it out and drive hard only to lose the ball to Take-away Ray again. This time he fakes a pass and pulls up to sink an outside jumper for two. And now we've got them playing catch-up, not sure how they lost control of the game. I start driving the ball inside, feeding Julius and Highrise and sometimes taking the shot myself, and

Coach lets Eddie come in a few times. He upsets the Raiders' rhythm, wrestling the ball out of their shooting guard's arms when he gets an easy rebound, proving he's earned Julius's nickname of Wrestler. But then his lazy bounce pass to Ray gets intercepted, and they come back to hit us with a full-court press and score three unanswered baskets before the buzzer sounds for the half. We go into the locker room up 40–32.

I tune Coach out as he tells us what a great game we're playing and assess my team. Take-away Ray and Julius are still hot and only have a foul apiece, but Highrise and Ricochet are tired and not running the court. Ricochet's got two fouls and needs to watch out—I tell him so as we run back onto the court. He nods, and it's Highrise who falls behind, letting the Raiders shooting guard get past him on a fast break to sink his shot. Then the guy steals the inbound pass and adds a layup. Suddenly it's 40-36, and they've got the ball again after Ricochet's attempt at a three-pointer falls short.

But now Take-away Ray's long arm snakes the ball away from one of the Raider forwards. He goes for the shot and misses, but Highrise finds his second wind and is in position to tap it in. Ray steals it again. Instead of driving to the hoop himself, he passes it out to me and I drive inside, then spin around and kick it back out to Julius, who goes up like he's more bird than human, hanging in the air, then letting the ball go so it soars over everyone on the court and lands for three. Ashley does a somersault and the girls chant:

"We play hot,
We play cold,

On the court
We explode!
Warriors! Warriors!"

The band bursts into song behind them as the Raiders take the ball out, but Ray steals the pass, flipping it to me, and I realize all over again how much I love basketball. Practice, drills, even pickup games give you no sense of what it feels like to run down the polished hardwood court, the ball dribbling beside you like it's attached to your hand by an invisible string, until you see the space open up for a pass to the open man to score, or until a path to the hoop suddenly appears as if etched by light straight through the confusion. It's just as thrilling to guard your man, see the uncertainty in his eyes, and know the exact moment to snake one hand in to steal the ball and whirl toward your own goal with it.

It's not just the cheers of the crowd or the thunder of the band, though that background swell makes a perfect counterpoint to the squeak of rubber on the court. It's not just the shouts of the players, the ball's thump off the backboard, its swish through the net—throughout it all, giving the game its shape and its rhythm, the pulsing beat of the ball.

It's that you're never alone on the court. You're part of a team that's bigger than the scattering of boys in the gym. It's a unique camaraderie—for once you're more than a gawky teenager. It's a glimpse of what it will be like to be a man among men, a man who can do anything he sets his mind to. You can win, even against guys who play rough with jabbing elbows and knees and don't respect the game.

At the start of the fourth quarter we've pulled farther

ahead, 58–47. Their center takes the ball out and Take-away Ray makes his move to intercept the pass—but this time the guy reads him. There's no way to draw Take-away into fouling out, so the big center fires a pass straight to him, smashing Ray in the face and knocking him to the floor, blood spurting onto the polished wood.

Guys on both benches are on their feet as whistles cut through the crowd's shouts, but no one actually crosses the sideline onto the court for fear of being ejected. Julius and Shooter go for the Raiders center, but I grab their jerseys, hauling them back. "Don't get thrown out of the game!" I yell at them. "Let the zebras take him out."

The refs do eject him, but they send Take-away to the locker room also, with a broken nose. He wants to get patched up and come back in, but he can barely see with tears and blood streaming down his face. "Win duh game fo' me, guys," he calls blurrily, his voice distorted by his smashed nose. "Sduff it down dere hole!"

The Raiders sneer as he limps out, holding a stained towel to his face.

"Are you going to let them get away with that?" Coach screams. "Get in there and win this one for Ray!"

As if to underscore his anger, the cheerleaders chant:
"Defense, feel it!
Bad pass, steal it!
Warriors own the game—
We'll make you sorry that you came!"

Shooter charges in with fresh legs. He's not as fast at stealing the ball, but they've lost their center and their sixth man plays like he's the only go-to man, not passing, trying to make every shot himself.

"Stay with me, guys!" I tell my team, and we're playing like five men with a single heart and brain. I distribute the passes, and Shooter surprises everyone with a couple of sweet three-pointers before they realize Julius isn't the only one who can score from outside the arc. When they start picking him up at midcourt, I slip inside, take a bounce pass from Highrise and kick the ball out to Julius on the outside corner, who puts it in for another three points.

The Raiders try throwing a few more elbows, hoping Ricochet will retaliate and foul out, but the refs are keeping their whistles hot and sharp. Ricochet hits his free throws, Coach sends in Wrestler a couple of times, and in the end the Raiders point guard fouls out, sending another new player onto the floor. As the seconds count down, their shooting guard attempts two desperation three-point shots. They both clank and we win, we win big, 74–61. We own the court.

I charge off the court with the team—my team—every member an extension of myself. I feel I've played my allotted part in the great scheme of things tonight. I feel more than triumphant, I feel this is what I'm alive for. This isn't any sort of jock escape from the realities of life—this *is* real life.

CHAPTER

10

If only you could hold onto that feeling forever. After the triumph comes the letdown—out of the celebration, into the night, with curfew reminding you to get home before it's too late.

Before we get to that stage, while we're all still high on victory despite Take-away Ray's broken nose, I tell them about the movie.

"Would that mean we'd have to work with the Turd?" Brittney asks, giving a little ladylike shudder.

"That'd be a fate worse than death, all right, Bright Eyes," Julius says, leaning back in the booth at the Pizza Palace, one arm around Brittney and the other around Keesha. He scored 32 points tonight, and he rules. "Anyway—who cares about the stupid projects? You sound almost as bad as Lesbo, Brainman." He makes his voice go all high and whiny. "'Oh, Julius, you are going to ruin my grade! Read this book about American generals! Look how the troops want their commander to rule the country! Look at what MacArthur tried to do compared to the beloved father of our country, George Washington!'"

He goes back to his normal voice while the girls are

shrieking with laughter and the guys are banging their root beer mugs on the table. "I say—if you know the point of the stupid assignment, then you do it, and I'll stand there beside you and look like I care. But don't ask me to rank a school project higher than making my moves on the court—no way that's going to happen."

"You're missing the point, guys," I tell them, taking a swig of soda. "If we're going to keep playing we've got to keep our grades up. We make our presentations right before the game with Jackson. A bad grade from Fortner could put any one of us on the bench that night. Forget everybody else in the class. We've got to score on these projects for the team."

There's a chorus of catcalls, but I wave them down. "We won tonight because we're a team who plays together—every player's there for every other player. We all know this assignment is a time sink and none of us wants to lose all our practice time on it. But if we help each other out on the presentations, we can blow Fortner away with awesome projects and still get in our hoop time. You guys help out with the movie—if one of you wants to do a bunch of posters for a mural or something, then the team shows up to pitch in with the painting. Whatever it takes."

Ashley pops a slice of pepperoni in my mouth and I munch it while the guys think about that. Part of me wishes she wouldn't do things like that, but part of me loves it. I can't imagine Amanda doing anything like that in front of the team.

"Posters is one thing, but learning lines for a movie is going to be a big job," Shooter objects. "How long is all this helping each other out going to take?"

I grin. "No lines, Shooter—it's a silent movie. You all just put on the moves, and we'll add the dialogue in little boxes. It'll be like running plays in the playbook, only there's no guard getting in your face. One afternoon—max."

They still look unconvinced, so I add, "Hey—would I lie to you?"

Highrise shakes his head. "On the court or off, Brainman tells it like it is. Okay, I'm in."

Before the pizza's finished they're all in, and I'm doing the casting in my head.

Ashley drops me off, with Highrise and Darla riding in the back, and I jog up the driveway to grab my ball and sink an easy two-pointer in the gleam of their headlights. The three of them cheer through open windows as the Bomb backs out and the lights cut a swath leading them back toward the main road. I dribble up to the garage, then drop the ball, watch it roll to a dead stop in the grass, and head inside.

Dad's watching TV, half asleep on the couch, but he sits up to check the time, then tells me what a great game it was before going upstairs to bed. I click the remote, flipping through the news for other area scores. Instead, I see the reporter, Natalie Hart, at the county courthouse.

NATALIE HART
Judge Lucian ruled late this afternoon on the last of the preliminary motions in the Daine murder trial, paving the way for jury selection to begin on Monday morning. The prosecution issued a statement that, in the

face of overwhelming evidence, the state expects the trial to be concluded quickly, but Mr. Daine's attorney paints a different picture.

> (New shot: a thin man who looks like a college professor standing in a crowd of reporters waving microphones at him; an identifying caption below reading: "William Rosen, Defense Counsel.")

REPORTER

What is your reaction to the judge's ruling that cameras may not be present in the courtroom during the trial?

WILLIAM ROSEN

It's unfortunate that the trial won't be televised so that more citizens can see justice served, but with or without cameras, despite all the technical evidence that the prosecution claims it is prepared to present, the fact is that my client is innocent of these charges. I believe that the jury will come to that conclusion when they hear the truth from our witnesses and see the gaps in the prosecution's case. Where did the gray fibers found at the scene come from? Where is the murder weapon? Most importantly, where is the real killer?

(Screen cuts back to Natalie Hart.)

NATALIE HART
The defense continues to insist that investigators made up their mind that Mr. Daine
was guilty and concentrated their efforts on
only gathering evidence that proved their
point, allowing the real murderer to remain
at large. Mr. Rosen told reporters that a
jury will realize that as the case is presented. He added that his client only hopes
that the seven months that have passed since
the murder isn't such a long time that it
will make it impossible for unbiased investigators to bring the real killer of the
Daine family to justice.

ANCHORMAN (voice-over)
Thank you, Natalie. Stay tuned for sports
and—

But I don't care about the scores anymore. I thumb the
remote and switch off the news, the good feeling from our
victory washed away by the question of who did kill
Amanda. Could it really have been her own father, after
all? She thought he was a great dad, when he wasn't fighting with her mother or working too hard. She never
seemed uncomfortable around him. In fact, she was thrilled
whenever he was home early enough to spend some time
with Cory and her. Even if she'd been doing something
with me, she'd dump me in favor of being with him. Not

that I was jealous, or anything. I mean—he was her dad. And he was even a hero after that drug bust!

But Amanda told me that day that things were worse at home. . . . Did that mean not just that her dad and mom were fighting more, but that she was actually scared of being around her parents—maybe even scared of her dad? Was that why she begged me to let her stay with me that afternoon?

Something the defense attorney says sticks in my head, about gray fibers found at the scene. I think back to that long afternoon, struggling for hours to make the perfect shot. The jogger who ran by had been wearing a gray sweat-suit, hadn't he? Or she? I shiver, even though the house is warm. Could that jogger have been involved in the killing? Then I think about all the joggers and walkers who turn around in the cul-de-sac on a daily basis when the weather's good. The police probably checked it out and found out the jogger was just some neighbor.

I shake my head in disgust. Maybe the defense attorney is trying to distract people from the facts of the case by raising questions that don't matter, the way I'm stressing out over an innocent jogger in order to distract myself from my guilt at letting Amanda go to the pool when I should have let her play ball with us instead.

"I've got traces of blood in the airway,
but no airflow behind it."

"There's a swelling in the belly.
I think he's losing blood internally."

"You, keep the head elevated to left lung level.
Increase the IV flow. You, get more Ringer's."

CHAPTER
11

Snapshot of Todd's house as Mom drives up: tiny buds on the flowering pear trees, hints of the white cotton-candy fluffballs of blossoms to come, azalea bushes still tangled sticks, but dotted with the promise of leaves and bright funnel-shaped flowers.

"Nice," Mom says, meaning: a lot like our own front yard.

Beyond the landscaping stands a neat ranch-style house with brick walls and a sharply sloping roof. The only weird thing about the place is that there are two front doors. Now I see why Todd told me to come in the door with the lion. One door is painted tan to match the shutters, and features a bronze lion knocker that seems to be snarling more of a warning than a welcome. The other door is painted dark brown, with a push-button ringer at its side. In front of that one, a sign announces Warren Pollian, Attorney-at-Law. I've seen doctors who have their office at home before, but not an attorney. Strange.

Mom's eyes pause at the sign, then light on me, and she smiles. "I just want you to know how proud of you I am," she says.

"Mom . . ." I feel the heat creeping up the back of my neck.

"I'm proud of the way you played last night," she barrels on, ignoring my embarrassment, "and I'm proud of the way you're tackling this project. I know how important basketball is to you, but school matters, too." She laughs, a little self-consciously. "I know I didn't want to hear anybody telling me that while I was in high school, and you don't want to hear it now. But I think this sounds like a good assignment and I'm glad to see you giving it your all."

More blushing, mumbling, then I'm finally released with my promise to call her on her cell when we're done. At least she didn't insist on meeting Todd and his mommy before letting me spend the day here.

As she drives off, I wonder if she misses playing the guitar at the craft fairs with Dad. She says she knows how important basketball is to me—what's important to her?

Then I'm climbing the front steps to the lion knocker and the door swings open to reveal Todd's cautious face. "Thanks for being on time," he says.

That surprises me a little. If I say I'll do something, I always do it. "Mom brought me," I say unnecessarily, and he nods, like that explains it, even though it has nothing to do with my being here when I said I would.

"Pretty nice place," I say, stepping inside and wondering if my high-tops are clean enough to walk on the beige carpet. "Have your folks lived here a long time?" I contrast our house (with its lived-in look from two hardworking parents and one teenage son) to the just-vacuumed look of this place, with its chrome and glass tables and pale upholstery. It's not expensive, imported furniture, I guess, but it's newer and shinier than our stuff. I guess lawyers make pretty good money. Of course, since Dad hand-carved our furniture, it's a lot fancier in its own way.

Todd shoots me a sidelong glance. "My brother and sister-in-law have lived here since they got out of school." He lays particular emphasis on the brother and sister part. "My brother's the Warren Pollian on the shingle—he got out of law school and Elise graduated from medical school about five years ago, and they got married after he passed the bar. I've been living with them for nearly three years now."

He doesn't volunteer why, and I don't press. Maybe his parents died or something. I just follow him up carpeted stairs that don't creak underfoot but don't have that warm gleam of polished hardwood, either.

And then I get a load of his room. Except for his black jacket hanging on a chrome chair back, it's all white: white walls, white carpet, white curtains, white desk, with a white bubble-top computer on top of it that looks like an R2-D2 droid.

Todd hits a key, and the flat panel screen comes alive. He gestures to a stack of paper in the white and silver printer tray on the otherwise empty desktop. "I printed out the series of magazine articles this morning, but the newspaper accounts don't print out as neatly. Do you want to read the printouts, or the news articles online? Or talk about the movie idea?"

He's staring at the screen as if the answer doesn't matter to him. I see a second chrome chair and turn it around so I can sit resting my arms along the top of the seat back. "I saw you cheering at the game."

He nods, ducking his head a little as if embarrassed at

being caught acting like an ordinary fan. But then he says, "I like basketball. And I liked the way you won last night. Congratulations."

I smile. "Yeah, we did win. We won big."

He grins. "You did." He gives up all pretense of watching his browser load the newspaper archives and turns. "So what happened?"

"So I asked them about our movie."

I sit there deadpan until he starts to laugh. "And they said? Come on, Brian—give!"

I laugh, too. "And they said they're all in."

"Yes!" Todd pumps one fist. I half expect him to high-five me, but we're not teammates, just partners. He points to the pile of printouts. "Well, if they're all in, we'd better get this movie ready to shoot. You want the magazine articles or the newspapers?"

"I'll take the printouts," I say, figuring he'd probably rather be the one using the computer, since it's his. "The real question is what we're supposed to have learned from the case. You know, what the point of the assignment is."

Todd's scrolling through a yellowed article on the screen. "Maybe just that everybody's in a rush to make sure outsiders get the shaft."

"Well, it's true that Frank was an outsider, but if he killed the girl and got punished for it, even if the case got rushed through court awfully fast, that doesn't mean he got the shaft." But that gets me thinking. Todd's an outsider—does he identify with Leo Frank?

Todd looks at me again. "What about the witnesses who lied under oath? And why did the governor commute Frank's sentence to life imprisonment instead of execution?

And why did Frank insist up to the end that he was innocent? Those magazine stories make it look like Frank got railroaded in court. I think we need to keep an open mind as to whether or not he actually killed her."

I nod, imagining the lynch party that dragged Leo Frank out of the prison farm. "It sounds like there was a lot of public pressure on the governor. Do the newspaper accounts say anything more about that?"

"You start on the printouts and I'll see what these say." Todd turns back to the screen. "And I've found references to some books that weren't in the school library."

He's gone out of his way to find all of the material so far. "Give me the list, and I'll ask Mom if we can stop by the public library on the way home," I tell him. "Then we can link up to go over them."

He nods, skimming the newspaper article. Then he sits back and frowns. "Maybe," he says slowly, "maybe what we're supposed to learn from this case is how the justice system works—or doesn't work."

"You mean, if Leo Frank got railroaded and was actually innocent, the justice system isn't working right?"

"Yes." Todd swivels in his chair toward me. "My brother Warren specializes in civil-rights cases. He's always saying that the way the justice system is designed is beautiful in its fairness, but people screw it up in action. Policemen have a gut feeling that somebody's guilty, so they arrest him without bothering to go over all the evidence."

He leans forward, getting into his stride. "Witnesses say what their lawyers tell them to say, whether it's true or not. Prosecutors are so determined to have a perfect win record in court that they slant the evidence. Sometimes they even destroy evidence, or hide it when they're supposed to be honest about it, or get witnesses to say what they want them to say instead of the whole story."

I suppress a twinge of guilt. I told the police the whole story about Mrs. Graidey and the mysterious jogger. At least, as much as I remembered.

But Todd doesn't notice. He just goes on, "And a lot of people can't afford high-price defense attorneys. But public defenders have such a heavy caseload and so little budget that they can't hire their own experts and challenge the prosecution. On one level, Warren says, it's individual people who get hurt, but on a larger scale it's everybody's civil rights that suffer. It's the Constitution itself that gets hurt."

I nod, making myself concentrate on our project. "So, if that happened to Leo Frank—if his civil rights were taken away from him and the Constitution got hurt—and your brother says it's still happening today, then we didn't learn anything, and history's still repeating itself."

"That's right." Todd slumps back. "I think that may be exactly what we're supposed to find out. Is the justice system all right, in spite of everything, or has it been damaged so badly that it can't be fixed?"

I swallow, thinking of Mr. Daine in jail. "Then what we need to find," I say slowly, "is exactly what went wrong in the Leo Frank case, and if there are other cases like that today—you know, cases where other innocent guys get railroaded."

Todd nods. "I'm sure I can find a database like that online. It's the kind of thing the American Civil Liberties Union would get up in arms about." He bookmarks his page, then enters in a new URL. While he's waiting for the site to open, he says, "You know who would have loved this assignment? Amanda. Talk about someone who got up in arms over a cause!"

I can't say anything.

Todd turns to me, his expression stricken. "Sorry—that just slipped out. I guess she's on my mind these days, with her father in the news, and not knowing what really happened. It's got to be worse for you—I'm really sorry."

I guess he's inviting me to say something, but it's none of his business how I feel about Amanda or her father, or anything. When I don't answer he says, quietly, "I miss her too, you know? I mean—not the way you do, but . . ." His voice trails off. "I just miss her. That's all."

It's stupid to feel jealous over somebody who's dead. I mean, he probably misses her because she was one of the few people who treated him like a human being instead of a turd. Anyway, neither of us can have her now. But I miss her too much to share the feeling with Todd.

CHAPTER

12

Mom is so shocked when I ask if we can stop at the library on our way home, she nearly runs a stop sign and has to slam on the brakes. And when we get there, she tells me there's no hurry getting back to the house—take my time—in spite of the fact I know she's got a stack of paperwork to do for Dad waiting.

But once in the building, it's harder than I expect. I take the list Todd gave me and fumble with the computer catalog. It should be Amanda sitting here, clicking on options, with me looking over her shoulder. I tell myself it can't be that hard to find specific books. People do it all the time, after all. But some are unavailable or at one of the university libraries. We'd have to go into Bloomington or Indianapolis to see them. One I don't see listed at all. When I ask a librarian, she says it's too old and they probably couldn't even get it through interlibrary loan, although she'll try if I want to fill out a request for it. I have no clue what interlibrary loan is, though I'm guessing it's a way for you to borrow a book from another library. But does it cost a lot? How long does it take?

Amanda probably knew all about interlibrary loan. I

used to come here with her when she was all excited about a book she wanted me to read, but I don't think I've been through the doors since she was killed.

But I do see one title listed as being on the shelves—a book that was published just last year, even though you'd think the case wouldn't matter to anybody by now. Scratch that thought, however—it still matters to Mr. Fortner. I write down the call number for the book and head downstairs where the nonfiction is. Now I'm lost in a maze of book spines with faded titles and tiny, barely legible labels with their own call numbers that seem light years different from mine. It's so much easier when a teacher just hands you a book—or when all I had to do was trail along after Amanda. She had a knack for suggesting books that really grabbed me. Or maybe I just liked them because she did.

"Is it—could it be—a jock? I didn't know you guys could read!"

I turn around fast, feeling faked out, and see Leslie with a stack of books. Obviously she knows her way around this place.

"Hi, Leslie." If she'd wipe the sneer off her face, she might be pretty—not so beautiful as Amanda, or even Ashley, but pretty. She'd need a major attitude readjustment, though.

"Hi, yourself," she retorts. "Why aren't you out with a ball attached to your brain?" She looks around skeptically. "Did Todd manage to drag you in here to do some work? I'll have to make him tell me how he does it."

"Actually, Todd's working on his computer while I'm here getting some books," I tell her, stung. "Where's Julius?"

Her eyes narrow. "You tell me. He's made it clear he wants nothing to do with this project, and Mr. Fortner says I'd better find a way to make him work or take a lower grade."

I sigh. "Look, treating a guy like he's dirt because he's an athlete isn't going to win you any points with Julius. Have you tried being nice and treating him like he's human? It's working for Todd and me so far."

"I don't want to win any points with Julius Malik!" she practically shouts. Then she looks around, like she's spooked she might get in trouble for making noise in a library. "I just want him to do his fair share of the project."

"Julius always does his fair share on the team," I tell her. "And we're all helping each other out on these projects, to make sure we all get through this with decent grades. So if you're not happy with Julius's contribution, maybe the problem is you—not him!"

For a moment Leslie looks ready to throw her stack of books at me, and I prepare to sidestep. Then she says, "You jocks—all sticking up for each other and acting like the rest of us are so far below you we're not worth your time!" The distaste in her voice is chilling. She's just a geek. What could any of the athletes have done to upset her so much? "You guys think you can get away with anything just because you get your pictures in the paper and college coaches beg you to come play for them—well, I'm glad Mr. Fortner sees through you, even if it costs me my grade. Because if it costs me, it'll cost Julius more!"

"Okay, okay! Why don't you just go check out your books or whatever and leave me alone to find mine?" She's not worth arguing with. But I make a mental note to warn

Julius he'd better get with the program. She sounds like she could get nasty.

Instead of leaving, Leslie takes a step closer to me. I almost step backward, deeper into the shelving, but then I remember she's just a girl, even if she has a heavy armload of books that could flatten my foot. She peers over them at the scrap of paper in my hand and snorts. "You're like all the other jocks, Brian. When it comes right down to it, you're stupid too. The 360s are over there, not in the 700s. You probably only feel halfway safe here because you're near the sports books." She shakes her head and turns away. At the far end of the aisle she pauses to look back. "I don't know what Amanda ever saw in you. She was worth ten of you."

Numbly, I watch her leave. Then I find my way over to the 360s and pick up the book I wanted. I stare at the cover. Another photograph of the lynched man, and one of the girl with blonde ringlets—she looks like the girl from my dream.

Help us.

How can I help her—or Amanda—now?

I know Mom's waiting on me, and I don't want to waste too much of her time, but if I go upstairs now she'll see something's wrong with me. Instead, I pull out a hard wooden chair, sit down at a library carrel, and start leafing through the book. I'm not taking in the words, though— just thinking about how uncomfortable the chair is. My desk chair is hardwood, too, but the way Dad made it the seat and back encircle me. I could sit there for hours. If I could keep still, anyway. I'd rather be in motion. I wish I had my basketball with me. Even just rolling it back and forth on the table might make me feel better.

I take a deep breath and start looking at the book more carefully. It's the same stuff, about Mary Phagan going to get her pay before the parade and getting killed instead, about the circus they called a trial, with the prosecutor suppressing evidence and rehearsing his witnesses to say what he wanted, even though some things weren't true. He prepared Jim Conley especially well, getting him to say that Leo Frank had girls in his office all the time and that Frank told him he'd killed Mary Phagan and ordered him to take the body downstairs. And he paid Conley for his testimony afterward, as well. Then there was the same stuff about the governor commuting the sentence. I flip past the riots, past the lynching, past the governor's abrupt escape from the state he thought he was serving.

There's a whole chapter on Mrs. Frank trying to get her husband pardoned after his lynching. She kept trying (and kept getting turned down) until her death. But the book doesn't stop there. The last chapter is about Alonzo Mann.

I have to stop and think a minute to remember that he was the office boy. He'd been working in the office that morning, but he left before Mary came in to get her pay. He just mumbled his testimony at the trial and wasn't even cross-examined. Apparently the lawyers on both sides agreed he was just a kid who hadn't seen anything important.

But he had.

Fourteen-year-old Alonzo Mann had seen the real murderer carrying Mary's body—not Jim Conley helping Leo Frank, like the prosecution's star witness had claimed, but Conley all by himself! Conley told Alonzo that if he said anything, he'd kill him, and when Alonzo asked his mother what to do she said he should keep quiet. She said she didn't want the family involved in the case. And his father assured him that Leo Frank would never be convicted anyway, so he should just forget what he had seen.

Alonzo was called as a witness at the trial, but nobody asked him if he'd seen anyone that day. Neither lawyer asked him anything about Jim Conley. And without his eyewitness testimony and his information about Conley threatening him, Frank was convicted.

Alonzo kept silent until 1982, nearly seventy years after the murder. Then, saying he couldn't live with his guilt at not speaking out, Alonzo came back to Atlanta and finally gave his evidence. He even agreed to take both a psychological stress analysis test and a polygraph test, and both confirmed he was telling the truth about what he had seen the day Mary Phagan was murdered.

The gray fibers . . . I keep thinking about Mr. Daine's attorney talking about them on the news, and about the jogger I saw that day in the baggy gray sweatsuit. Apparently Alonzo didn't think his evidence would have made a difference at the time, not compared to how dangerous it would have been to speak up. But it could have saved Leo Frank. Could my seeing the jogger be more important than I thought?

"Brian?"

My head snaps around, but it's not Leslie again. It's Mom, looking worried.

"I thought you must have gotten lost down here," she tries to joke, then gauges my expression more clearly. "Are you all right?"

I open my mouth, then close it. I don't know whether to nod or shake my head. "I—It's—it's this history project. I just found something totally unexpected in this book."

"Oh!" She looks relieved, and even laughs a little. "Well, that's good, isn't it?"

I can nod at that. "Yeah, I think it's really good. I think I just found out what the point of this whole assignment is."

As we drive home, I try to call Todd on my cell phone, but he's not there. His sister-in-law promises she'll tell him I found something exciting in my research. She sounds as pleased as Mom about the way we're working on the project. But I don't know if exciting is the right word. I think it's more like scary.

"I've lost all pulse and pressure.
I think he's gone."

"We are NOT giving up. Keep working!"

CHAPTER

13

Sunday morning I find myself sitting in Dad's wood shop, feeling the warmth of the sunlight streaming through the dome. I haven't wanted to spend much time in here these last months, not without Amanda. But I think about what Todd said—how much she'd like this assignment. So even though it feels a little weird, I take the library book out to the wood shop, maybe like sharing it with Amanda's spirit or something.

We don't go to church on Sunday—that's usually when Mom and Dad work on the accounts for the business. Amanda's mother was big on taking the kids to church, but afterwards Amanda would come up here and we'd sit together and play guitars or just watch the patterns of sunlight and shadow dance above the dome and talk. I can still hear her voice. "This is the way to worship the Almighty and give thanks for His creation."

I pass by the main worktables, dragging one finger through the dust—plain old gray dust, instead of the rich-scented wood dust I remember from when I was a kid. Dad hardly ever has time or energy to work in here anymore. Is that what happens to everyone? You only have so much time, so you end up spending it doing what other people tell you you're good at, best at, and so what if you really care about something different, something you're only okay at but you love? I don't think it's supposed to be that way.

I pause at the foot of the steps leading to the carving tower. Sun spills down the stairway from the roof's glass dome, a cascade of dust motes floating in the rays of light. I squint upward, nearly blinded. As shifting branches cast their shadows, I can almost see the edge of Amanda's skirt swirling across the opening above me. I climb into the sunlight, holding the book. *Todd was right, Amanda—here's a cause for you, a wrong to right. And what about me? Did I really see something important the day you were killed? Did I do enough in telling the police? Should I do something more? I don't want to be like Alonzo Mann.*

Dear God, if You've got Amanda safe beside You, please— can You, or can she, help me see what to do?

A roaring engine shatters the hope that God or Amanda is going to answer. Who's got a loud ride like that around here? I drop the book on Dad's carving bench and head down to the door, half relieved at the excuse to get out of the place, and half chilled at the thought of a stranger in our cul-de-sac (*another stranger, this one drawing attention to himself, not like that other one*). I'm totally unprepared for the motorcycle stopping in front of my garage door. The rider gives the engine a final rev, kicks the stand down with one black boot, dismounts, and turns toward me, faceless behind a helmet visor as shiny and impenetrable as an oil slick, and taller under the hoop even than Julius.

I walk forward, feeling strangely like the sheriff meeting

the gunslinger in a western, wishing I had a six-gun and feeling silly for the wish. Then the rider smoothly sweeps off his helmet, sets it on the back of his bike, and bends to catch up my basketball. He turns, bouncing it once to get a feel for it, and goes up for a jump shot that sweeps neatly through the net for three points. He grins, and the faceless rider is transformed.

"Todd?" I hear the incredulity in my own voice.

Paul and Matt Francis from across the street dash up, far more fascinated by the gleaming silver and black bike than the perfect basketball shot.

"Give me a ride!" Matt demands.

"No," howls Paul, "me first!"

Before I can warn the twins that Todd's not like Julius so they better clear off, Todd drops down on one knee to bring his face closer to the twins' level. "You like the bike?" he asks, his voice friendly instead of aloof.

Both boys nod enthusiastically. Matt tentatively runs one hand across the handlebars the way he'd stroke a fierce, beautiful creature. Paul reaches for the shiny helmet.

Todd lifts it first, and holds it above the little boy's head like a crown. "Gee," he says, sounding regretful as he lowers the helmet and the sun-bleached head disappears into its depths. "I think it's a little big for you."

"I don't need a helmet," Paul objects.

"I tell you what," Todd suggests. "Why don't you ask your mom if it's all right for you to ride my bike without a helmet? If she comes over and tells me yes, then we can all go for a ride."

The twins' faces fall, but they both understand. And they're not mad at Todd for not giving them rides, the way they get mad at me when I tell them to get lost while the guys are playing a half-court game.

"How fast can you go on this?" Matt asks, pausing at the foot of the driveway.

Todd stands up and grins down from his height. "Faster than the wind," he assures them. The two boys beam up at him and dash back home, making vroom-vrooming noises as they ride imaginary motorcycles across the street.

"You're a born diplomat," I say. As Todd smiles, less openly than for the kids, I add, "And that is one impressive bike," and he lights up again. "I can't believe you never bring it to school—people there would be as wowed as the twins." I'm thinking they wouldn't pick on him so much if they could label him something cool, like a biker.

"Considering how they treat me at school," he says dryly, "I'm not sure my bike would survive the experience. I've put too much work into it to just stand back and watch it get trashed."

He's got a point. I scoop up the basketball and add, "Well, you're a born player. Why didn't you try out for the team?"

Todd's face closes. He shrugs. "I like playing ball, but I'm not much for team sports. Sorry." He doesn't sound the least bit regretful. "Elise said you called and sounded pretty intense. So what did you find in the books that got you so revved up? Oh—I found some excellent cases that are such clear railroad jobs they've even been on those TV investigative reporting shows."

I'd almost forgotten about the other cases he said he'd be looking for. "Great!" I say automatically. "But this book—I could only get one of the titles on your list—we'd have to go to the university libraries for the others, and one of the books was out of print and they didn't even think they could get on interlibrary loan. But the other was . . . surprising."

That's when I realize the book's still in Dad's wood shop. I can't see how to tell Todd he's not wanted in there, so I figure we can just get the book and come on down. But when he follows me inside he stops, looking up toward the tower. "This is beautiful," he says softly. Then he sneezes. "And dusty."

"It's my dad's workshop," I explain, climbing the stairs. "He used to spend hours carving in here, but now his construction business eats up so much of his time he scarcely gets in here at all."

Todd looks around the circular tower, taking in the way the round worktable in the center is lit by the dome above so that no matter what hour of the day you start to work you have natural light. He touches the back of the work seat that's mounted on a track to circle around the table at the slightest nudge and nods. "Very sweet," he says softly, almost reverently. Then he sees Dad's tools hanging in their places. He looks up at me. "Your father must be a real artist."

I nod. "He was—he is, but he doesn't have much time for carving these days."

Todd shakes his head. "That's a crime." Then he sees the book. "So what's the revelation?"

He's standing between me and the stairs, so I can't just lead the way back down. "The other books were written a long time ago, not too long after the murder happened. But this one was published last year, so it's got newer information. I marked the place—read it for yourself."

He glances at the work seat, but chooses not to sit in it and instead leans against the door jamb. I'm not sure whether he's thinking that's Dad's seat, or merely that it's too dusty. But it doesn't matter. In less than a minute he straightens up. "Alonzo Mann saw Conley carrying the body all by himself! He knew Leo Frank had nothing to do with it." He stares at me over the top of the book. "He knew the truth, and never said anything until he was in his eighties—when it was too late to do any good at all."

"Remember, the kid was only fourteen," I point out. "He said Conley threatened to kill him if he told, and he was scared. And his mother didn't help. He asked her what to do, and she said not to tell."

"Fourteen isn't that much younger than we are," Todd says flatly. "He was old enough to be working full-time—that means he was old enough to make up his own mind about what to do. And he knew he should have told. That's why he felt guilty all those years and left Georgia and never came back. He was punishing himself."

"That's a little harsh," I tell him.

"I just don't understand how anybody could do that," Todd says, his dark eyebrows drawn together in a frown that looks like a cross between disgust and total noncomprehension.

"It's not like she was someone special to him," I point out.

Todd's looking at me strangely. "So what?" he asks.

"I mean—it's not like she was his sister, or his girlfriend, or something." Even in my own ears, it sounds a lot like trying to make excuses for really messing up.

"But it's not about her," Todd says, carefully enunciating each word as if he's explaining it to a very small, not very bright, infant. "Mary was already dead." As if I didn't know. "Alonzo couldn't have changed that, but he could have gotten justice for her. Instead, he was responsible for Leo Frank's death. He could have prevented that, but he didn't say anything. That's why he felt guilty all those years. He didn't get justice for either one of them." When I don't answer, he adds, "And he deserved to feel guilty, too. There's no excuse for what he did."

"He was scared of Conley. And he didn't think it was up to him—he expected the system to do its job and find the real killer, like it's supposed to work." I demand, "Haven't you ever been afraid?"

Todd looks at me, eyebrows raised into inverted Vs. "Afraid? Me? I used to get beaten up almost every week of my life until I got this growth spurt. I've been stuffed into lockers more times than most people get on buses. In fact, unless my memory deceives me, more than a few of those times were engineered by your jock pals."

I duck my head, remembering. It always seemed like a stupid kid prank. I never did it to him myself, and I know I could have told the other guys to lay off and they might even have listened to me, but I deliberately tried to ignore what was happening. I didn't want to get involved in something that might put me at odds with my teammates. "Sorry," I mutter.

"I survived." Todd shrugs. "Of course, I made it that last time only because your girlfriend caught hotshot Julius in the act and then yelled at you to come let me out until you gave in and decided to play hero—" He breaks off, his neck flushing. "Oh, man—open mouth, insert foot. I'm sorry, Brian."

Had I wondered why Julius and the other guys shut Todd up in his locker? Maybe it's because, when he's not being a one-man spokesman for truth, justice, and the American way, Todd is an insufferable prick. Amanda never thought so, of course. That's why she made me let him out. Julius just shook his head and loped off, but she stared at me with those accusing brown eyes that wouldn't let any crime pass. . . .

I feel as if the air has left the carving tower and I'm underwater, drowning in her accusation, then I make myself breathe again. I'm not the guy who locked Todd in his locker—I'm the one who let him out, that once-upon-a-time day not so long ago. I didn't want to get involved, but Amanda caught sight of me and called me and I came, like always, even though I wish she wouldn't put me on the spot. I can still see her staring hard at me until I make Todd tell me his locker combination through the grates in the metal door, until I spin the dial and let him out, until she turns her gaze into warm brown sympathy for him, and lets me off the hook. Is she looking down at me from heaven with that unrelenting expression, accusing me now of not helping her?

"Brian?"

The voice comes from a long way away, farther than beyond a metal locker door. Todd's voice, concerned. "Are you okay? Really—I'm sorry. It was a stupid thing to say."

I shrug. "It doesn't matter. You were right, on both counts. Amanda stopped the guys from bothering you when she could, and she was my girlfriend. That doesn't mean I want to talk about her."

"You should," he says quietly. "You've changed since last year, Brian. It's like part of you died with her. She had a lot of friends who miss her. You should keep her memory alive in you by talking about her with them, instead of shutting out everybody and everything except basketball."

And what would Todd Pollian know about loving someone and losing her? Even if his words do come too close to Julius's advice for comfort. I glare at him. "Well, you should fight back! Why did you just let the guys shove you into your locker like that?"

"Does not fighting back make it all right?" He gives me a crooked smile.

"No—but if you'd ever fought back, guys would have stopped picking on you."

He eyes me more seriously. "Do you really believe that?"

I guess I do. But maybe it's not the whole truth. When I don't say anything he says, "I don't believe in violence. I mean—I don't believe in meeting violence with more violence. Fighting back just makes things worse. So I won't fight."

I frown. "But you have to fight for what you think is right! If somebody's picking on you, you fight back and they leave you alone. Or do you like sucking it up, or like being a martyr, or something sick like that?"

His face closes. "No, I don't. And I do fight back, but not with my fists. I fight with words. I fight by doing the right thing, or at least doing things the way I think is right, and apologizing when I'm wrong."

I understand what he's saying on one level. But I don't understand it on another. Fighting back his way didn't make anyone leave him alone until he got so big he intimidated everyone even though he wouldn't fight. I don't understand this guy. And I don't want him in the tower one minute longer. This is my place and Amanda's. There's no room for Todd in it.

As if he reads my mind, he suggests, "So—you want to work in the house instead?"

"Sure," I tell him, relieved. I grab the book and brush past him quickly, leading the way out of the wood shop.

CHAPTER

14

When I open the front door to the house, Todd's eyes widen again at the sight of the gleaming hardwood entrance with the stairway right in the middle, leading upstairs to a landing that branches off into my parent's bedroom and office. The stairs divide the ground floor, with the kitchen and dining room on the right, and the living room and my bedroom on the left. The rooms aren't big, but the effect of the two-story entrance gives you the feeling you're in a much larger house.

"Wow. This place is—impressive."

"Dad built it himself, like the workshop." I tell him how Dad blocked out the shape and got the walls and roof up so we could move in while he finished it. He started with the first floor so we had a kitchen, places to sleep, and space for him to work on his plans. Then he built his workshop, and finally he finished the upstairs. "I was just a kid at the time, and it was fun living in an unfinished house that was still changing all around you."

Todd cocks one eyebrow. "Yeah? And what did your mother think of cleaning and cooking in an unfinished house?"

I realize I've never really considered that. She just put up with it, but I can't remember her getting angry. "She never complained," I say slowly. Then I remember those were the days when she and Dad still went to craft fairs with his guitars. "Actually, I can't remember her worrying too much about cleaning. She seemed to have fun planning things out with Dad."

He studies me a moment, then smiles. "Sounds like nice parents."

"I guess," I say, shrugging. They're just my parents—I love them, but I don't especially think about them being nice.

Todd's eyes drift over the cabinets that flank the halls leading to my room and the kitchen. The one on the kitchen side has a bunch of stuff Mom has collected over the years, everything from family photos to candles shaped like castles and dragons to tiny wood carvings Dad has made her—miniature mice playing guitars for dancing rabbits and squirrels and chipmunks. The cabinet on the other side holds my basketball trophies—all the way from the little trophies every kid on the youngest youth basketball teams gets up through Most Valuable Player trophies from basketball camp and playoff trophies.

Todd straightens up to his full height. "That's impressive, too," he says, nodding toward the assortment of little bronze figures on their marble stands.

"Thanks," I say. I know I sound a little short, and add, apologetically, "I was going to put them on a shelf in my room, but Dad wanted to put them out front. It's neat, but it's kind of embarrassing, too."

I point out the way to my room, then go into the

kitchen for some water and Gatorade, but Todd follows me. "How come your room is down here instead of upstairs?"

I let him choose what he wants from the fridge. "It was supposed to be upstairs, but I'd spent so long in that corner down here I liked it. And Dad said a guy needed some freedom." Upstairs there was a master bedroom for my parents, a room that should have been a nursery for my baby brother or sister, and an office for Dad. But the baby never came, and sometime after Dad started up the contracting business, Mom turned the nursery into her office to handle his paperwork. Not that Todd needs to know any of that.

We head over to my room on the far side of the staircase, and he stops in the hallway again, pausing to look through the open doorways into the dining room and living room. "This place is really something," he comments, studying the trophy white-tailed deer Dad has mounted in the living room along with a smaller deer and a good-sized elk he got once on a trip out west. "And it has really big heads."

"Yeah, Dad's got this group of friends—a couple of guys he knew in high school, and some guys who own some wild hill country in Kentucky. They get hunting licenses, and Dad pulls out his rifle and cleans it, and he takes a long weekend down there every fall. They all sit around and tell stories and don't shave." I grin, thinking Dad always comes home from those weekends looking happier and more like the way I remember him. "Dad usually bags something, and we have venison for a while, but that one's special. It's a perfect one-shot kill that he'd tried to make for a long time."

Todd doesn't say anything, just looks at the deer for a

while. Finally I ask him if he's ready to get to work, and he nods, distant again, and follows me into my room.

I look around at my half-made bed with its threadbare basketball pillowcase exposed, the open closet door, notebooks and papers and sports magazines scattered on my desk, the hamper with its lid up so I can sink shots (only clothes lack the perfect spin of a basketball, so they don't all go in the hole, and loose T-shirts litter the carpet around the base). "If I'd known you were coming I would have cleaned up," I try to apologize, remembering his uncluttered room. I shove the closet door closed, slam the lid on the hamper, and try to push in a few half-open dresser drawers, which is tough since I just stuff my underwear and shirts inside.

Todd smiles. "That's okay. Even Elise tells me my obsessive neatness is unnatural, especially in someone so closely related to Warren." He studies the basketball posters and framed photos of the team up on my walls. Then he sees my guitar propped in the corner. He drops his pack on my bed and eyes the guitar. "Very nice work," he says, admiration clear in his voice. He reaches for it, then draws his hand back, as if remembering I'd clearly wanted him out of the wood shop.

"Go on," I tell him, and he lifts it carefully, turning it around in his hands to examine the carved inlays.

"Dad made that," I say, thinking how Amanda and I used to sit side by side with our guitars. We both play, but with her songbird voice it was real music, not just the thin strumming I do alone. The polished wood is dusty now, and when Todd plucks a string it's badly out of tune.

"Sounds like you don't play much."

I shake my head. "I'm not that good on my own."

He sets it down gently, not saying anything.

Somehow, knowing about Alonzo Mann makes the Leo Frank movie all fall into place. "I was thinking we should use everybody to film the murder and then the inquest and trial," I tell him, clearing off a workspace on my desk. "Then we can tell about Governor Slaton and the prison farm, and use actual photos of the lynching. But let's not film the ending until after they leave—then we can make me up to look really old, so I don't look anything like my role in the first part of the movie, and cut to the 1980s so you can film me giving Alonzo's testimony. That way they'll be surprised like the rest of the class when they see the movie."

"Good thinking!" Todd smoothes my bedspread over a few lumps and sits there, pulling a notebook out of his backpack. We work out the casting and plan how we'll direct everybody so things can move as quickly as possible during the shoot. I don't want the guys to get bored and start something with Todd that will ruin the project. Even if I thought it was a waste of time in the beginning, I really want to do this right.

"Since Alonzo is more important now," Todd says thoughtfully, "we need someone to play him as a kid. But it needs to be someone who looks younger than the rest of the cast."

I think about Julius's brother, but he's too young.

"What about one of those little kids from across the street?" Todd asks. "They'll be on top of us anyway, and if we get them involved it might keep them under control. The height difference will make it clear that Conley's an adult and Alonzo is a kid."

I nod. "Bribery—that's very good thinking."

Todd grins. "I have my moments."

We plan out simple costumes and where we'll shoot the movie—some of it in the cul-de-sac, some of it in my house. "I can mask the backgrounds afterwards and put in something else, more like a courtroom," Todd explains. "It's getting the actors to do the right thing on camera that matters." And that's my job to deliver. I hope I can keep them moving in the right direction on camera as smoothly as they do on the court.

Satisfied that we've got the movie under control, we stop by the kitchen to toss the plastic bottles into the recycling bin, then run into Dad on our way to the front door. The tired expression drops from his face and he straightens up, smiling.

"Hey guys, taking a rest from shooting hoops?"

"We've been working on the history project, Dad. This is Todd Pollian."

Dad reaches over and pumps Todd's hand. "Glad to meet you, son. Good to see you boys going back outdoors, too. You can't spend all day inside on schoolwork. You've got to practice to stay sharp—Brian knows that."

Todd smiles faintly as he disengages his hand. "Nice to meet you, Mr. Hammett. I saw the work you did on Brian's guitar. You're a real artist."

Dad smiles at him, but it's a sad smile. "Thanks, son. But that was a long time ago—more of a hobby than an art, I guess you'd call it."

Todd doesn't answer, but his eyes drift toward the trophy buck in the living room.

"I see you've noticed my prize buck," Dad says, his voice prouder. "I drilled him in a perfect brain shot—just dropped him like a puppet when you cut the strings. A group of us go hunting, you see, and one of us, Jake Bernard, was a sniper in the military."

"Dad," I say, trying to interrupt the flow before he can get started. I've heard this story so many times I can recite it, and I'm guessing from Todd's earlier reaction to the buck that he doesn't want to hear it in all its gory detail.

"I know you've heard it before," Dad says, chuckling, "but your friend hasn't. Give your old man a break and let me tell it one more time, okay?"

Todd doesn't say he'd rather ride his bike off a cliff, so I sigh and let Dad go on.

"We'd sit around the campfire at night, and Jake would tell us how he'd wait, perfectly camouflaged, his rifle zeroed, the sights clear, waiting for a good target, and then—wham! He'd pull the trigger and make the perfect brain shot. The body just collapses when you do that, and the victim doesn't even feel anything."

A shadow crosses Todd's face, but he stays silent, and Dad doesn't notice, because he's coming to the good part of his story. "All the guys kept trying to take their buck with that perfect shot, but they'd miss. Jake would tell us it takes lots of target practice, but who's got the time to do that year-round? Still, I'd try to get out to the range and shoot as often as I could. And then, one season, I make it! I make the perfect shot and bring that deer down instantaneously. You can see the hole in the forehead—the taxidermist wanted to hide it, but I wanted to see it."

Todd nods, looking at the buck. "The perfect shot," he

says quietly. "That's very impressive."

"It sure is," Dad agrees heartily. "Do you hunt with your dad, son?"

Todd turns to Dad. He looks at him like they're from different planets. In some ways, they are. "With my father?" he asks blankly. "Go hunting? No—I guess we never did that." He glances at me. "Do you take Brian hunting much, Mr. Hammett?"

Dad shakes his head, and the heartiness goes out of his voice. "No—you'd think he'd love getting out there in the woods with his old man, wouldn't you? But he's always got practice during hunting season." Then the sadness fades and he looks proud again. "Not that I mind—he's the best, you know."

"Dad," I moan.

Todd sees the mortification on my face and raises his eyebrows. But all he says is, "Yes, sir. He's a terrific point guard."

"So," Dad says, "you look like you could shoot a mean hoop with that height, but I don't remember you from the team."

I start to answer, but Todd just shakes his head. "I'm not into team sports," he tells Dad, like he told me earlier. "I shoot hoops on my own sometimes, and I watch the game, but I'm not on the team."

"You're not?" Dad repeats, clearly at a loss as to why anyone Todd's height and build wouldn't go out for the team. "What do you do?"

Todd considers this. "Well, right now I'm concentrating on just making grades to get me into college. In the future—I'm thinking maybe I'll write. Maybe movies. That's what Brian and I are doing for our history project, shooting a movie."

"Oh." Now Dad's the one looking at Todd like he's from a different planet.

"It was very nice to meet you, Mr. Hammett," Todd tells him politely. "And congratulations on your perfect shot."

Dad smiles again, on safer ground now. "Have Brian bring you around next fall—we'll give you some venison if I bag another one."

Todd doesn't answer right away. Then he says, "Thanks for the offer, Mr. Hammett."

I follow him outside. "You really are a diplomat," I tell him as he straddles his bike and prepares to buckle on his helmet.

Todd lowers the helmet and grins. "You're right. Not only am I a pacifist, I'm a vegetarian."

Time stands still for a moment, then we both burst into laughter, almost like friends.

But Alonzo's too-late testimony about Conley stays in my head, and I'm frowning again when I come inside.

"What's up?" Dad asks.

"I don't know," I say slowly. "Dad—remember the day Amanda was shot?"

His face gets a closed look, almost like Todd. I know it's something we all sort of agreed to stop talking about, because I used to wake up from horrible dreams of gunshots and screams. I just played more ball so I was tireder when I went to sleep, and tried not to think about never seeing Amanda again. But I need someone to help me figure out what this all means—if it means anything.

"Remember that jogger I told the policeman about?" I

ask him. "I didn't think it was any big deal, but the more I think about it I remember I almost hit him when one of my jump shots bounced off the backboard. I tried to apologize, but he wouldn't meet my eyes."

Dad nods. "Sure, I remember your telling that officer about a jogger you couldn't really describe. But there are lots of joggers around here. I'm sure he checked it out, Brian. It was probably just someone down the block you didn't recognize, or someone visiting a neighbor."

"I know. I guess that's what I figured at the time. But—" I shake my head. "On the news they were talking about gray fibers, and never finding the clothing that matched them, and this jogger was wearing a gray sweatsuit with the hood pulled up. What if —"

Dad cuts me off. "Let's not jump to conclusions, Brian. Did you see any weapon? A gun?"

I shake my head. "No, but it could have been under the sweatsuit."

Dad studies me. "Are you sure you didn't see the jogger's face at all? Could you describe him—or her?"

"Whoever it was wore sunglasses and didn't even look at me," I try to explain, even though it sounds stupid. "But what if the police just assumed it was a neighbor and didn't check it out? Should I call them to remind them? The officer gave us a card with his name and phone number. Or should I maybe call Mr. Daine's attorney?"

Dad sighs. "I threw the business card away, Brian. Look, you don't want to get involved in a police investigation if you're not sure. You don't want to waste their time on false leads, for a start. And you don't want them marking you as some kid who's just trying to get attention, or even start treating you like a suspect yourself." There's a trace of bitterness in his voice, and I know he's remembering the craft fair theft. He straightens up, shaking his head. "It would be different if you'd definitely seen something you were sure about—but this is so vague."

"I know, but . . ."

"Is it the news stories about the trial?" he asks, like he's suddenly figured it out. "It's been in all the papers and on TV. Have you been seeing Amanda's father in court?" His voice softens. "Look, Brian, I know he looks terrible, and you've got to feel sorry for him."

Is that it? Do I just feel sorry for him because he's somebody I know personally, somebody I'd see and wave to, and talk to when he was home and I was over at the house? Actually I didn't see that much of him. Amanda came over to our place, especially to Dad's workshop with me, as an escape from home. I didn't go over to her place nearly as much, except when her parents were gone and she was babysitting Cory. It was like she wanted to keep her life there separate from our time together. She didn't want me to buddy up with her parents. She didn't even want to talk much about them. Was she trying to hide the fact that there was something strange about her father, something that could erupt into murder?

If Dad was accused of something and arrested, I'd more than feel sorry for him—I'd be outraged. If it were someone else I knew pretty well and liked, say, the twins' parents across the cul-de-sac, I'd feel sorry for them. But the truth is—I really don't know Mr. Daine all that well. The ones I feel sorry for are Amanda and Cory and their mother, and there's nothing I can do for them.

Then I remember Todd telling me that Alonzo should have gotten justice for both Mary and for Leo Frank, but he didn't. That was what haunted him all those years. But I told the police about the jogger—isn't it a little arrogant of me to think that I could get justice for Amanda, all by myself?

As if he reads my mind, Dad goes on, "Don't get it into your head that you can take matters into your own hands with the police."

"But what if Mr. Daine is innocent, Dad?"

He frowns. "I don't pretend to know what really happened, Brian. Mike Daine always acted like a good guy, even if he always seemed to be too busy to be very social. And we were all real proud of that drug bust he made last year. I've got to admit—he seemed an honest cop who cared about doing his job right." That's high praise from Dad. "I'd have expected to see him in the witness stand testifying against somebody accused of murder, not on trial for murder himself. But things aren't always the way they appear."

I nod, wondering if that's closer to the reason I'm feeling so uncomfortable about seeing the jogger. "You're right about that. In this history project we're working on, this kid saw the real murderer but was too scared to tell the police or the lawyers, and this poor guy who only *looked* like he was guilty ended up convicted and hanged. I guess I started wondering if I should say something more about the jogger, and let somebody else decide if it's important."

Dad's face clears and he nearly chuckles. "I understand—you're getting all caught up in this thing for school. You *want* to see parallels between what you're studying and your own life, but I think you're stretching here. Keep the history in the past—and keep your head in the present, okay?"

He's probably right. Mr. Fortner has us looking for ways that history repeats itself, and I'm just looking too hard. If the jogger were important, the police investigation would have found out. It's their job to see justice done, not mine.

"What are you doing?"

"It's no use. He's flatlined."

"Keep going!"

CHAPTER

15

The next couple of weeks fast-forward past me. I'm not the only guy on the team revving up for Mr. Fortner's project. Like substitutes helping out in a hard-driving game, we take turns helping each other—we even pitch in to help the cheerleaders who ask. Ashley's paired with Glenn, a quiet guy who would disappear into the background except for his blue-streaked hair and the dozen or so piercings on his nose and eyebrows and ears. He's short enough that he still gets shut in his locker sometimes, if anybody notices he's there.

At first he's really nervous having us around, but it's clear he's at a loss how to make Ashley get a handle on their project, and we're his last hope. They've got the secret investigation of Martin Luther King Jr. Back in the 1960s, the FBI was afraid the civil-rights activists might do something violent or dangerous, despite the fact that King was so big about peaceful demonstrations. So they spied on him and other civil-rights sympathizers, and put together a secret report on them that went out to all the state and local law enforcement offices.

"It's all about names," Glenn says tentatively. "Lists of

names." When we don't look enlightened, he explains, "Databases."

I begin to see where he's going. He wants to show that what we learned from the FBI lists is how the government can gather names to make a database, and keep it secret from the public but available to the law-enforcement agencies across the country. Then those agencies can use that information, just because they have it, to make somebody look like a criminal just because he once went to a meeting or something and got his name on a list.

Ashley jokes, "If body piercing ever becomes illegal, you're toast."

Glenn doesn't smile. "That's the point."

Some of the team helps Ashley make posters showing how the FBI lists evolved into criminal databases and then evolved into databases showing terrorist suspects. Glenn has made a list of the kids in class, and the rest of us help him come up with every little thing they've done that could sound suspicious, even if it's not, then set up a computer database to generate a printout.

Ray's stuck at home for a few days, thanks to that broken nose from the Raiders. It gives him some extra time to think about his topic. He and Phil Winters got assigned the Battle of Niihau. A Japanese pilot who'd bombed Pearl Harbor crash-landed on this island, and this family killed him when he broke into their house. They weren't in the army or anything, so were they heroes, or had they taken the law into their own hands? The guys decide to stage a trial where the class is the jury and has to decide what's vigilantism and what's the constitutional right to bear arms and use them. We all agree to help them act out the parts of the people on the island.

In fact, all the students who thought they were getting a liability when they got a partner who was a cheerleader or played ball are surprised to find they've actually got the whole team helping them out. We're all going to be pretty familiar with each other's projects before the class presentations ever begin—but Mr. Fortner's bound to be surprised by what a bunch of jocks can do.

Julius pitches in on everybody else's project over the next couple of weeks, but he shrugs off my warning about Leslie. "Old Lesbo has a thing about jocks," he tells me. "I'm sure not going to scrape and bow and promise to read some book just because she tells me to!"

"Well, you're going to have to work with her somehow," I tell him. "You know Mr. Fortner said it had to be a team effort—and we can't afford to have you benched right before the game with Jackson if you end up with a lousy grade."

He laughs. "I've got an idea for a presentation—Lesbo can stand up there and read her report, and I'll set up a hoop by the blackboard. Every time she makes a point, I'll slam dunk the ball to emphasize it."

I can't help laughing along with him, but I wish he'd get serious. His folks aren't going to be any happier than we are if he doesn't get a decent grade from Mr. Fortner. Funny—I know I'm not the best player on the team, but Dad's going to be more thrilled if I get a basketball scholarship than if I get a good grade. Julius really is star material, and his parents could care less whether he plays ball after high school or not. They're proud of him, and they come to every game and cheer him on, but they're way more excited about his grades in math class than his game statistics. Sometimes I think kids aren't always matched up with the right parents.

By the time the guys show up at my place for the filming, though, everybody thinks teamwork on the projects is a great idea. And the consensus is if they could put up with Phil and Glenn, the group can tolerate Todd as well. Before he gets there, I tell them the main story and the casting.

"I'm going to play Leo Frank," I start.

Catcalls from the team: "You mean, we get to lynch you? That's not so smart, Brainman."

"Yeah, right, guys—we're using the actual photographs of the lynching for that part, so you'll have to pass." I press on over the groans. "Highrise, you get to be the prosecutor, so use your height to look like a noble and righteous public servant." More catcalls. "Ray, you get to be the defense attorney." He draws himself up to his full height, too, and tries to look like a serious lawyer. "Ricochet, you'll be the governor. And Julius—you get to be Jim Conley, the star witness for the prosecution."

Keesha pouts. "Is this an all-male film or what? I thought you said you needed us, too!"

"We do," I assure her. "You girls are going to be the rest of the star witnesses—and, Darla, you get to be the murder victim!"

The news is met with suitable gasps and whistles. Then I explain how the cheerleaders will be the factory girls who testified that Leo Frank came onto them, and Brittney will play Mrs. Frank.

Ashley takes my arm. "Are you sure you don't want Brittney to be a factory girl instead of me, Mr. Frank?"

"Ha, ha," I say weakly. "Don't worry, Ashley, there's no chance of any romance on film—I get to spend all my time in jail or on trial."

"So who's the Turd?" Julius asks.

"He's the cameraman," I tell them. "He's the one with the digital video camera and the computer, so that makes sense. Now let's scope out the costumes."

The girls giggle over the semi-old-fashioned dresses Mom helped me dig up, and the guys put on the suits I asked them to bring, all except Julius. I've borrowed some work clothes of Dad's for the opening, and then an old suit of Dad's for the trial. With padding they make Julius look bulkier and stronger, more like a guy who could kill a little girl, though I don't tell him that. I want him to be as surprised as everyone else by the end of the movie.

We're all ready when Todd's motorcycle cruises into the driveway. I can tell the bike takes everyone by surprise. It's a real status symbol for a guy who has no status whatsoever in their eyes.

"Now I get the black," Brittney says, smiling a little. "He's kind of a hunk on that bike."

"Like the Turd would stand a chance with you, Bright Eyes," Julius mutters, and the other girls smother their giggles.

Matt and Paul come tearing over at the roar of his engine, just as Todd predicted. But Matt's so self-important about his role in the movie that he's on his best behavior, and Todd makes Paul his special assistant, holding props and fetching camera batteries and memory cards from the carrier on Todd's bike.

Aside from a few turd jokes that Todd pretends not to

hear, the filming goes perfectly. Both the team and the cheerleaders follow directions, and once they get the idea that they can strike exaggerated poses like in old movies and they really don't have to say anything, they have a great time. We shoot the scenes outside the pencil factory against the brick wall of Matt's house. We shoot Leo Frank's arrest in my dining room, and then Mom lets us move furniture so we can use the wood paneling in the house for the courtroom.

She's so pleased at seeing me taking schoolwork as seriously as basketball that she even digs out some cash for pizzas as the afternoon goes on. Either she talks to Todd or just hedges her bets, because one is vegetarian and one is plain cheese, so he's not stuck trying to eat around pepperoni or sausage. I'm almost surprised there aren't any vegetarian cracks from the team, but nobody seems to notice.

Matt and Paul stuff themselves with a couple of slices, but they run out of energy after a while and wander on home. By the time we're done shooting, everybody's beat. Mrs. Malik comes to pick up Julius, Keesha, and Shooter, and Ashley piles the rest of the crowd into her car. Once they've cleared off, Todd helps me put away the remains of the pizza.

"That was nice of your mother," he says.

We look at each other for a minute, then I grin. "This is going to be such an awesome movie!"

He laughs. "I didn't believe they'd come through, but you really got them to deliver. Is that the way you do it on the court, too? No wonder you're the team captain."

"Well, you're the one behind the camera."

We go on for a while like teammates sharing the glory,

then Todd stretches. "Okay—ready for your closeup?"

"I guess."

I change costumes and Mom helps with makeup to get me looking old, while Todd watches through the lens and makes suggestions. Then we shoot the scene where I return to Atlanta as old Alonzo to tell the truth about seeing Jim Conley with Mary's body. It's late afternoon by then, and Matt comes back to play the scenes we didn't film earlier, the young Alonzo asking his mother (played to perfection by my own mom) what he should do and taking her advice not to say anything. His father volunteers to stand in the background, taking my statement, since Dad isn't home yet, and then it's done. The movie's all on those little memory cards.

I feel kind of strange, almost like the letdown at the end of the season, when you realize you don't have another game for months.

"You look like the last game of the season is finished," Todd says, eerily accurate as he mounts his bike. "Cheer up. We've still got to edit this thing and do the text boxes and lay down the music track. It's not over yet."

For some reason, that makes me feel better. I head inside to tackle the cleanup. When I roll up the sections of newspaper Mom laid out on the dining room table while she was doing my old-age makeup, I see the headline: PROSECUTION PRESENTS EXPERT WITNESS BALLISTICS TESTIMONY IN THE DAINE TRIAL. I glance at the article.

"Firearms expert Rick Logan concluded his testimony about the shooting of the Daine family, unchallenged by the defense. Jurors seemed engrossed as Logan testified that each victim was killed by a single, perfectly placed shot from a .380 caliber handgun. 'This is clearly the work of a shooter with professional expertise,' he explained, 'the sort of expertise that police officers gain on the pistol range.' The prosecution was quick to point out that Officer Daine had qualified on the target range while shooting his personal firearm, a .380 special, although Daine has consistently claimed that he sold the handgun some time before the murders."

I look across the hallway to Dad's prized buck, dropped with a single perfect shot. Maybe Amanda's father really is that good a shot. If so, he could have killed them, like the prosecutor says—a chilling thought, but it would mean I don't need to worry about whether I should do anything more about the jogger.

I stop myself in the act of crumpling the newspaper. The prosecutor wants people to buy into his reasoning: just because Mr. Daine is a police officer, he can shoot well enough to make three perfect shots, therefore he actually did shoot his family, and therefore he's guilty. But that reasoning doesn't hold up. Even if Mr. Daine could make a perfect shot, that doesn't necessarily mean he actually did make those three perfect shots to kill his family, does it?

I wonder if Alonzo rationalized his continued silence with the same circular reasoning: *Oh, well, if Mr. Frank had made advances to the other factory girls, maybe he came on to Mary Phagan and killed her when she resisted him. Maybe he really was guilty. So maybe what I saw wasn't what I thought it was—maybe it's not worth telling anybody about.* Yet even if Frank had made passes at girls, how does it follow that he would have killed one girl who wasn't interested in him?

Thinking that way let Alonzo off the hook way too easily. He knew he'd seen something important.

If I buy into the prosecutor's reasoning, then I can tell myself the jogger I saw wasn't important and I don't have any more responsibility. I told the police, what more do I have to do? But doesn't that let me off the hook too easily also? If Mr. Daine is innocent, like Leo Frank, then maybe the jogger is more important than anyone realized.

Or is the prosecutor right this time, even though the lawyer prosecuting Frank was wrong? Maybe Mr. Daine really does know how to make a perfect shot, and maybe he had reasons I don't understand that made him decide to kill his family. Can that be why the defense attorney didn't challenge the expert on the stand? Is that why he didn't point out that just because you know how to do something, there's no proof you're actually going to do it?

CHAPTER

16

I try not to think about Amanda's father and focus instead on gearing up for Friday's game against the Spartans. Coach is getting really excited, now that the victories are stacking up.

"You guys can go all the way to the championship," he tells us at practice. "It's up to you now. Don't let up for one second—we need to win every one of our last games!"

The effect is spoiled a little by his dropping his clipboard and his dog-eared *High School Coaching Bible*, but we don't laugh. We're too hot this season. Julius isn't the only one expecting to see scouts in the bleachers as we get closer and closer to making the playoffs. For a second I let myself fantasize that Dad's right: I could get a basketball scholarship, and then... But somehow I can't see what happens after that. Even if I do get a scholarship to play ball in school, where do I go from there?

That's too far in the future to think about now. Keep your mind on just winning this game, I tell myself. Beat the Spartans before you plan out the rest of your life.

Playing the Spartans in their gym that Friday takes every bit of our concentration. They take their strongest defender off the bench to guard Julius, willing to sacrifice some of their own scoring if they can shut him down, but Julius simply dishes off to me if he can't take the shot, and I get the ball to Ray or Ricochet for two, or do a fast layup myself. When Julius can fight through his man to get air space, he makes high arcing three-pointers as if the Spartan guard is playing in slow motion. By the half, we're up 42–31.

The Spartan coach must read them the riot act in the locker room, because they come out looking like they're on fire. They try to muscle us as soon as we cross the center line, or squeeze us along the baseline so we can only get trash-shot two-pointers. But sooner or later, the twos add up. Even though Wrestler comes off the bench to fight off a few of their scoring drives, they're hitting enough threes to bring the score up to 58–49. It's clear the refs don't like the elbows flying, though. They start sending us to the free-throw line.

That's one thing I love about the game—the fairness. Guys break the rules, the zebras call foul. A lot of teams don't spend enough time practicing free throws, so they can't take advantage of the foul shots, but I make sure we drill free throws in practice, and I'm not the only guy on the team who shoots at home for hours. We make over 80% of our free throws, and those points add up, too. On top of that, the Spartan players start fouling out before the third quarter is over, and we get back our momentum.

As soon as the tough defender guarding Julius is benched, we go into high gear. Take-away Ray seems to intercept every Spartan pass near him and dodges inside their lines to steal their dribbles. He only draws two fouls and his grin is bigger than his swollen nose. Ricochet plucks a rebound off the glass on the defensive end, then drives the full length of the court, weaving between guys until he sinks the shot. Some of the Spartan home crowd is screaming for a goaltending call, but our fans go wild.

As Take-away feeds me the ball again and again, I distribute the passes so the Spartans never know who to guard. Ricochet takes it strong to the hoop, Highrise glides in for his share of layups, and Julius drains jumpers like he's all alone. Each sweet swish sounds like magic, and by the time the buzzer ends the game the score is 76–62. We win fair and clean, and really whoop it up as the fans pour onto the court, lifting Julius onto their shoulders, lifting me, too, as captain, but I tell them to raise Ray instead. Take-away Ray and Joyous—they're the men tonight.

The Maliks pound Julius on the back, almost speechless with delight. For two university types, that's not their normal condition. All Mr. Malik can do is keep repeating, "I am so glad we didn't have to leave before this game—I wouldn't have missed this for anything in the world!"

That's not quite as fanciful as it sounds, since Julius's parents are flying to Europe late tonight. His father is delivering some paper at an international conference in Germany. The organizer had wanted them to leave earlier today, but I guess the Maliks wanted to see Julius play more than they wanted to get to the conference early.

Before I can tell them to have a good trip, my folks are there, Dad swooping me off my feet into a giant bear hug. "You did it!" he's shouting. "You're going all the way to the championship, Brian, and after that you can write your own ticket anywhere!"

I want to tell Dad the team did it, but he can't help being proud, I guess. Mom's beaming at me, too. To her, I'm keeping basketball and schoolwork in balance again, like I used to do last year, so she's happy.

In the midst of the confusion, Julius punches my arm. "I've got to hit the showers so I can take the Prof and the Scribe to the airport," he tells me. I grin. He's even got nicknames for his own parents. He adds, "But let's party tomorrow, okay?"

Mrs. Malik says, "Not too much partying while we're gone, young man!" But she's joking, proud of him, happy.

"When the cat's away," Julius teases her, then lopes off to the locker room, getting pounded on the shoulder by the rest of the team as he goes.

It's an almost perfect night.

It would be perfect if Amanda and Cory were here to cheer the win. In spite of the crowd spilling out of the bleachers onto the court, I keep seeing this empty space where the two of them should be, and their silence makes a hollow blank in the midst of the other cheers. Every time I think the ache is a little less, guilt washes over me again, reminding me that if I'd only let them stay with me that afternoon, they'd be alive today, sitting there in the bleachers, cheering the way they should be.

But I don't want to sour the night for my folks or my team. I hug Mom and Dad and grab a loose ball, dribbling into the locker room, high-fiving the guys and replaying the highlights until we're sated with victory and the empty feeling fades into background numbness.

*"Flatline now at 2 minutes 30.
We're almost out of time."*

CHAPTER

17

I'm just about to head in to bed on Saturday night when the telephone rings. Sometimes you just can't wait to pick up the receiver because you've got a feeling it's good news. Sometimes you're afraid to pick it up without really knowing why. This time my hand hovers over the receiver. It's too late for anyone to call with good news. But it'll wake Mom if it keeps ringing—Dad's probably already heard it. He's a light sleeper.

"Hammett residence," I say, finally grabbing the receiver.

"Brainman?" There's a note of panic in Julius's voice.

"Yeah—are you okay? Where were you today? We kept waiting for you to party and we called, but you didn't pick up."

"I'm in the city—my parents were flying out last night."

"Yeah, I know. Did their plane get postponed?"

"I wish! Stop talking, Brainman, and listen. This is a pay phone. I'm at the jail on Yorick Street and Meridian. You got that? The police picked me up for making a left turn. I got lost getting out of the airport and I got off the interstate to get back on going the other way, but all the streets were one-way or dead ends and I got completely turned around—man, they arrested me for being lost in some ritzy whites-only hood and making a wrong left turn! I've been in jail!"

His voice is rising in hysteria. "Calm down, Julius, what can I do? You want me to get your folks? Where are they staying?" I have no idea how to call Europe, but I'm sure I can figure it out.

"No!" Julius practically screams in my ear. Who, then? I doubt he wants me to call his grandmother and scare her in the middle of the night. She's looking after his little brother, but Julius is staying at home so it's easy for him to make practice and the games. I don't know what I'm supposed to do. I can feel my breathing speed up—now I'm getting hysterical, too.

"The police finally said I can go," he's trying to explain. "But some adult has to come in and get me—I don't get it, but they won't let me go alone. You got to get your dad to come get me, and I mean now! I can't stay here another night, Brainman." Now his voice is breaking. What have they done to him?

"Okay. I'll come."

"No—aren't you listening? Your old man has to come! It's got to be an adult!"

"I got that—don't worry. I'll bring him. You're going to be okay, Joyous."

There's silence, and for a second I'm afraid we've been cut off. Then he says, "Just come. I'm counting on you, Brainman." The line goes dead.

"What's wrong?" Dad says as I drop the receiver back into its cradle.

"It's Julius," I tell him. "Something's happened—we've got to go to the city to get him."

"Slow down there a minute," Dad says. "Now tell me from the beginning."

I run through the story as best I can. "So we've got to go now! Don't you see?"

Dad's not looking at me anymore. He's looking off into space, like he's seeing a different world full of new possibilities. "I know you like Julius," he says slowly, "but it sounds as if he's really gotten himself in trouble this time. I don't think we should get involved, Brian," he says finally, avoiding my eyes.

"Not get involved?" I demand, incredulous. "But he's my best friend!" As if he doesn't hear me, Dad stubbornly keeps staring off into space.

I reach out and grab his arm, trying to make contact. "Come on, Dad—you know what it's like to be accused of something when you didn't do it! Julius isn't a trouble-maker—he doesn't mess with drugs or hang with gangs or do anything—ever. I don't care what the police said about him—it's not true—you know Julius! You know it can't be true."

Finally Dad looks at me. And I can see in his eyes how he sees me stepping into Julius's place if he's forced out of the picture. Dad's always wanted me to be the best player, the guy who gets his name in the paper and gets the scouts watching his perfect shots, the guy that every father wants for his son. He's always wished I were Julius, with some other guy passing to me so I could make the perfect shots—and now he's thinking I might get my chance in the spotlight.

"You don't want to get involved, Brian," Dad says patiently, his voice almost condescending, as if he still sees me as just a little kid who can't fathom the complexities of adult decisions. But I'm beginning to understand that complexity all too well. "You want" (he means, I need) "that basketball scholarship. Do you think Coach Guilford is going to recommend you if he thinks you're a troublemaker? You go out there tonight—get your name in the paper hauling him out of jail—everybody's going to associate you with whatever Julius got himself into."

"Dad, he didn't get himself into anything! He's in trouble, but it's not like he did anything." My words seem to be bouncing off my father like ghost balls off an indifferent backboard. "You think people don't already associate him with me, after all the years we've been friends and teammates and—"

"That was before he got himself into this mess," Dad says, unmoved. "Now it's high time you got some distance between the two of you." His eyes shift, a little unfocused, as if he can see some sweet play I've missed. "Maybe with that. . . ." He doesn't say the n-word. He almost says it—I can see him tasting it on his tongue, a word that he might toss out, not thinking much about it, with his construction crew or his hunting pals, but never with his son—and he swallows it at the last minute. "Maybe with that boy out of the picture you'll get your chance at last, Brian, your chance to really shine on the court. Just be the star I know you can be, and you'll get that scholarship."

He's nodding at his own vision, not even realizing that I'm not paying attention any longer. If I could stuff my fists in my ears and start humming like Amanda to drown out his words, I'd do it. But I can't waste any more time, not when Julius needs me.

I could hear in his voice that Julius is hurting and scared—and I think he's holding on, counting on me to get him out of there. I need to come up with some responsible adult to bail him out if Dad won't. Then I remember Todd telling me his brother's a lawyer. I can't believe I hadn't thought of him earlier. I turn my back on my father and head for the phone.

"Brian! What do you think you're doing?" he demands.

"Okay," I tell him, without looking back. "So you don't want to get involved. That's your call. But somebody's got to do something, and I think I know somebody who'll help."

"Go on," he says, his voice smug. "Call Coach. He'll bail out his player, all right. Then he'll wash his hands of him."

I pause, my hand on the receiver. Calling Coach never even crossed my mind. Why? I know Coach'll be furious if he finds out Julius got arrested, even if it's unfair. He still thinks grades and conduct matter more than playing ball, and he's always resented the way Julius does the minimum work to pass in subjects he doesn't care about. To be honest, he's always resented Julius, period—the way he's so good with the ball in his hands, and the way he won't even pretend to care about grades or anything else. I know there's something wrong with Coach's attitude, and I don't like it, but I've never challenged him about it.

Now, though, it's clear Dad's right—Coach won't like me getting involved tonight. He won't like me getting involved with the police, and he won't like me helping Julius.

Maybe I've always understood how Coach feels about Julius, someplace deep inside. Maybe that's why I've never challenged Coach about the way he treats Julius. I didn't want to cross him. Maybe part of me even agreed with Dad that it was okay for Coach to act that way, since Julius refused to play by his rules.

For the first time, it occurs to me that up till now I've bought into Dad's way of looking at things on some level so deep and instinctive I never even realized I was doing it. How can Dad be so right about what Coach will do, and so wrong about how I should deal with it at the same time?

Will Todd's brother react the same way as Coach and Dad? But I can't just leave Julius where he is.

The image of Amanda and Cory and their mom lying there until Mr. Daine got home comes into my mind. I know they were already dead—but I can't get the idea of their being so alone out of my head. I should have checked on them when no one came out to shoot baskets, or to tell me about the afternoon at the pool, or anything. I should have let them play with us to begin with. I don't see how I can change what I did then, but I know I can't leave Julius in jail alone tonight.

I leave the receiver in its cradle, go into my room, and barely keep from slamming the door. Even without looking at Dad, I can see the faint smile on his face. He thinks he's taught me something tonight. He has.

I pick up my cell phone, punch in Todd's number, and push Send. It only rings twice before a man's voice snaps, "Pollian residence." He doesn't sound pleased at being called so late.

"Ah—this is Brian, Todd's partner on the history project," I stammer.

"What? Do you have any idea what time it is? Todd can't come to the phone at this hour." The deep voice, eerily like Todd's, sounds extremely annoyed.

I take a deep breath and force myself to sound like I know exactly what I'm doing making this call, when I'm actually still trying to figure out how my world has spun out of control. "I know that, sir, and I wasn't calling Todd, actually. I was calling you about a legal matter." When the man doesn't answer, I add, "An emergency."

"What is it?" His voice is still sharp, but the edge doesn't sound as angry.

I try to explain succinctly before he decides it's just a crank call after all and hangs up. "Our classmate, Julius Malik, was arrested in the city for making a left turn in an all-white neighborhood. He didn't do anything—he's just a black kid who got lost in the wrong place. Maybe they should have given him a ticket, but they never should have arrested him! But his parents are in Germany at some kind of academic conference, and the police are holding him at the jail on Yorick Street—Yorick and Meridian, he said. They won't let him go until a responsible adult comes to get him. So—" I run out of words. "—I was hoping you would."

In the pause I can hear voices in the background. His wife, the doctor, maybe? And Todd, still awake? "I take it your parents aren't responsible enough to collect this boy?" the man asks, a little wryly.

"My dad doesn't want to get involved," I admit, reluctantly.

After another pause, he asks, "But you do?"

"Julius is my friend. He didn't do anything." When he doesn't answer, I burst out, "Todd said you believed in civil rights! He said you fought for everyone to get a fair hearing, not just people who could pay for big expensive lawyers! He said—"

A chuckle interrupts. "Okay, I get the picture. That sounds like Todd in his Don Quixote rant. Sancho, my horse!" He sighs.

I start to explain the details that Julius gave me, but he asks, "Are you on a landline?"

"What?"

"Are you talking on a telephone with a wire plugged into the wall, or a cell phone?" he asks.

"My cell phone."

"Then don't say any more," he tells me. "I take it Todd knows where you live? I'll come get you on the way to the jail. You can fill me in on the details as we go."

I almost sag against my desk with relief before I pull myself together and assure him that Todd knows the way. As soon as I hang up, I grab a pair of khakis and a clean shirt, and change so I'll look respectable enough to rescue my best friend.

When I get back into the hallway, Dad's in the living room watching late-night TV. Good—I hope he can't sleep after what he's said. I reach into the hall closet for my team jacket, and he turns around, then stares at me like I've turned into a stranger. "Where in the world do you think you're going?"

"One of my classmates has a brother who's a lawyer," I explain briefly. "He's on his way right now."

"You're not going anywhere with any lawyer," Dad says quickly, getting up and moving as if to block my way to the front door.

"Dad," I tell him, pacing my words evenly, "you're wrong this time. What I'm doing is right, and I'm not backing down." Before his shocked expression can turn forbidding, I brush past him and out the front door to tilt at Don Quixote's windmills with Todd's brother.

CHAPTER

18

A dark blue sedan is pulling to a stop under our driveway light as I run down the front steps. I hurry toward it before Dad can follow me outside, and the passenger front door opens. Todd climbs out of the front seat, a spiral notebook in his hand, and into the back. "You sit with Warren so you can tell him exactly what happened while we drive," he tells me.

I'm surprised he came, considering how he and Julius feel about each other. But maybe Warren wouldn't come without him, not knowing me. Anyway, I'm just as glad he did, because I don't feel all that comfortable just taking off with a strange adult.

"Hi, Brian," Warren says, backing out of the driveway while I'm still buckling my seat belt. "Sorry about cutting you off, but cell phones are monitored constantly. The courts have held that cell phones broadcast directly into the air, so you give up your Fourth Amendment right to privacy by using one—the police don't even need a court order or warrant to listen in. I didn't want you to say anything that might compromise my ability to get your friend out of there." He's already reversed and is heading away from the cul-de-sac. "Todd's filled me in on most of the background—your project together, who Julius Malik is. I just need a little more information from you. Is he a troublemaker?"

"No!" I'm surprised to hear Todd's voice join in with mine.

I see a grin cross Warren's face in the faint illumination of the dashboard lights. He looks as remote as Todd usually does until he smiles. "He's your best friend and Todd's worst enemy, but he's not a troublemaker. That says something about his character references, but I'm not sure what."

"I wouldn't say he's my worst enemy," Todd comments from the backseat.

That's probably generous of him. I explain how important Julius is to the team, and about his parents being in Europe for the conference.

Warren asks, "If the police pulled him over, would Julius give them some lip, make them think he was trouble, part of a gang, doing drugs, or anything at all?"

I shake my head decisively. "No way! He's proud of himself, but he's not rude to adults—well, not adults he doesn't know, anyway."

"What does that mean?"

"He can be rude to teachers, sometimes," I admit, thinking about Mr. Fortner. "But if he smarted off to the principal, or to a policeman, or someone like that, his parents would ground him for the rest of his high school life."

"What do his parents do?"

"Mr. Malik is a professor at Butler University, in the political science department, I think. He's always going on about politics and the government, anyway. And Mrs.

Malik writes books—you know, the kind that get endorsed by important people and win literary awards and stuff like that." I've never read one of them.

Warren chuckles. "So what is this famous family doing in little old Willisford?"

Behind him, Todd laughs shortly. "Folks could ask the same question about you and Elise."

I tell Warren, "Julius said something about his parents wanting him to grow up somewhere other than the city. I think they'd lived in big cities all their lives and didn't like them much." When Warren doesn't answer, I ask, "Why are you in Willisford?"

He sighs. "I suspect Todd's pinpointed the similarity, all right. We wanted someplace peaceful to live—no gangs while our kids are growing up, no drugs, no violence in the schools." Todd shifts on the seat behind us, but says nothing. "So—Julius is the perfect kid?"

Todd and I both laugh at that. "Nobody's perfect," I tell Warren. "But Julius is okay. He's not too crazy about schoolwork, but he's fair, he's honest—he's a good player." That about sums up Julius Malik, and that should explain why there's no way he deserves to be arrested for getting lost in the wrong neighborhood.

Warren drives on, thinking. Ahead of us I can see the city lights getting brighter. The two-lane road has turned into four lanes. "All right," Warren says. "I'm going to make a call, and I don't want to hear a sound out of either one of you while I'm on the phone. I'm not joking—the law is serious business." He pauses. "Is there anything else you need to tell me? I know Julius is your friend, Brian, but is there anything else I need to know about him, anything the police might try to use as a justification?"

I can hear that Warren really means it. But I don't think he's asking about things like not wanting to work with Leslie or stuffing Todd into his locker when he could get away with it. I shake my head. "I don't think so." But just to be on the safe side, I look back over the seat. "Todd, you see him differently than I do—what do you think?"

Warren glances up at his rearview mirror, probably looking at Todd's expression. But all Todd says is, "He can be an arrogant jock, but there's no law against that. And without a basketball I can't see how he'd come on so hard that the cops could think he's any sort of criminal."

"Okay." Warren gets out his cell phone and punches in numbers.

"I thought you said not to talk about it on a cell phone," I remind him.

He smiles swiftly. "Since I'm calling the police, it doesn't matter if they listen in. And sometimes you want to broadcast information on a cell call." Before he connects, he says, "Remember, not a sound. I don't want to give the impression this is a group of kids on the way to break their buddy out of jail."

I'd laugh, but this is too serious. I just sit tight and listen.

"Yes, this is Warren Pollian. Who am I talking to?" I hear a soft rustling of paper in the seat behind me and realize that Todd's taking notes. "Officer Wainright? Are you the senior duty officer? No? Then who is the senior duty officer? Officer Connor. Please connect me with him."

Todd's pen scratches across paper while Warren waits.

"No, Officer Wainright, I will not call back later. I am

en route to pick up my client, Mr. Julius Malik, and I will speak with the senior duty officer now, or you will be speaking to the press tomorrow to explain why you deliberately obstructed a minor's right to counsel."

Traffic picks up as we get closer to the city. Warren waits for a few moments, then says, "Is this Officer Connor? You are the senior duty officer tonight? My name is Warren Pollian and I am Mr. Malik's attorney. Has my client been charged with anything?" His voice is brisk and businesslike.

"That wasn't what I asked, Officer Connor, and you are perilously close to a constitutional violation, for which you will be personally liable. Has the prosecutor or the D.A. charged my client with anything? Officer Connor, 'not yet' is 'no.' You have held my client for twenty-four hours without benefit of counsel, and I believe that exceeds your authority. Be quiet, Officer Connor. I am on my way to pick up my client right now. I should be at the jail within fifteen minutes. Either you have Mr. Malik ready for me to pick up, along with all copies of his paperwork, any questioning you engaged in without his counsel being present, and copies of any files you have created concerning him, or I will be on the Federal District Circuit Court Judge's doorstep to get a writ of habeas corpus at eight in the morning, then I will go directly to serve it—which will give me plenty of time to alert the news media to meet me there so that you can explain to the good people of this state why you incarcerated an Indiana High School All-Star and Mr. Basketball candidate."

We're on the interstate now. There are exits to the left and right, and traffic is rushing by even at this hour. It's no wonder Julius got lost.

"That's what I hoped you'd say, Officer Connor. I will see you shortly." Warren clicks off his phone, and Todd applauds from the backseat.

"Wow," I say, amazed. "You ran right over them."

Warren nods, but he doesn't look happy. "Todd, write down that Connor told me the police claim they are refining their evidence and planning to bring an indictment shortly."

"What?" I can't believe they told him that. "An indictment? For what?"

"For nothing," he says flatly. "They have no intention of charging your friend with anything, but I'm sure they've been trying to frighten him with that threat since they picked him up. That's doublespeak for 'We don't have anything on you but we think you must have done something so we're going to hold you until we find out what. Or until we cook something up.'"

"But—but that's wrong!" I splutter.

Warren glances at me. "Yes, it is. But that's all too often the way the police do things. They get a feeling about someone, and then make up their minds to find the evidence to prove it. That can't come as a complete shock to you, Brian. From what Todd tells me about your project on the Leo Frank trial, it's what you've already uncovered in that case."

"I know, but . . ." My voice trails off.

"But it's a lot tougher to handle when it's happening to somebody you know personally," he says, more kindly.

A few moments later he changes lanes, then takes the next exit. When we get to the parking lot beside the jail he says, "You two come with me, but don't say anything to

anyone except me. Todd, keep taking notes. Brian," he hesitates, "don't lose your temper inside. They may have
roughed your friend up some. But he doesn't know me and
Todd's not exactly his best friend, so I need him to see you
so he knows we're on his side." He takes a deep breath.
"This isn't going to be fun, guys. But let's do it."

He gets out, takes a suit jacket from the backseat and
pulls it on, then straightens his tie, smoothes down his hair,
and seizes his briefcase. He looks like an opposing coach—
formidable. I wish I'd brought a sports jacket instead of my
team jacket.

We follow him inside, passing a young officer in a crisp
uniform on his way out. He looks up and smiles at us. Then
he takes in Warren's and Todd's hard expressions and whatever confusion and anger must show on my own face. His
smile falters, and he ducks his head and hurries on. Warren
strides past him to the high counter and says, "Warren
Pollian to pick up my client, Mr. Malik. I believe Officer
Connor should have him ready."

The officer behind the counter keeps writing for a moment, then slowly raises his eyes to meet Warren's. "If you'd
like to have a seat, Officer Connor will be with you in a little while."

"And you are ... " Warren reads the man's name,
"Officer Klein. Well, Officer Klein, either produce my
client or I'm on my way to the District Court Judge for the
habeas corpus."

To my surprise, he waits about two nanoseconds, then
pivots and heads back out to the parking lot. Todd follows
and I fall in behind them, heart thudding.

"Wait—Mr. Pollian! I didn't ... Roy?" There's a

distinct note of panic in the man's voice.

Warren pauses at the door but doesn't turn around.

Barely a moment later a different voice says, "Mr. Pollian? I'm Officer Roy Connor. If you'll step this way, we have the paperwork on your client ready for you."

Warren turns, measures the officer silhouetted in the fluorescent light, and comes toward him. "Is Mr. Malik ready?" he asks.

"He's yours as soon as you complete the paperwork," the man says. It's a black corrections officer. I can read the name "Connor" on his uniform. He looks at me and Todd, eyes narrowed. "And these are?"

Warren says, "My associate, Todd Pollian, who is making a record of this meeting, and Brian Hammett, the captain of Mr. Malik's basketball team, here to ascertain my client's condition."

That's news to me. But the officer doesn't challenge us again, just leads the way into an office. A few other officers pass us in the corridor. A couple of them look back and forth from Connor to Warren, apparently worried. None of those guys want to meet my eyes when I look directly at them. But most of the officers smirk when they see us, and stare at me as if daring me not to look away first. I don't take the dare.

Warren sits down opposite a metal desk in Connor's office, sorts through the paperwork, and asks, "Where are the transcripts of your . . . interviews with Mr. Malik?"

The officer smiles. "I'm just the corrections officer, Mr. Pollian. The arresting officer keeps all the preliminary paperwork to file at the police station."

Warren rolls his eyes while Todd writes furiously. "Was

Mr. Malik interrogated here?"

"Well, we provided an interrogation room, but it was a police detective who questioned him, not one of my officers. . . ."

When his voice trails off, Warren locks eyes with him. "Who was that detective?"

Connor shakes his head. "As I said, it wasn't one of my men, so I don't—"

Warren cuts him off. "You have a log, Officer Connor. You know it and I know it. So let's cut to the chase right now. I want to see that log, and I want copies of the videotapes and transcripts of the interviews."

"I'll get the log ·for you," the officer says. Then he spreads his hands. "And I would be happy to oblige you with the other materials you want, but I'm afraid that's simply not possible, because they're not in my keeping. You'll have to file a request at the police station."

Warren stands up and slams his briefcase shut. "Let's stop playing games, Officer Connor. Do you want a 1984?" I have no clue what he's talking about, but the officer turns an ashy color under the fluorescent lights as Warren leans forward. "I'll have you in Federal District Court Monday morning for violating my client's constitutional rights, and you know that the law will hold you personally liable."

When Officer Connor doesn't answer, Warren says, "But it would simplify things considerably, and will also go a long way to restoring public confidence in your department, if you choose to be part of the solution instead of part of the problem by contacting the arresting officer personally." He takes a business card out of his breast pocket and hands it to Connor. "Fax them to this number and then mail hard copy and the tapes. If my office does not receive them within seven working days, I will proceed with a 1984."

The officer clears his throat, then takes the card and drops it on his desk without looking at it. "Right." He turns to a file cabinet and flips through folders, then pulls one out. "Here's the log." He shoves it at Warren and barely gives him time to find the right entry before saying, "Come this way to the holding area and you can take your client out of here."

Warren takes his time copying down the information he wants and putting it into his briefcase while Officer Connor waits impatiently in the doorway. We follow him down the corridor into a larger room. Most of the room is separated from our end by bars. There must be a dozen guys on the far side of the bars, standing around, sitting on benches, or leaning against the wall. More than half of them are black. The weird thing is that they're not fully dressed. They're just wearing undershirts, or no shirt at all, and pants or jeans, without any belts, and socks. A few are barefoot.

Connor calls out in a booming voice, "Malik! Get on the red line!"

And then I see him. Julius stands up from a corner where he was huddling, arms wrapped around his legs. One jeans knee is torn, and he's not wearing any shirt. He comes forward uncertainly, then sees me and hurries.

"Stop right there, boy!" Connor shouts. "I said on the red line. The rest of you, back against the wall."

The other men behind bars make a show out of lazily moving back a little way. Connor unlocks the gate and motions Julius forward. "Come on, Malik. I haven't got all night."

Julius steps through the gate like he can't quite believe he's out of there, and Connor points to a counter. "Get on the white line at that window, boy."

I bristle. How can a black cop talk to a black kid that way?

When Julius takes his place on the line, another officer behind the counter throws a paper bag on the floor. It lands at Julius's feet. "One step forward and sign here, boy," the officer says, holding a clipboard out through the window.

Julius starts to step forward, but Warren says, "One moment, Mr. Malik." His voice is mild, but he sets down his briefcase, reaches for the paper bag and pries open the staples sealing it. "Let's inventory the contents before you sign for them, just to make sure nothing has disappeared."

Julius's eyes flicker from Warren to me to the officers surrounding us. I nod, trying to signal him that it's okay to trust Warren. One by one, Warren takes Julius's clothes and the stuff he must have been carrying in his pockets out of the bag and checks them with Julius, giving him time to get dressed along the way. By the time Julius buckles his watch back on his wrist and counts his money and the IDs in his wallet and pockets it, he's standing taller.

Warren nods. "If everything is accounted for, Mr. Malik, you can sign for your possessions now." He takes the clipboard away from the cop leaning through the window and hands it to Julius. Then he turns to Connor. "And where is Mr. Malik's car?"

Connor smiles. "In the police garage, for safekeeping."

Warren sighs patiently. "And for examination by your

drug enforcement team, I'm sure. Where is this garage, Officer Connor?"

Connor says, "The impoundment lot is right behind the police station, but I'm afraid it doesn't open until seven a.m."

I hear a soft sound from Julius, like a half-swallowed whimper. Warren puts his hands in his pockets and looks up at the ceiling. Then he shakes his head. "No, Officer Connor, I'm not wasting any more time playing games with you. We both know the impoundment lot can receive cars twenty-four hours a day, and can release them twenty-four hours a day as well."

His voice grows steadily louder. "Please remember I am talking about a constitutional violation where you are responsible in your personal capacity and the venue will be Federal District Court? I suggest you call over and get Mr. Malik's car out here now, this moment, and we inventory it and check that inventory against the digital photographs of it, or you will find yourself explaining your actions to a Federal District Judge. Do we understand each other?"

There's a pause. Connor finally says, his voice tight, "I'll see if we can't release that car tonight."

"Now, Officer Connor," Warren tells him. "Not later tonight."

"That's right."

The crowd of men in the holding area behind us erupts in cheers. One of them yells, "Way to go, my man! You let me know who your lawyer be, bro—I can use me a hard-talkin' lawyer who can take it to the mats with the man!"

Warren spends some time going over the Malik's BMW with Julius. Why would the police strip it looking for drugs?

Do they think every teenager is somehow mixed up with drugs? Or just black kids like Julius?

Finally Warren nods. "All right, if you're sure everything is in order, Mr. Malik, let's get you back home."

He turns back to Connor. "Remember—those transcripts within seven days, or you'll receive the judge's order."

Connor nods. "Yeah, I hear you, Mr. Pollian." Then he leans forward. "Good-bye, Malik—you drive safe now, you hear?" He smiles when Julius flinches backward from him.

Warren is still holding the car keys. He holds the passenger door open for Julius. "Thanks for your concern, Officer, but I believe I'll drive my client out of your city tonight."

When Todd starts the engine in his brother's sedan and we finally pull out of the jail's parking lot, I feel like I'm the one who's been liberated. I turn to Todd. "What exactly was going on in there?"

He smiles faintly in the glow from the dashboard lights. "The police and the corrections department play sort of a tag-team game to keep the prisoner away from you. Warren called Connor on the game by threatening him with a special kind of lawsuit that would leave him holding the ball all by himself."

We follow Julius's car for a while in silence, until the city lights recede behind us and there's nothing but white headlights cutting through the empty night. Finally I say, "Your brother sure is something in action."

Todd nods. "He believes in standing up for what's right. It runs in the family. We just all have our own way of doing it."

Does it? I don't say anything, but I think about all the times the guys used to rough up Todd for being different, and he just took it. Was he standing up for what was right by not even trying to conform, even though he wouldn't fight back? I think I like Warren's way better. And then I think about Todd living with his brother and sister-in-law, and wonder what his parents' way of standing up for what's right was. I have the feeling that the answer would go a long way toward explaining why Todd's always the odd man out, but I don't know how to ask.

We get to Willisford and trail the Maliks' BMW to Julius's house. The second Warren parks the car, Julius jumps out, takes the keys, and practically races up the driveway and inside the house without a backward glance. No thank you's, no see you around—nothing. Todd puts the car in park and slips out of the driver's seat into the rear as Warren walks up, frowning.

He slides in and sighs. "I think you're right, Brian. Your friend didn't do anything except get lost. But something happened that he's not telling. He said all he wants to do is pay the ticket and forget about the whole mess. I told him that they'd violated his rights by holding him in jail without any evidence of a crime, but I couldn't get a peep out of him beyond they checked the car and asked him some questions. Now he just wants to pay the ticket and get everything behind him before his parents get home. Something doesn't add up."

"I'm not sure," I say slowly, "but I think he's embarrassed about it. Maybe he doesn't want his folks to know that this happened at all. They're so proud of him—maybe he thinks if he pretends it didn't happen he can forget about it and everything'll be the way it was before."

"Unfortunately," Warren says, shifting into drive to take me home, "it doesn't work that way. Once they mark you as a potential criminal, you have no choice but to fight for what is right—at least, if you want your life back."

CHAPTER

19

Night dissolves into early morning. Even after a late night, a day's not off to the right start without shooting practice. But after I've warmed up and sunk some free throws, the door opens. I see Dad walking down to join me. He's wearing sweats and rubbing his arms a little like it's cold, even though it's not bad for the end of February.

He doesn't say anything right away, and neither do I. I just dribble down the driveway, then move in and hit an easy layup.

Behind me Dad claps, then grabs for the rebound. I don't chase it. He bounces it a couple of times, then shoots. It clangs off the edge of the rim and rolls down the driveway. I reach for it, drive back to the goal, and pop in another quick layup.

"No question who's the ball player in this family," Dad says, chuckling. He reaches for the ball again, takes longer setting up, and scores this time. "Though your old man's not hopeless."

I retrieve the ball, not wanting to banter with him, still smarting from his betrayal last night. But it's one thing to mouth off to your father in the dark of the night in the middle of a crisis, when your temper's burning that pure, white-hot rage from knowing he's let you down. It's not so easy to say the same things in the crisp morning's light when he's standing there, reaching out to you.

I guess Dad can tell I don't want to fight, but I'm not willing to meet him halfway either. He sighs. "Look, Brian—about last night." He lets the words hang there, but I don't pick up on them the way I retrieved the ball. I just stand there bouncing it, listening to the thudding rhythm, waiting for him to finish what he's started. "I guess you got Julius home all right?"

I nod, not volunteering any extra information.

Dad shoves his hands into the pockets of his sweatpants and exhales a frosty breath. "I'm glad." He pauses a minute, then says, "I'm glad you didn't listen to me. . . . I'm glad you went and got him. It was a good thing to do." He looks up at me, almost bemused. "You're a good kid, Brian. I'm proud of you, being the way you are, seeing the right thing to do and doing it." He searches my face, then shakes his head. "I only worry, sometimes, you'll charge ahead and do something that seems right to you, and only later see it's a mistake."

I can't help myself. The words just burst out. "How can it be a mistake to do the right thing?"

Dad smiles at me, a little sadly. "I know that sounds completely ridiculous to you, and it is crazy. But the truth is that if you get associated with the wrong sort of people—"

"How can Julius be the wrong sort of people?" I demand.

"There's nothing wrong with Julius," Dad says quickly. "But he got arrested. That means he's in some police database somewhere." He shakes his head. "You don't know how it works in the real world, son. They've got databases for everything, and a police computer in Indiana talks to an FBI computer or a Homeland Security computer in Washington, and suddenly a cop sees Julius driving a couple of miles over the speed limit in Ohio, runs his license plate, and finds out he's listed as some sort of suspicious character."

I shiver a little, thinking about the database project Ashley and Glenn are doing. I didn't quite get it at the time, but this is what Glenn was trying to tell us. It's a real threat.

"And if you're associated with Julius and the arrest," Dad goes on, "you can wind up in a database, too."

My head snaps up. "But that's not legal! That's not even fair!"

"The world's not fair, Brian. It's not like a basketball game." Dad shakes his head.

That's when I remember the gleam in his eye last night at the thought of Julius being out of the game. "It's not really about being associated with Julius and getting stuck in some database, is it, Dad? It's about basketball, about Julius being off the team and me being the best player."

Dad's eyes slide away. Finally he says, "I shouldn't have said that, you're right. I'm sorry. I just get caught up in hoping, and for a second there, it seemed like maybe Julius really had done something and deserved to be arrested and it could be your chance. . . . " He breaks off and sighs. "But that's not the way it should be. You can shine without anybody else stepping out of the picture to give you an edge."

"Then why did you say it?" I press.

Dad's silent for a while, and I just hold the ball, not

even bouncing it. "You'll understand when you've got a son of your own, Brian. Every father wants his son to get the breaks—to get the chances—he didn't have." He shrugs helplessly. "You don't even know how you lost those chances, how they slipped away. You're going along, and you take one wrong turn, and you think it's just a kind of temporary detour, and you'll be back on track any moment." At first I think he's talking about Julius, but then I realize he's going somewhere else completely.

"Then that detour becomes your life, and it's too late to find your way back to what you want to do." He gives me a tired look. "I don't want that to happen to you, Brian. You do something because you think it's the right thing, and maybe it's a good thing right then, at that moment. But it knocks you off track, and you just can't ever seem to get back on." I wonder what Dad has done that he thinks knocked him off track. Is it the decision to stop making guitars and open the construction business? Can't he just go back to carving, if that's what he really wants to do?

Dad looks at the backboard, then down to the ball in my hands. "You're good, Brian. You're so good. I want you to have everything I missed out on. I want you to live your dream, not get lost on some detour and see everything you wanted disappear in the rearview mirror behind you."

And because I feel sorry for him—because I love him, even thinking that he's wrong about so many things—I turn, put the ball in the hole, as sweetly as sinking a free throw, then catch it, pass it back to him, and ask, "Hey— you want to play a game of HORSE?"

His face lights up like it's Christmas, and he says, "You're on."

CHAPTER

20

The rest of the weekend zips past in a blur of speed-dialing Julius on my cell phone over and over. His phone just rings until the automatic voice mail takes over. I keep leaving the same message. "Hey, man—are you okay? It's Brian, call me." But he never calls. Highrise and Ricochet show up in the afternoon, and we mess around in the driveway, but it's not so much fun with three guys.

I don't see Julius until Monday morning, when he's strolling down the school hallway as if nothing unusual happened over the weekend, except that he's got his arm around Keesha, and she's got this huge smile on her face. I've known for ages that she's had her sights set on Julius, but he never had time for her before. He's always been hot for Brittney, but he's never walked down the hall with any girl, making some sort of public announcement that she's his exclusive property. So why suddenly be so public about hanging with Keesha?

When I see Keesha disappear around the lockers into the girls' room, I grab Julius to ask if everything's okay. "Didn't you get my messages? The guys were over playing ball, and they wondered where you were."

"I was with Keesha." He darts a fast look up and down the hallway. "You didn't tell them anything about—you know, did you?"

"Of course not! But you ought to tell them yourself."

He looks at me like I'm crazy. "No way, Brainman! I don't want anybody to know! And I wish you hadn't brought the Turd with you."

"He'll keep his mouth shut," I tell him.

"He'd better!"

"And, anyway, it was his brother who got you out."

Julius doesn't answer right away. Finally he says, "I thought your dad could do it."

I shrug, embarrassed for my father. "You know how he is—the king of not wanting to get involved unless it's basketball."

Julius glares at me. "But this is basketball! I'm this team, Brainman!"

"You're the best player on the team, but you're not exactly the whole team," I point out. I try to turn it into a weak joke. "Which has nothing to do with my dad's chronic refusal to do anything to upset the balance of his universe."

Keesha re-emerges from the girls' room and looks from one of us to the other. "What's wrong?" she asks.

"Nothing," Julius says, giving her a fast hug. "Just Brainman running on at the mouth." And he almost drags her down the hallway in the opposite direction. She shoots one uncertain glance over her shoulder at me before they turn a corner and disappear.

"Touchy, touchy," a voice says behind me. Todd's standing there, watching the spot where Julius told me off.

"You haven't told anybody, have you?" I ask.

He shakes his head. "No one's going to hear a word from me. Warren made it clear from the start that I had to keep quiet about anything I heard concerning his legal work. He's pretty easygoing about my living there, except for that one, relatively major, point."

"That's a relief." We turn and head down the hall together. "I just can't understand what's going on. I couldn't get hold of Julius all weekend and now he's acting so different—strutting around with Keesha and not wanting to talk to me at all."

Todd looks at me shrewdly. "Wouldn't you be embarrassed if you got arrested and treated like dirt and hadn't done anything wrong?"

"Sure! But I'd be angry too."

"Oh, he looks like he's angry, all right. I'm glad we've already shot the movie. I wouldn't want to get too near him anytime soon. He looks like he'd have trouble remembering I don't fit in my locker anymore." Then he asks, "So when are we going to finish this project? We've still got to lay down the music and write the presentation script."

"Right." My mind's more on Julius than Leo Frank. "When's good for you?"

"Anytime you're not playing ball," Todd says, grinning. "I've already written a draft of the text boxes to put with the silent movie, and I've got an idea about the music."

"What?"

"If you can tune that guitar of yours, why don't you bring it by and we'll lay down some folk music that gives the feel of the old South? I've got an electric keyboard that feeds right into the computer, and we can mike your guitar." He swings his backpack around and pulls out a couple of music books. "I've marked some pieces I think would work. It's not hard music." He must pick up on my ambivalence. "Unless you don't want to use your guitar," he adds.

"No, it's fine," I say, taking the music. "I'm just out of practice." I shrug a little sheepishly. "I never really played with anybody except Amanda, and she could make up for me."

Todd smiles. "Well, I'm not too bad on the keyboard, so it should work out all right then. If you can make it one afternoon this week, I can probably get Warren or Elise to drive you home. Or the weekend would work, if that's better for you."

"Let's do it Saturday," I tell him. "We've got games Tuesday and Friday, and I need time to practice—guitar as well as ball."

"Don't worry," he says cheerfully. "Your fingers will remember the chords, even if your mind doesn't. But they might hurt. Soak them after you practice, so they won't stiffen up and get in the way of your game."

I remember thinking that Todd might not be such a bad partner after all. Now I think I was lucky to get him. We're going to end up with the best project in the class.

—————

If only team practice would go as smoothly as working with Todd on the movie. Coach is afraid we'll be too cocky after beating the Spartans, and he drills us hard to remind us not to ignore fundamentals when we go up against the Cougars on Tuesday. He's right, but the guys want to feel good about themselves, and he ought to let them.

After what feels like the ninety-ninth iteration of layups on the same pass-shoot scenario, we're all wanting to get loose and use our moves, and he doesn't want to let us. Julius is the one who blows up first. He races through one final drill, then grabs the ball, flies downcourt, stops, fakes out an imaginary defender at the top of the key, and goes up to sink it hard. He sprints in to grab the ball before it hits the floor, races outside and shoots again. Unbelievably, the ball clangs off the rim, but he's already under it, takes it out to the far side, and shoots again, his moves almost manic.

One by one, the rest of the guys stop drilling on the other side of the gym and turn to watch. Julius moves like he's burning up from within, in snappy jerks instead of his usual smooth grace. He's taking chances and sinking most of his shots, but not all of them, and the more he shoots the harder he pushes himself. This is no cool-down shooting free throws. He's fueling a fire.

"That's enough!" Coach yells, blowing his whistle, but Julius doesn't seem to hear. He just keeps running and shooting, breathing hard in time to the rhythm of the ball. "Stop that, Malik!" Coach shouts. "Stop that this instant!"

Julius may need to burn off heat from the weekend, and the court may be the only safe place for him to let loose, but he's scaring the other guys, especially the kid, Wrestler, and that's not helping the team at all. Julius is even scaring me, and I know what happened. On top of that, he's infuriating Coach, which isn't going to improve the guy's shaky coaching at all. I'm the team captain. I move in on defense, not trying to stop him, but going for the ball when it falls through the net, and lunging out of bounds with it before he can grab it back. He reaches for it anyway, but I mutter, "Quit it, Joyous—you're freaking the team out. Get a grip, man."

His hands are already on the ball, but he stares at me, almost snarling as if he's facing a guard on a really vicious team. Then, slowly, he registers it's me. His hands drop to his sides, and he looks around at the rest of the team like he only now realizes he lost it.

"What in the world did you think you were doing out there?" Coach demands, his face red.

Julius looks like he's about to say something he'll regret, so I bounce the ball hard a couple of times, then send him an easy bounce pass. "He's just pumped for the game, Coach," I say. "We all are. And, you know, after the drills we've got to let the excitement out somehow. That's all."

Coach looks around at us. The other guys are nodding, following my lead even if they're not sure what's going on. Julius just stands there, watching the ball as he bounces it hard against the gym floor.

"You can get so pumped you forget your fundamentals," Coach says finally. "That's what the drills are all about."

"Sure, we know that," I tell him.

"Okay then." He looks around at us uncertainly, as if he knows he hasn't gotten to the heart of the matter but isn't sure where to go next. Then he asks, "So how are these famous projects coming along? You're all going to get good grades on them, and you're keeping your grades up in your other classes, right?"

"Coach, the projects are so awesome Mr. Fortner is going to give every one of us an A," Ray assures him. The others chime in with updates, and he looks pleased. I don't volunteer anything about the movie, to mask the fact that Julius is still silent. He's holding the ball under one arm now, just looking down at the floor. Coach looks like maybe he's going to ask him about it, then either thinks better of it or gets distracted when Wrestler asks for help working on his free throws while the rest of us cool down and head for the showers.

"Have you done anything on your project?" I ask Julius. "Can we help out?"

Julius shrugs. "Ask Lesbo. I don't care about the stupid project. I told her I'd stand up there with her, and if she gives me something to read I'll read it. But it's a waste of time. Nice, clean white history. Why didn't Fortner ask somebody to research what we learned about the black civil rights movement, or something relevant like that?"

"Good point," I agree. Even though Julius knows perfectly well that Ashley and Glenn are working on the FBI investigation of Martin Luther King Jr., since we helped them with their database presentation, I think it would just make matters worse to point that out to him. I've never heard him go on this kind of racial tirade before. He's always acted color-blind. At least, he did before the police got hold of him. "Come on, man—it's just schoolwork. What difference does it make what the teachers assign? We do it, we keep our grades up, we play ball."

Julius grabs his towel and mutters over his shoulder, "Sometimes playing ball isn't enough. Sometimes you feel like you've got to do something more or just explode. And you don't need to be wasting time on prissy school assignments about history that don't matter to anyone except some white teacher."

I let him go because I have no clue how to answer. I know how it feels to want to explode—that's how I felt when I found out Amanda was dead. But I've made playing ball be enough. I made it be everything, until this history project got in the way. Maybe Julius hopes he can make Keesha and playing ball be enough now.

I hang back in the locker room, but Julius is waiting for me outside, one arm hugging Keesha's neck like he's choking her, only she doesn't look like it hurts, just like it's a little unexpected. "Come on, Brainman," he calls. "Time for pizza."

I don't feel like pizza. I feel tired. I just want to get away from everything for a while, so I shake my head. "After we beat the Cougars tomorrow," I promise.

Julius shoots me an angry look, then pivots Keesha around. "Come on, girl," he says. "We don't need him."

She hugs him around the waist as they walk away, and I can hear her saying, "It's okay, Joyous. I think he just wanted some time alone, you know? Or maybe he figures we want some time alone." I can't hear what he answers.

CHAPTER

21

I barely walk a block before I hook a ride home with Paul's and Matt's mom. She's been out grocery shopping, and lets me take the front seat while the twins squeeze in around the bags in the back. While they settle down, she tells me again how much they loved helping make the film. "It was really nice of you to let them participate." I just thank her, without trying to explain that Todd was the one who figured out that was the easiest way to deal with them.

"Good luck against the Cougars tomorrow night and the Eagles this Friday!" she tells me as she drops me off in our cul-de-sac. The twins scream, "Go Warriors!" and I grin and wave.

But right now I don't want to think about the Cougars or the Eagles or basketball or Julius. I want to get away from the feeling that things are moving too fast around me. The season's rushing to its end, Julius is rushing in some direction that I can't understand, Dad's rushing me down some road he thinks is the right one for me because he's afraid he lost the one that was right for him. Mom's rushing back and forth between me and Dad, trying not to make him feel worse about refusing to go to the jail to get Julius at the same time she's trying to show me she's proud of me both for getting Warren to help my friend and for making up with Dad the next morning. And from the newspapers over the weekend, I think the prosecution is rushing toward the end of its case against Mr. Daine. I just want to get away from it all and slow down until I can get a handle on what I'm supposed to do about everything—about anything.

Without stopping to pick up my ball and shoot some quick hoops, I go to my room, get my guitar, and head out to the wood shop. The stillness settles over me and my footsteps on the stairway sound hollow, like footfalls in an empty gym, a sound that's at once lonely, yet filled with memories and also with the promise of future games. When I sit down in Dad's carving room, up at the top of the tower, it's as if Amanda sits beside me with her own guitar in hand. I can hear her teasing me that my fingers are long enough to make perfect chords, but what in the world am I doing with those choppy strums? I don't mind. She's the musician. It's enough to accompany her.

I tune my guitar, amazed at how easily it comes back to me, then run through the fingering on the folk songs Todd has marked. My fingers really do remember their positions on the frets, and the guitar feels comforting cradled in my arms. But when I try actually playing the songs, the strings cut into my fingers and my hands fumble. Echoes of Amanda's laughter fill the room. "So play with me," I say softly. "Help me get it right."

More than just hearing her play the lead, so all I have to do is follow her, it's as if I can feel her fingers resting on mine, helping me find the rhythm. I close out the world rushing past outside the tower and play, following the guitar's sense (*Amanda's sense*) of the way the music should sound. Above, the shadows change shape until I realize it's time to go in for supper. I put the guitar down reluctantly and discover my fingertips are throbbing. I'll have to soak them, as Todd warned.

Mom and Dad are in the kitchen. He's stirring garlic slices in butter, and the smell makes my stomach gurgle as if it hasn't been fed for days instead of hours. When I come in he dumps a bowl of snap beans into the skillet, and the sound of their sizzling fills the room. "I heard you playing when I came home," he tells me over his shoulder. "You sounded good."

"Thanks. It's the guitar you made me, though, more than my playing." We never talk about my using the wood shop since he doesn't work there anymore. I figure he'll tell me if he wants me to stay out of his space. I almost wish he would, since it might mean he wants to get back to working there himself.

Mom smiles at me and passes me a bowl of mashed potatoes. "It's good to hear you making music as well as playing ball," she says.

Dad looks torn between being pleased I'm using the guitar he made and worrying that I should have been playing ball instead, until Mom catches his eye. After giving the beans another stir, he catches her from behind and puts his arms around her for a quick squeeze, and tells me, "Yeah, you sound good."

I put the potatoes on the table and go wash up while Mom brings in the lamb chops and salad, and Dad dishes up the green beans. While we eat, I assure them that we're ready to take on the Cougars and carefully avoid the subject of Julius. Dad doesn't ask about him, and Mom doesn't mention him, either. For a change we just slow down and have a peaceful evening.

After supper I tackle the homework I didn't finish in study hall and finally head into the front room to catch the news. I'm not sure whether I'm hoping for news about a breakthrough in Mr. Daine's trial or just watching for some local sports news. I catch the end of some moronic sitcom and wait it out, soaking my fingers in a bowl of an aloe mixture that old Coach Ritter told me how to make. It used to drive him crazy that I wasted my fingers on the guitar, but he finally decided it would be easier to show me how to cope than to keep trying to talk me out of it.

Finally, the canned laugh track fades out and the news anchorman appears, managing to look both friendly and serious at the same time.

ANCHORMAN
In the Daine murder case today, former Willisford police officer Michael Daine looked outraged as he listened to damaging testimony from one of his fellow officers, Claude Recks. Natalie Hart was on the scene.

   (New picture: red-haired woman standing on the courthouse steps, microphone in hand.)

NATALIE HART
The prosecution's earlier forensic witness

testified emphatically that the shots that killed Caroline Daine and her two children came from a .380, and were consistent with a handgun that Michael Daine owned. Although the defense attorney argued that the handgun in question had been sold some time before the killings, he did not dispute the fact that Mr. Daine had, indeed, owned a .380 and had practiced with it. He implied, however, that Mr. Daine was an indifferent shot with his handgun and could not have made the single-shot kills. Today the prosecution presented a witness who challenged that idea, police officer Claude Recks.

(New picture: camera rests on a uniformed man striding down the courthouse stairs, holding a thin file folder in one hand and looking regretful but determined.)

NATALIE HART (voice-over)
Officer Recks testified today that Michael Daine had often shot on the police range with other officers and was an excellent shot. He spoke to reporters after the court recessed for the day.

(The uniformed man stops at a small podium crowded with microphones and faces a group of ·reporters; camera zooms in on him and an identifying caption below reads "Officer Claude Recks, Outside County Courthouse.")

OFFICER RECKS

I'd like to read a brief statement. I've worked with Officer Daine for years, and I believe he is an honest cop. But I was called in to court to testify that he's a good shot. I know he is, because he's proved that on the range time and again. Because I knew the Daine family well, because I played with those kids, I was one of the first officers on the scene.

(Camera pulls in for a close-up of OFFICER RECKS'S face.)

I cannot and will not ever say that Officer Daine shot his family last August. My business doesn't lie in deciding who's guilty or innocent. My business lies solely in finding evidence, and the ballistics evidence conclusively proves that a good shot committed these murders. It wasn't easy to testify against my fellow officer in court today. I didn't do it because I wanted publicity from you people. Frankly, that's the last thing I want. You face a hundred crossroads and you have to choose which way to turn. It's my business to make the right choice, even if it's a painful choice, in making certain that the state is in possession of accurate evidence.

NATALIE HART
(voice over image of OFFICER RECKS)
Officer Recks is not the prosecution's last witness in what has become a lengthy trial, Peter. Despite the defense's insistence that Mr. Daine disposed of his .380 prior to the killings, and the prosecution's inability to match a murder weapon to the bullets recovered from the victims, the prosecutors feel their evidence proves beyond a reasonable doubt that Mr. Daine had the means to commit these murders.

(Camera cuts back to NATALIE HART on the courthouse steps.)

Although the prosecution insists it has proved opportunity, the defense is sticking with the alibi that Mr. Daine was playing basketball when the murders occurred. Even prosecution witnesses confirm that Mr. Daine was at the gym with his team, but they admit that he was not on the court the whole time and could have slipped out without anyone noticing. This evidence leaves one element of a murder case that the prosecution has yet to address: motive. They intend to begin

calling witnesses this week to show that Mr.
Daine had reason to want his family dead.
Back to you, Peter.

My fingertips are puckering in the bowl. I lift my hands
and dry them deliberately before clicking the remote to
switch off the television. What possible motivation could
the prosecution think Amanda's father had to kill her and
Cory, and his own wife?

I can't bear to think about it. Instead, I remember
Officer Recks questioning me after the bodies were found.
I wonder about his testimony today that Mr. Daine was
such a good shot—good enough to make three shots in a
row like that. I try not to think about how it would feel to
look at your own family and pull a trigger to end their lives.
That's not the question. I remind myself that even if Mr.
Daine really could make three perfect shots in a row, that
doesn't mean he actually did it. But it does mean there's a
lot I don't know about him, and maybe one of the things I
don't know is why he might have wanted to kill his family.
And maybe that means they're trying the right man after
all, and the jogger I saw had nothing to do with it, like Dad
said. Except—Dad has been wrong about a lot of things,
lately. I can't help wondering if he's wrong about this, too.

I find I can't bear to think about that, either.

"I'm going in. Get me the
chest-cracking kit now."

"Are you qualified for this procedure?"

"It doesn't matter. I'm here,
and I'm the last chance this kid's got."

CHAPTER

22

The week blurs past in a haze of practicing: practicing free throws in the morning before school, practicing with the team in the afternoons, practicing the guitar when I get home from school. Beating the Cougars is barely a blip in the rush of time. Keesha must have talked some sense into Julius, because he cools off enough to follow Coach's game plan. But he's wired at practice the rest of the week, like there's some dragon inside of him that's itching to get out and scorch all of us.

Friday game night comes up before I know what to expect from him. He follows the drills in practice, but he's been striking poses and making faces behind Coach's back. By the time we face the Eagles, I don't know what he'll do on the court, and that worries me. Our team works together because we know each other. When Ray gets the ball to me, some part of my brain instinctively knows my guys' moves. If I can't predict where Julius will be, how can I get him the ball when he's open, and send it to Highrise or Ricochet when he's not? And his parents aren't back yet. I'd feel better knowing they were in the stands, watching over Julius.

The Eagles charge out onto the court, acting like they own it even though it's our gym. Their cheerleaders and road fans whoop it up, but when we run out our fans let us know we rule. I glance up to see Mom and Dad clapping and waving, and catch Todd's eye as well. He's sitting alone up near the top of the bleachers, clapping for our team. He waves two fingers in my direction in a casual salute. I wish I could feel as calm as he looks. But I can see something burning in Julius's eyes that looks like the dragon's about to break loose.

It happens almost immediately. We open with a fast break. Julius takes the ball down the court and stuffs it for the opening score, then steals the ball and adds an immediate layup. Our fans are cheering and he's got a wide grin across his face, almost manic. The Eagles put the ball back in play far away from Julius, but Take-away Ray gets the ball and kicks it to me. I see Highrise is open, but Julius is waving and I know he's hot, so I whip him the ball. He pivots and shoots—and hits from 30 feet.

Now the gym's rocking. People are on their feet on both sides, cheering Julius or screaming for the Eagles to defend against him. Keesha signals the girls and Ashley does a series of somersaults as the others sing out:
"We play hot,
We play cold,
On the court
We explode—
Warriors are gonna win!"
The Eagles rush upcourt to get past him and sink a three-pointer, but when Ricochet inbounds to Highrise, Julius doesn't even give him time to get it to me to set up

the next play. He dodges in front of me, signals Highrise to pass to him, then crosses the court with big strides to shoot long again. But this time he misses. We weren't expecting the shot, so Ricochet isn't in place for the rebound—there's nobody there except a flock of Eagles. Our fans groan.

The Eagles race upcourt again, make three crisp passes, and score before our guys can set up any kind of defense. Their fans are cheering as Ray takes the ball out, but Julius streaks up the court and cuts in front of me to grab the ball, determined to make his shot this time. I can see the other guys looking at me, confused. The Eagles close in on Julius but he shoots anyway. I catch my breath, because no one is under the basket for the rebound, but this one goes in for three. Julius pumps his fist in the air as the Eagles take it out. But Take-away Ray intercepts the inbound pass and gets it to Ricochet, who passes directly to me this time. Julius is in my face almost immediately, grabbing for the ball. In the confusion an Eagle fouls me and Coach signals for a time-out. We head over to the side before I shoot my free throws.

"What do you think you're doing out there, Malik?" Coach demands when we gather by the bench.

"Winning the game," Julius retorts. He grabs a paper cup of water, acting like he doesn't care when some sloshes over the brim, and chugs it.

"You're hogging the ball," Coach tells him flatly. "You play with your teammates, or you sit on the bench! Do you understand me?"

Julius locks eyes with him for a long, defiant moment before nodding. "Sure, Coach. I understand you."

"And you." Coach turns to me. "What are you doing letting him take charge? You're the point guard—you control the plays on the court. Now do your job or you can both ride the bench the second half!"

"Yes sir," I mumble, knowing he's right.

"We play as a team," Coach orders. "Remember that!"

The other guys nod, halfheartedly, not knowing what's going on. We run out and the ref blows the whistle to signal the end of the time-out. He announces I have two free throws and hands me the ball. I close my eyes so I don't have to meet Julius's burning glare. I look down at the line, to set my position, then bounce the ball the way I always do before I take my shots, feeling its rhythm as much as hearing it. A free throw is easy, if no one's watching. It's just practice and keeping your focus. It gets harder when both sides are screaming at you in a gym.

I ignore the noise and open my eyes on nothing but the basket, waiting for me. But Julius has me more shaken than I realize, and the first shot rattles around the rim before stuttering through the hoop. The ref brings the ball back to me and blows his whistle again. I bounce it once, twice, ordering myself to focus, then shoot again. The ball teeters on the rim, but finally falls through the hole before the Eagles break for it and race us down the court to their goal.

Julius manages to contain himself during the rest of the first half, letting me control the flow and signal for Shooter and Wrestler to come in to give the other guys a break and keep the Eagles off balance. But I can feel Julius's eyes burning into me whenever I pass to anyone other than him. I can't understand it—sure, what happened was bad. But he's got Warren on his side, and when his parents come back they'll be furious with the police, not with him. He's got to get past it. Or did something more happen, something he's not telling me?

But I don't have time to think about it, and I can't ask Coach to bench him long enough to cool off. The Eagles slide into a zone defense, and I need every player ready to shoot. We hold onto our lead, but by halftime everybody's strung to the max.

"Why aren't you getting the ball to me more?" Julius demands as we head into the locker room at the half. "You want points, you want to beat them big, you get me the ball!"

"You're not the only one putting points up there," Ricochet interrupts, glaring at Julius.

"You be right about that!" Julius retorts, and he sounds funny, like he's trying to talk black or something. He's never talked like that before. "And if the rest of you guys clear out and give me some room, I be racking up so many points the Eagles be dead!"

The rest of the guys stare at him as if he's talking Chinese all of a sudden. "We're a team, Joyous," I say, trying to remind him that it's a game he used to enjoy playing, not a war. "If you keep the ball, the Eagles are going to guard you so tight you won't be able to do anything with it."

Coach goes even farther, screaming at us that we're not playing as a team, calling Julius a ball hog and telling Ray he's playing like a girl against the Eagle point guard because his steals are down.

We listen numbly and jog back out on the court. This half, I'm determined not to let Julius ball hog, and he senses it the first time I get the ball and pass it to Ricochet for a neat layup.

"That should have been my shot," he hisses at me as he runs downcourt. He ducks in front of Ray and grabs the ball, then runs it blindly back to the goal, not even looking to see if anyone's open. He shoots as the Eagles close in, but it clangs off the rim. If it weren't for Ricochet's inside game we'd be sunk, but he's in place for the rebound. Julius doesn't thank him. We stay ahead of the Eagles, but after Julius keeps three more balls he should have passed off, Coach takes him out of the game.

Furious, Julius storms off the court and kicks a chair leg before dropping heavily into it.

"You'll sit there until you remember this is a team sport!" Coach tells him, just as furious. "And if you don't, you'll stay on the bench for the rest of the season—yes, even with Jackson coming up!"

Julius keeps his mouth shut, and Shooter runs onto the court, looking tense, but he settles into the rhythm of the game after a few minutes and we're clicking as a team for the first time this evening. I keep the ball with Ricochet and Highrise for a few plays, letting them take easy shots, and when the Eagles stop worrying about Shooter I pass to him for a beautiful three-point jumper, showing them we still have an outside game even without Julius.

When we go into the showers, the 83–75 score doesn't begin to give the idea of the game tension. Coach gives the game ball to Highrise, saying he managed to keep his head out there, and implying he's the only one who did. Julius looks furious, and even though we won I feel defeated. We don't even bother celebrating, just head out in different directions after our showers. Julius leads the exodus with Keesha, roaring off in his parents' car. I'll be so relieved when they get back home this week.

Ashley drives me home, hinting about going out for pizza, or maybe going somewhere to park, but I shake my head. "I'm sorry," I tell her, then don't have the words to tell her what I'm apologizing for.

She pulls into my driveway, shifts into park, and sits there looking down at her hands in her lap for a minute. Then she kind of leans against me, still looking down, her smooth hair resting under my chin. I put an arm around her, without meaning to, and she fits in my hug unexpectedly well, warm and soft. All-the-way Ashley, Julius calls her. Would she . . . ? She turns her face up to mine, and my body bends by itself until my lips brush hers. I will myself not to think about the crime-scene house with its forever darkened windows behind us, and the girl I love who's gone now. Instead, I wait for the electric explosion to go off inside me, even without the fireworks overhead, but nothing happens. After a moment I straighten up.

Ashley says, "I'm sorry. I know I'm not Amanda, and I won't ever be. I guess you're going to have to figure out for yourself how to get past her memory."

I'm surprised at her understanding. I hug her again, swift and tight, and let go. "Thank you," I say, and she nods. As soon as I'm out of the car, she backs the Bomb into the cul-de-sac and drives away.

I walk into a darkened house, with nothing except the outdoor lights left on. It's no real surprise, because I know Mom and Dad expect me to be out with the team after the win, but the empty darkness adds to my sense of letdown. I feel my way into the kitchen through the shadows of the familiar hallway and get out some Gatorade. The light from the refrigerator illuminates the stack of newspapers for recycling, and the sports section is on top. I pick it up, looking for some sort of distraction, and beneath it I see the main news section it had hidden. The front-page headline adds the final touch to the day: PROSECUTION IN DAINE CASE RESTS and in slightly smaller print beneath it: WITNESSES TESTIFY ABOUT POSSIBLE MOTIVATION FOR MURDERS.

I swig the Gatorade, then carry the paper into my room and switch on the reading lamp over my desk. I spread out the paper on top of the clutter of magazines and notebooks and begin to read.

"Two final witnesses for the prosecution testified today that Officer Daine had had sexual relations with them, following the four other witnesses the prosecution had previously put on the stand this week. But the final witness stunned the courtroom by saying that she and Officer Daine had discussed marriage, if only he were free to do so."

I close my eyes, seeing Amanda begging me to let Cory and her play with us that afternoon, telling me in that low, troubled voice, "Things aren't so good at home right now." Had her father asked for a divorce? Had her mother refused to give him one without a fight? But surely her mother wouldn't just pack the kids off to the pool if something that dramatic had happened!

"Under cross-examination by defense counsel, Ms. Brenda Pitfield (an earlier witness) explained that the intimate relations she had enjoyed with Officer Daine were not serious on either part. 'It was just a fling,' she told the jury, blushing slightly. 'The uniform was, well, kind of exciting, and when he made it clear this was a one-time thing, I thought, well, why not?'

"But Ms. Anne Riley's testimony was more damaging, as she revealed under direct examination by the prosecution that she had been with Officer Daine on numerous occasions. When questioned by the defense, however, Ms. Riley explained, 'Sure, we talked about getting married someday, but it was just one of those things you say to someone you're having a good time with: wouldn't it be great if we could get married someday? But you both know it's not going to happen, and you don't really want it to, because it wouldn't be the same if you were married.'

"Ms. Riley also clarified that she had had relations with Officer Daine 'on, perhaps, three or four occasions.' Prosecutors had implied that their relationship had been considerably more long-term. The prosecution objected but was overruled. On redirect, the prosecutor attempted to get Ms. Riley to confirm the earlier interpretation of her testimony. The witness appeared to laugh as she said, 'Well, three or four are numbers, so that would be numerous, wouldn't it?' Nevertheless, the prosecution felt confident enough that they had proven motive for first-degree murder, opportunity, and means. The defense will begin presenting its evidence next week."

Suddenly my chest feels like it's exploding with rage—rage at the prosecutors, rage at Amanda's father for being so stupid as to sleep around like that, rage at Julius for the way he's acting, rage at the police who arrested him, even rage at Amanda for leaving me to deal with all of this alone. I rip the newspaper into tiny pieces, not caring that

Amanda always insisted it was so important to recycle. I bury the shreds in my wastebasket and wish I had something else to rip apart. But there's nothing, and I end up just switching off the lamp with a violent twist and falling into bed, listening to my heart pounding like the basketball Julius dribbled with such fury on the court. Somehow time dissolves into morning without any detours into the angry dreams that hammer me in the dark.

CHAPTER

23

I can't concentrate on the Leo Frank movie. It takes every ounce of control to act normal while Mom drives me to Todd's house with my guitar in its case and my backpack stuffed full of sheet music and research notes. By the time I climb the stairs to Todd's room, my eyes are burning and I can barely focus on his draft of the text boxes. Laying down the music tracks is even harder. I try to tune my guitar, but my hands are shaking so badly I can't pluck the strings.

I watch Todd plugging in his keyboard and adjusting the feed, and try to take deep breaths to get control of myself before we lay down the music we planned. He's focused on setting up his equipment and never even turns around to look at me, so his question comes as a complete surprise.

"What's wrong?"

It can be a lot easier to talk to someone's back than to his face. Before I realize I've started talking, I'm telling him everything about the prosecutor bringing up all these affairs he claims Mr. Daine had, acting like it was obvious that any guy who'd sleep with someone other than his wife would be ready to kill her, just so it would be easier to sleep around some more. "I know Amanda told me that things were worse between her parents, but people get divorced because a guy sleeps around—not murdered! It's not even like Mrs. Daine had a lot of money and he would have gotten that. The prosecutor can't tie it all together—he's just throwing mud and hoping enough of it's going to stick that the jury decides Mr. Daine must have done it because they don't like him."

Todd sits down in his desk chair and runs one hand up the length of his polished black-and-white keyboard, looking thoughtful. "Well, in order to prove murder you have to prove motive, and husbands who are having affairs have been known to kill their wives. He's even admitted he slept with those women, so—"

"So what?" I'm practically shouting at him. "This guy at school—" (I don't say this guy on the team, since it's Ray's private problem and none of Todd's business who the guy is.) "—his father's slept around, and his mom didn't wind up dead. She threatened to leave her husband, and he begged her not to go and actually cried, so she stayed— even when he went out and did it with someone else! They're still all living under one roof, and nobody's dead. If every guy who slept around was locked up because people believed adultery always leads to murder, there wouldn't be any room in the jails for real criminals!"

"That's not the point. Why are you so positive this guy's innocent, anyway?" That kind of rocks me, because I'm not certain he's innocent. I just know this isn't the way to prove anybody guilty. When I don't answer, he shrugs and says, "Well, if the prosecution feels this establishes motive, then it makes sense for them to bring it up."

"No, it doesn't!" I can't believe this guy. "Don't you get

it? Sex is one of those things that scares people! That's why the prosecutor told everyone in the Leo Frank case that he'd come on to all the girls working for him in the pencil factory and made it sound like he'd raped Mary Phagan when she'd never even had sex! If you smear a guy's character by claiming he had sex with someone he shouldn't— even if it's not true, like with Leo Frank, even if it doesn't have anything to do with the case, like with Mr. Daine, then people start to believe he's capable of doing all sorts of terrible things."

Todd swallows. "You're right that people have strange ideas about sex," he admits, a little unsteadily. "And the prosecutor lied about Leo Frank. But apparently this prosecutor *is* telling the truth about Mr. Daine's affairs."

"So that makes him a murderer?" I shake my head. "What happened to you making such a big deal about civil rights and the beauty of the justice system? If you believe that sleeping around makes you a killer, that's like thinking being gay makes someone molest little boys, or being black makes a guy dangerous to white people, so the police were right to arrest Julius!"

Todd has gone white. His fingers spill loosely across the keyboard, and it almost slides off his lap before he fumbles to catch it. Maybe I'm finally getting through to him.

"Sex and race—they're just ways of labeling someone who's different to make him sound like he must be a criminal even if he hasn't done anything," I say flatly. "I'd have thought you, of all people, would know better than to jump to conclusions based on unfair assumptions."

"You're right." Todd's voice is barely above a whisper. Then he asks, "How did you know?"

What's he talking about? When I don't say anything, he almost repeats himself. Almost, but not quite.

"How did you know I was gay?"

I feel the heat rise, burning my throat. I didn't know. Or did I suspect that's what set him apart, and just not want to admit it to myself? I grope for something to say. "Is that why you left home?"

"That's why my parents threw me out," Todd says quietly. "My father's a minister—very conservative, very traditional. When I realized I was gay, I was honest about it. And my parents practically went crazy. First they put me through all these prayers and cleansing rituals." His voice shakes a little and I don't ask what he means. "And when I told them those feelings weren't going away, my father told me all about tough love and standing up for what was right, even if I was his son. He told me I was an abomination and I'd given myself to Satan, and my mother told me I was worse than the beasts in the fields. Then they told me as far as they were concerned, I wasn't their son any longer."

"Todd . . ." For the first time I want to put a hand on his shoulder, like I'd squeeze a teammate's shoulder to let him know he's not alone, he's got friends. But I can't do it. I don't think he wants me to touch him. Or maybe I don't want to touch him even though I want to do something.

"So I called Warren from a pay phone and he came and got me." He smiles without humor. "My father already thought lawyers were the scum of the earth and women should be in the kitchen, not in the operating room, so he didn't approve of Warren and Elise anyway. Funny how easy it was for him to turn his back on his kids so he could minister in absolute purity to his flock."

"Has he gotten over it now?" I ask tentatively.

Todd looks at me for a moment, then shakes his head. "They're just down the road a few miles, close enough I didn't even have to change schools when I moved here, but neither of them have spoken to me in two and a half years."

There's a pause, but I can't think of anything to say. I can't imagine my folks ever being so disgusted with me, no matter what I did, that they'd cut me off like that.

"So Warren and Elise took me in. I've always had summer jobs and we'd all gotten a little money from Gram's estate when she died, so I'm not much of a burden on them. I don't spend much money on anything except the bike and my computer stuff." He shrugs. "It's working out okay."

He stares out the window. "So, does knowing that make you look at me differently? I mean—we've almost finished the project. It doesn't matter if you want to go back to cracking jokes about me with your team."

He keeps staring into space, as if he really doesn't care how I answer, but I hear an undercurrent in his voice, a tension. How I answer does matter to him. Two months ago I wouldn't have heard that, and I wouldn't have cared if I did. We haven't exactly become friends, but I don't want to hurt his feelings, any more than I'd want to hurt Julius, or even the least important player on the team. I don't want to lie to him, either.

"I *do* see you differently," I admit. He stiffens and I shake my head. "No—I mean, I've always had the feeling there was something different about you, and it's bugged me, not knowing what. Now I know. But it's like knowing Julius is black. I'm not. I won't ever be. I won't ever know what it's like to be black, or to be—gay. But once we got past driving each other crazy, I've liked working with you. I'm not going to pretend I don't know you anymore, once the assignment is over." Now that I've said the words aloud, I realize I'm not just trying to make Todd feel better. I mean what I'm saying.

"And your parents were wrong," I add. "I mean—it's unfair assumptions again, isn't it? Except it hurts more when it's your own folks. A lot more."

He doesn't answer. After a moment, I finger a little riff on the guitar and realize I'm not blind with rage anymore. I guess the injustices are piling up too high to feel enraged. All I can do is deal with one thing at a time. Getting the team through the game last night, laying down the music with Todd, finishing this project. I flip to the first song he marked and play the opening. "Want to start with this one? Let's see if you can make me sound halfway good."

He adjusts the keyboard, positions his hands above the keys, and says quietly, "You sound good without any help."

CHAPTER

24

Just—one thing
at—a time.
One—by one
fix—them all.

I listen to the rhythm of the ball as we go through the motions of the lopsided half-court game in my driveway Sunday afternoon, still only five players where there should be six. Still no Julius.

One thing at a time, I remind myself. I've got the project under control, or Todd and I do, anyway. I've learned to deal with Todd—or, at least, I'm learning. As I dodge to guard Ricochet, I catch sight of a rusty deck chair tipped on its side on the corner of Amanda's front porch, but I shut it out. I can't think about Amanda yet. Maybe it's not time yet to deal with that. Maybe it's time I figure out how to deal with Julius instead. The first thing is getting him through Mr. Fortner's project, because if he doesn't pass history he's not going to be playing even if he gets his act together on the court.

I reach out and snag the ball as Ray lobs a soft bounce pass to Highrise.

"Guys—anybody have any idea where Julius is today?"

There's dead silence. After his performance on Friday, I don't think the guys miss him all that much. But he's one of us, and I know we need him. "Look," I tell them, "he's having a tough time right now, and he needs our help. For a start, there's this project—I don't think he's done any work on his at all, and we've got the presentations coming up next week."

They don't say anything, just look at one another. Then Highrise shrugs. "I don't know anything about him having a tough time—he sure hasn't bothered to fill us in. And he hasn't asked any of us for help on his project. Maybe Leslie's taking care of it for him."

"You know it's got to be a joint effort, Highrise," I remind them. "Fortner will flunk Julius flat out if he thinks he didn't do his share—and that leaves him benched for Jackson on Friday."

Shooter swallows uneasily as that sinks in. He loves charging in for the save, but the idea of starting for Julius and playing the whole game probably spooks him.

Ray taps the ball out of my hand, pivots, and shoots. Swish. He lets Ricochet grab the ball and turns back to me, hands on his hips. "So what? It's not like Julius has been such a great asset on the court this past week. And he's not here for us today."

The others nod, and I can tell Ray's put into words what they've all been thinking. So I make a tough decision. I promised Julius not to tell anybody, but sometimes you have to speak out about things instead of keeping your mouth shut.

"Remember the night he drove his folks to the airport?"

I tell them about his call and getting him out of jail with Warren, ending with, "This is just between us, guys—it's team business, nobody else's. I'm not even sure he's had a chance to tell his folks yet."

"So that's what's been eating Julius alive," Ray says quietly. "It looks like he wants to fight back . . . and if he can't fight back in a law court, he can't do anything but fight us on the ball court."

I'm impressed. The take-away artist understands more than I'd have guessed.

Then Highrise says, "The Turd knows?"

I nod. "Yeah, and he knows how to keep his mouth shut, too. He's proven that."

"Hard to admit it," Ricochet says, "but old Todd's turning out to be pretty much an okay guy."

I don't say anything about Todd's admission he's gay. I don't guess the guys would react as badly as his parents did, but there are limits to the way my team defines an okay guy. Anyway, this is about Julius, not Todd. "So I think we need to cut Julius some slack and take some of the pressure off him, by making sure he gets this project done, to start with."

"So what's the plan, Brainman?" asks Irv.

They're all looking to me for the answers, now, just the way they do on the court. "I was thinking maybe we surprise him after practice one day this week," I tell them. "You know, set out for pizza, but wind up at the library. The real problem is getting Leslie there too." I explain about running into her in the library myself. "She really hates jocks. I don't think she's going to be too thrilled if we ask her to meet us there, no matter how nicely we go about it."

The guys look at each other. Ray suggests, "Kidnapping?"

We all laugh, but I have to say, "Man, she's just the type who'd do something nasty, like press charges."

"Too true," Shooter agrees.

"Not us," Ray says. "The girls."

"Get the girls to kidnap Leslie Lesbo?" Ricochet cracks up. "Oh, that's rich, man!"

Ray grins, looking pleased with himself. "Hey, if anybody can fool Leslie into doing things their way, it's Bright Eyes Brittney."

I get the ball from Ricochet, feeling better now that we've got a plan, and dribble toward the basket.

Step—by step,
you—just do
what—you can.

I shoot a soft layup and recover it as it drops through the hoop. "Monday may not give the girls enough time, but we don't have a game this Tuesday. How about then? It still gives us a week to help Julius and Leslie put together a cool project in time for the presentations."

Everybody nods. We circle, hands outstretched, clasping in the center, as if getting ready for the opening tip-off. "Team!" Or brothers. Or, even, friends. As long as we stand by each other off the court the way we do on it, we can do anything we set our minds to.

"I need more light.
A little further with the rib spreader."

CHAPTER

25

All my hopes that Julius is going to get over his run-in with the city cops dissolve when I see his moves on the court Tuesday afternoon. All through practice, anger at Coach simmers just below the surface as he goes through the motions of dribble, pass, dribble, shoot—anger driving the ball hard on the court, hard off the backboard. And when we stop at the library instead of the Pizza Parlor, that anger burns holes into us.

"You got no right dragging me to this book barn and telling me what to do about my business!" he yells at us on the front steps of the library.

"It's team business!" Ray yells right back, before I can say anything. He glares at Julius. "We've got to stick together, man—and you've been letting us down, blowing up at Coach at the game last week, and acting up on the court every day. Now you're going to get benched for grades if you blow this project!" His voice softens. "And you can't— you just can't let that happen right before Jackson. We *need* you, man. The Warriors *need* you."

I can see Julius trying to hold onto his anger and failing. At last he shrugs and mutters, "It's a stupid project."

"Of course it is," Highrise tells him, punching him on one shoulder. "Schoolwork equals stupid work, doesn't it? None of us would have gotten it done without Brainman. It was his idea for us to all help each other out."

I grin a little, embarrassed. "Hey—we're a team. What works on the court works off the court."

"Only in your dreams, man," Julius says, an edge to his voice. "But, okay, let's get on with it. I ain't no research genius and I don't plan to turn into one, so I don't see what I can do about this army commander thing, but if you've got a plan, let me in on it."

"Well, you're a math whiz," I point out. "What about something to do with statistics? Maybe you could figure the odds on a general who becomes king, or dictator or whatever, setting up a good government or ruining his country. Then you could contrast that with the odds on a general who disbands his army, like Washington, but gets elected to public office, still contributing positively, or something like that."

I can see Julius is finally intrigued. But Leslie is a lot less enthusiastic about the plan when Ashley and the others show up with her in tow. "I don't believe this!" she practically shouts, or at least says as loud as she's willing to talk in a library. "What were you jerks thinking? That I'd just go along with your crazy jock conspiracy? Well, think again—because I don't believe in cheating!"

"*You* think again," Julius says, charging at her. "I don't cheat!"

"Stop it." I step in between them. "It's not cheating, Leslie—you and Julius do the brain work, the rest of us only help with the busywork for the presentation. Mr. Fortner told us we could all draft classmates to help with that part of the project. Todd and I made a film, and everybody was in it to help us out. We all pitched in to work on the ballots for Ray and Phil's project, and to help Glenn and Ashley set up the database." To my surprise (and relief) Ashley flashes me a quick smile. I guess she's not angry about the other night.

The others start to tell Leslie about their projects and how we've all helped each other, and she finally shrugs. "Enough, already. But Julius better do his share, or I'm out of here." She shoots him a murderous look over my shoulder and I know it's never going to work if she hangs on to that attitude.

Before Julius can retort, I tell her, "Fine!" I ignore the looks of shock on the other faces. "If you don't trust Julius to do his share, then get out," I dare her. "Julius shows up with his project and tells Mr. Fortner you refused to work with him. Even if you claim the same thing, we all back up Julius. So maybe he doesn't get a great grade either, but you'll be in trouble, too. And it'll be your own fault." I let this sink in. "Or you two can figure out how to get along for as long as it takes to finish this thing, and then go back to hating each other. Julius is willing to put up with you. It's your call whether or not you can do your part and work with him."

I can tell Leslie hates the idea, and she hates me, but she finally says she'll work with him. Julius tells her about the statistics idea, and she reluctantly admits that it will show Mr. Fortner that he contributed so it will get them both a better grade in the end. The rest of us agree to help make posters of different generals—with a little brainstorming, Julius and Leslie come up with the idea of making "Wanted Criminal" posters of generals who used their armies to help them form military dictatorships in other countries, and award certificates for American generals like Washington and Grant and Eisenhower, who kept the ideals of democracy alive.

By the time we've planned out when to meet to make the posters, and tried to make sure that Leslie and Julius can get through this without killing each other, I'm exhausted. I'm also a little unnerved by the way Keesha looks when Julius throws an arm around her shoulder and tells her he's going to come up with some special plan for the two of them to celebrate the end of the projects together. She almost looks a little scared of being alone with him, when I know she used to try to come up with ways to get him alone. I wonder if I ought to say something—but that's more than I can deal with right now. Running the team through a game is a breeze compared to dealing with Julius these days.

When I get home, even the tantalizing smells of olive oil, garlic, spinach, and Mediterranean herbs can't drag me into the kitchen to see what Dad's cooking. Right now, I've barely got enough energy to flop down in front of the TV and take in the news. But the lead story wakes me up.

ANCHORMAN

After four weeks of testimony, the prosecution in the Daine murder trial rested its case this morning, and the judge called upon the defense to produce its first witness. Natalie Hart reports from the courthouse.

(Camera cuts to the familiar red-
haired woman standing on the courthouse steps.)

NATALIE HART

The defense seemed taken by surprise at the
timing, Peter. The defense attorney, William
Rosen, asked for a recess until after lunch,
which the judge granted. Then the defense
called to the stand the guard who deacti-
vated the security alarm at the gym where
Michael Daine played basketball that afternoon, and then reactivated it after the game
was finished and everyone had left the
building. The guard's evidence seems to be
the first step in drawing up a timeline for
the jury that establishes Daine's minute-by-
minute whereabouts, in order to dispel the
prosecution's argument that Daine had the
opportunity to leave the gym.

(New picture: camera follows a thin-
faced man who looks like a college
professor, shuffling down the courthouse stairs, a fat briefcase dangling
from one hand.)

NATALIE HART (voice-over)

After court recessed for the day, Mr. Rosen
spoke briefly with reporters.

(The attorney stops at the same podium
Officer Recks used last week; camera
zooms in on him and an identifying
caption below reads "William Rosen,
Outside County Courthouse.")

REPORTER (off camera)
Once you've got the timeline set up, what
experts will the defense call to refute
prosecution claims that Mr. Daine's handgun
was the one used in the shootings?

WILLIAM ROSEN
We're not calling any firearms experts—we
don't need to refute any prosecution claims
because their so-called ballistics evidence
means nothing in the face of an iron-clad
alibi.

DIFFERENT REPORTER (off camera)
Does that mean you'll be calling witnesses
who can lock down the time of the murders
and definitively place Officer Daine at the
gym at that moment?

WILLIAM ROSEN
That is exactly what I mean.

ANCHORMAN
(Picture shifts back to news desk.)

Well, it sounds as if the defense is going
to be relying solely on proving an alibi.

NATALIE HART (voice-over)
That's correct, Peter. According to Mr.
Rosen, the prosecutor's claims of infidelity
and the mere fact that Mr. Daine at one time
possessed a firearm of the same caliber used
in the killings are simply circumstantial.
If Mr. Rosen can prove that Daine was at the
gym the whole time, jurors may well acquit
him of all charges.

"You see?"

I turn to see Dad standing in the doorway, looking at the TV screen. "The lawyer didn't need you for his defense. That jogger you saw—neither the prosecution or the defense said anything about him. He wasn't important after all." When I don't answer, he adds, "Now, come on in to supper."

Both Mom and Dad look worried that I'm so quiet, even if they can't agree whether it's because I'm studying too hard or playing too hard. They don't say it out loud, but I know they're also wondering if I'm missing Amanda too much with the case in the news all the time. I guess they don't want to put it in my mind if I'm not already having more nightmares about it, but at the same time they want to be there for me if I need them. I haven't told them I'm dreaming about the killings again since I started working on the Leo Frank project.

"Stop worrying," I finally say, savoring the spinach's

sweetness before swallowing. "It's almost over—next week Todd and I give our presentation, next Friday we beat Jackson, then it's on to regionals." I don't say anything about the case almost being over, too.

Dad grins at me and Mom smiles, and I tell myself all I have to do until then is hope that Todd and I pull off our presentation, hope that Julius manages to keep his cool until his parents and Warren deal with the cops, and, most of all, hope that William Rosen can prove that Mr. Daine was playing ball that whole August afternoon, and identify the jogger. Because I think Dad's wrong. I do think the jogger is important. If so, then I can see why the prosecutor wouldn't want to bring it up as part of his case, because it points away from Mr. Daine. But they're always saying on TV that both sides have to share their information—that means the prosecutor has to tell the defense attorney about the jogger. And the defense will use the information, I'm sure of it. I push away the nagging question of why the lawyer never got in touch with me about it. Probably they found a better witness, someone who saw the jogger's face. The attorney is just taking one thing at a time, like me.

CHAPTER

26

The rest of the week, the team closes ranks around Julius. Normally the guys run interference for him on the court. Now they also run interference in the hall and classrooms so he won't lose his temper over some freshman getting in his way or anything. And we're all looking out for him at practice.

Coach seems to be keeping an eye on Julius, just waiting for him to blow up again. He's almost acting like he wants Julius to back him into a corner where he has no choice but to cut him, or at least bench him until the play-offs. Coach wants to win, but it's as if he wants to do it without Julius.

Coach Ritter liked Julius. He was willing to cut him some slack on grades, especially since Julius always keeps his math grades up. Even then Coach Guilford seethed about it on the sidelines, always reminding us he's a guidance counselor first and an assistant coach second. He still hammers on all of us to keep our grades up. Sure, he'll get us an extension if we need it, but he makes it clear we better do the work in the end if he's going to put his rep on the line for us. The only player who's ever let him down, if you can call it that, is Julius.

Last year our English teacher, Mrs. DeWitt (Julius called her DimWit) dumped this big essay on us right between Thanksgiving and Christmas. The season was already going strong and we hated the assignment, but we all turned something in, except Julius. He calculated his grade point average in that class and said he could pass without it, so why bother? But old DimWit said the essay was mandatory. No essay, no pass. Guilford convinced her to accept the paper after Christmas, then he read Julius the riot act, and made him swear to do the paper. He ticked Julius off, so when we got back to class in January he turned in a dumb essay that could have been written by a mentally challenged fourth grader.

Coach Guilford never forgave him. He's not about to give Julius a break now. If you ask him he'll say he's not prejudiced—it has nothing to do with Julius being black, just with him being a slacker in school. But Joyous isn't a slacker. When it comes to math and basketball, he's simply unbeatable. Maybe he just doesn't like having to compete in other things where he might come in second best. The whole team knows Coach is already down on him, so this week we make it our business to prevent the two of them from ending up in a head-on collision. That works pretty well until game day.

The Blazers are already out of the running for regionals, but that doesn't mean they don't care about beating us. And it's a home game for them, so we don't have the bleachers packed with Warrior fans. They even have their band set to play full volume every time our cheerleaders try to go into a routine. We start out okay, with Julius sinking a perfect jump shot early in the first quarter. But the Blazers play on the edge, talking trash and throwing their elbows when the zebras aren't looking. They're called a few times, but they get away with it often enough to keep trying. I can count on Ray keeping his cool, but Ricochet gets rattled and begins missing easy shots, which fires up the Blazers.

After Ricochet blows an easy layup and fails to get the rebound, Julius shifts his playing gears. Instead of letting me dish the passes and keep the game under control, he turns it into a one-man show, a replay of last week. He darts in, grabbing the ball before Ray can get it to me, playing recklessly and shooting from impossible distances and angles. He misses two, three shots, but then sinks a 35-footer and quickly intercepts a Blazer pass.

Coach sends Shooter in for Ricochet, who slumps on the bench, flushed with shame, but Julius doesn't back off. He rushes down the court, blowing past Highrise and Shooter to take the shot himself, only to be fouled by a Blazer. But instead of keeping his mind in the game and taking his free shot, Julius's hands clench into fists and he rounds on the guy who ran into him.

I signal Ray and we get between them under the guise of turning Julius to the free-throw line and psyching him up.

"Cool it, man," I say in a low voice. "Get the points and keep on playing—you throw a punch on that jerk and you're out of the game!"

"Just dial it down a notch, champ," Ray tells him. "We're all behind you, so don't let those guys get under your skin."

As the Blazers line up along the foul lanes, one of them mutters, too low for the zebra to hear, "Aw, does little baby player need his mama to tell him to play nice with the big boys?"

Julius's nostrils flare and his chest heaves as he catches his breath in fury.

"Stay loose, Joyous," Ray tells him. "All that Blazer baby can do is talk trash. We're winners, let's act like it."

Julius hits his free throws, but after that he uses his own elbows and trash talk against the Blazers. Coach tries sending Wrestler in, but even our tough guy is no match for their brawn and attitude. As soon as they find he can't hit free throws reliably, they practically taunt him with fouls. By the time we go in at the half we're down by six.

"What has gotten into you guys?" Coach explodes in the locker room. "I know you've all had a lot of pressure on you with these history projects, and I'm proud that you've worked on them as hard as you've worked on the court." He carefully avoids looking at Julius as he says that.

"But those kids are street punks—don't let them drag you down to their level! Ray—get the ball to Brian, not Julius." Take-away wipes his face with the bottom of his jersey and nods.

"Brian—you decide who's open and get him the ball. Ricky, Stu, Irv—once you have the ball, you shut your ears to those punks. Take your shot or get the ball back to Brian." Ricochet shakes his head in disgust, as if he knows all this and can't understand how they're getting him so flustered, but Shooter punches his shoulder in encouragement and Highrise says, "Right, Coach."

"Eddie, when you go in concentrate on staying on your man, getting the ball, and—just hand off to Brian. Don't even try to pass or shoot to draw another foul!" Wrestler flushes dark red and seems to shrink on the bench.

"And Julius—stop playing some fantasy game! You're the mathemagician. Crunch the numbers and remember—the odds of your making those long three-point shots are worse than one in three. That brings *down* your scoring average! You got that? Stop hogging the ball and get it to Brian. He's the one with the cool head out there, not you!"

Julius shoots me a dangerous glare, and I wish Coach hadn't put it quite that way. Unfortunately, Coach sees the look, too.

"Don't blame your poor performance on your teammate!" he shouts at Julius. "Get your head out of your butt and start playing like you're part of a team, instead of the only guy on the court! If you don't, we lose and it's on you."

Julius's face contorts like he's going to tell Coach exactly who he'd like to blame for losing, but the ref comes in to tell us it's time to get back on the court. I grab Julius's arm and lead him out. "Chill, Joyous," I practically beg him. "Keep your head in the game and don't sweat Coach."

I keep talking, as if enough words flowing over him could wash his anger away and leave him calm again. Behind me, I hear the guys talking to Coach. At first I figure they're just trying to calm him down, too—then I hear what they're saying, and my heart sinks.

"He's having a really tough time right now," Ricochet is saying earnestly. "He got arrested for doing nothing—just for being black, and he had to get a lawyer and fight the police and everything."

"It's just giving him a short fuse," Highrise tries to explain. "And the Blazers are jerking his chain. But he'll get through it—we'll get him through it."

They think Coach will understand and cut Julius some slack, maybe even get protective of him, because Coach Ritter would have. But Coach Guilford isn't like that. When I told them it was team business, I meant they should keep it just among ourselves, the team. Old Quitter may have walked out on the school for a better contract, but he was part of the team while he was here, in a way our guidance counselor will never be. I start the second half with a cold, sick weight choking me, slowing me down.

Sure enough, the next time a Blazer trash-talks Julius and gets fouled for it, Coach pulls Julius. He makes it look like he's got to save Julius, with four fouls, in case he needs him at the end of the game, but I see the faintest gleam of satisfaction playing around the corners of his eyes, and I'm sure he's thinking: I knew you were trouble all along, boy, now you're going to pay for it.

Julius never comes back in, and we lose to the Blazers, unbelievably, 78–75. That still leaves our season 22–2 so far, with only one earlier loss to the Lions. But it's a bad omen a week before we face Jackson.

===

By the time we get back to town it's late, but when I get home to watch the sports news, I wish I'd gone somewhere with the team. Not only does Jackson coast to an easy victory over the Raiders, but the news anchorman closes by turning to Natalie Hart to recap the lead story.

NATALIE HART
(seated at news desk beside anchorman)
It certainly was a dramatic ending to a
tense week in court, Peter. Former Officer

Daine took the stand today and told the jury
that he was sorry about his relations with
other women, but insisted that they didn't
mean anything, and he loved his family very
much. He testified that he was in the gym
with friends at the time of the murders,
playing basketball and watching his teammates play.

    (Camera shows a collage of photos of
    Amanda, Cory, and their mother.)

            NATALIE HART (voice-over)
Officer Daine finished his testimony by saying that he wants to find the real murderer.
He said, his voice breaking, that he only
hoped it wasn't too late for investigators
to follow all of the evidence and bring the
killer to justice.

            NATALIE HART (close-up)
Then Officer Daine stunned the courtroom by
announcing that he believed the murders were
revenge killings related to his work in law
enforcement.

                ANCHORMAN
    (camera frames both him and NATALIE
    HART at news desk)

Has the defense produced any testimony to

support such a claim?

NATALIE HART (shaking head)
No, Peter, not a word. And defense attorney Rosen declined to answer any questions after court today about a possible revenge motive. But prosecutors suggested that this late mention of a mysterious revenge killer could be a desperation red-herring ploy to create reasonable doubt in the minds of the jurors.

ANCHORMAN
Any idea what the defense has planned for next week, Natalie?

NATALIE HART
Mr. Rosen said that Officer Daine would be his last witness. So I think we can look for the prosecution to begin its cross-examination on Monday, probably exploring this revenge motive as well as the defendant's character. Then the attorneys will go directly to closing arguments. We can probably look for the jury's verdict before the end of the week.

I stare at the stupid commercials with their sickly sweet music and canned laugh track, with no idea what they're supposed to be advertising. What is this revenge killing motive? And what does she mean by saying Amanda's father is the last witness?

Somehow, I realize, I've decided that Amanda's father couldn't have killed his family. No matter what other mistakes he's made, I do not believe he could be a murderer. Which makes the jogger even more important—especially that gray sweatsuit. There's something about the gray sweatsuit that's bothering me, something more than the gray fibers they found in Amanda's garage, but I can't put my finger on what it is. . . .

When the defense attorney said he had all the evidence he needed to clear his client, I was so sure he meant he had a witness who could ID the jogger and place him at the murder scene at the same time Mr. Daine was on the court at the game. Without that witness, how can the jury be positive Mr. Daine didn't sneak out of the gym and shoot his family?

A tiny voice inside me whispers, *maybe you're the only one who saw anything.*

Not possible, I tell it. The jogger was there in plain sight.

But people miss things in plain sight all the time. . . .

Well, maybe Dad's right and the police checked out the jogger and it wasn't important.

But what if the police didn't bother to investigate because they were only looking for evidence against Mr. Daine? What if the jogger was actually the revenge killer Mr. Daine was trying to tell the jury about?

Then it's up to the defense attorney to bring up the evidence, not me!

What if the prosecution hid the report of what you told the police, like Todd's brother said they sometimes do, and the defense attorney doesn't know? Do you really want to carry that evidence inside you for the rest of your life, like Alonzo Mann?

I rub my head with the heels of my hands, not sure whether the TV is giving me a headache, or whether it's leftover humiliation from the loss, or whether it comes from the nagging fear that the jogger is, indeed, very important, and I'm the only one who knows about him.

CHAPTER

27

The headache's still with me when I get to Todd's house on Saturday to put the last touches on our project. I've done my sections of the script and he's finished matching the music tracks we laid down together with the filmed scenes, but I can't focus on putting them all together.

"What's going on?" Todd finally demands. "We've got to give this presentation in a couple of days, remember? Your mind's a million miles away."

I shake my head. "Sorry. I just—I'm having trouble concentrating."

He sighs. "Obviously."

"Did you watch the news last night?"

He frowns. "Yes. Car bombings in the Middle East, more insanity in Washington, an earthquake in India . . ."

"No—the local news."

"Oh." He looks away. "The Daine trial. I didn't think you wanted to talk about it." When I don't say anything, he adds, "I'm surprised the defense isn't putting up more of a fight—and I don't know if putting him on the stand is such a good idea."

"People want to hear him say he didn't do it," I point

out, even though I agree with him.

"Sure, but he's a cop," Todd says. "You saw them in action when Warren got Julius. It's as if the badge and uniform make them look down on the rest of us. Most of them have this arrogance—I don't know if the arrogance makes them want to be cops, or if it comes with the badge. But it's scary. I don't think he made such a good impression on the jury, even though he told them he didn't do it. And that revenge killer theory, coming out of the blue like that—I don't think the jury is going to buy it. The prosecution is probably going to try to push him on cross until he blows up or says something cocky he's going to regret."

I study Todd. "Did you know Amanda's father?"

He shakes his head, which makes his on-target analysis even more amazing—he's really got Mr. Daine pegged. He looks back at the script. "You've got some good stuff here," he says. "I've researched some other cases, and I thought we could take turns doing the narration."

Sure, I think. Good plan. But the words don't make it out, and he looks exasperated. I ignore his irritation and ask, "What do you think happens after you die?" I'm not sure if I'm asking him, or myself. "I mean, do you think Amanda's looking down on her dad's trial and waiting for the police or jury or somebody to punish her killer? Or do you think she doesn't even exist anymore? Or maybe she's an angel or something and doesn't care about what's happening down here on Earth. I don't know."

Todd looks out the window. "My parents would say that you go to heaven after you die, if you're a God-fearing Christian and washed clean of your sins," he says dryly. Then he shrugs. "Me, I'm not so sure. I don't think it's that simple. I think it's more like what we read in *Hamlet* last year in English—an undiscovered country. You don't know until you get there. But you make up stories about it to make you feel safer, because you know you'll wind up there in the end."

I remember reading *Hamlet*. Mrs. DeWitt had us read the play aloud, even though most of us sounded dumb reading Shakespeare. Amanda read Ophelia's part, her voice lilting musically even before the character went crazy and started singing. Todd read Hamlet's part, reluctantly, but without tripping over the lines. Most of the team were guards and gentlemen of the court, but I read Laertes, who fights a duel with Hamlet and kills him accidentally because Laertes is too dumb and earnest to know he's fighting with a poisoned sword. The story's all about death and revenge. Basically Hamlet spends the whole play wondering what he should do about the guy he thinks killed his father, and not being sure enough of his evidence to do anything. In the end, he gets practically everybody he knows killed because he takes too long to make up his mind.

I shiver a little at the thought.

"What's wrong?" Todd asks, half smiling. "You don't strike me as the sort of guy who stresses out over what happens in the afterlife—you've got a long time to wait for that." When I don't answer right away, he adds, more serious, "Or are you worried about Amanda's spirit, or soul?"

I start to shake my head, then shrug. "I'm worried about Amanda, Mary Phagan, Leo Frank, Amanda's dad—everyone, I guess. Life and death. Making the right decisions while you're alive—like why did it take Hamlet so long to decide to get his revenge on King Claudius for killing his father? And why did it take Alonzo so long to decide to speak up about Mary's murderer?"

Todd nods. "I know. It makes me angry, too."

"No—it's not that." I'm groping for the right words. "I don't feel angry so much. I feel . . ." I shrug a little. "Well, sad, I guess. And . . ." My voice kind of drops. "I guess, kind of guilty."

Todd looks taken aback. "Why? You haven't done anything."

And that's the point, isn't it? I haven't. The real question is, why am I telling Todd? Maybe it's just that I have to tell someone. "I thought *Hamlet* was stupid when we read it last year. All that agonizing after the ghost told him who the murderer was—why didn't he just do something? But then Amanda was killed and, well, I haven't done anything."

"Unless her ghost came and told you that the killer wasn't her father," Todd says, "I don't think you ought to feel guilty."

"No, her ghost isn't haunting me. But—I think maybe I did see something." And I find myself telling him about the jogger I saw that afternoon.

Once I get started I can't stop. It's as if everything's been out of balance in my life since last summer. It's more than feeling like something inside me died because Amanda died. Something inside me died because I didn't help Amanda before she was killed, and I haven't helped her since by making sure the police followed up on what I saw. I've been so focused on basketball—maybe it's because I hoped if I did the right things on the court, where the game is fair, then I'd find a way to do the right thing off the court, only things don't seem to be fair on the court anymore, either.

Todd listens without saying anything, until I run out of words. I feel an overwhelming sense of relief. Maybe what I've needed all this time is to confess. But if I'm hoping for forgiveness, Todd doesn't offer any.

"You've got to tell someone," he says instead. "Now. Before the defense rests."

I stare at him. "Haven't you been listening? I did tell someone. I told the cops." I shrug a little. "When I didn't hear anything more about it, it felt almost like a sign that it wasn't important. And I can't see how the jury's going to believe some teenager over all these experts."

"They'll believe an honest teenager as easily as they'll believe an arrogant police officer," Todd says.

"Yeah, right."

"Brian, you've got a better chance of being listened to than most guys our age." When I look at him, surprised, he rolls his eyes. "Come on—you're the one the rest of the team looks to for leadership. Even kids who aren't jocks listen to you. You don't throw your weight around, but you could if you wanted to."

"Yeah, well," I mutter, embarrassed. "I mean, teenagers are—well, manageable. But grown-ups . . . They've got this—aura of power. I'm not sure I'm ready to handle that yet."

Todd stares back, unblinking. "Don't you get it?" he asks. "Being a teenager—that's just a stage we're passing through. Life won't always be as simple as dealing with other teens. Most of those morons don't get that yet, but I thought you did."

When I don't say anything, he goes on, "We're going to have to stand up to, or face down, grown-ups for the rest of our lives. Sure, the first face-down is the hardest..." He gets that closed, looking-inside expression. "... whether it's facing your parents or facing someone else who doesn't want to listen to you." Then he looks straight at me. "You can't pretend you don't have the guts, Brian. I know you do. It's okay to say it's hard, but that doesn't change the fact you have to do it."

I look away. "But if I make a big deal about the jogger and the defense attorney makes the police find out who it is and it turns out to be some innocent person and I'm responsible for getting him or her arrested or hauled in for questioning or something, people around here are going to hate me! I've got to live here, too."

Todd considers that only briefly, then shrugs. "Not forever. You'll go to college and be a hotshot, then you'll get drafted by the NBA and you'll never see this town again, except for family get-togethers and maybe your twenty-fifth high school reunion or something."

That stops me. It's what Dad's always wanted, for me to leave Willisford and make something of myself, be some sort of national star. But is it what I really want? I hear myself asking, "You're leaving when you graduate?"

Todd practically snorts. "I'm out of here so fast it'll be like a tornado heading east."

Amanda always planned on leaving, too—like a tornado heading west, I guess. But I'm not sure that's what I want, even if everybody else thinks I should. I feel my way through the idea. "But suppose you want to stay here—if you stir up a big controversy or something, and you're wrong—or even if you're right, how can you face everybody again?"

Todd stares at me. "You *want* to stay here? In this blip on the world's radar screen? Why?"

Because this is my home, I think, but I don't say it. It's not reason enough. I'm not even sure it's the real reason. "I don't know, exactly, but I think I do." I shake my head before he can tell me I'm an idiot. "I'm not sure about anything, okay? What if Mr. Daine really is guilty? What if it really was just some innocent jogger, and the police find him and investigate him and ruin his whole life because of something I said?"

"That is not your decision to make!" Todd snaps. "You saw what you saw, and it might be important. You have a responsibility to call the defense attorney and tell him, and let him investigate it and decide whether you saw the murderer or someone who's not important to the investigation."

"But I don't know what I saw!" I burst out. "What if I'm wrong? What about that stupid woman who heard those Arab guys joking in that restaurant on the anniversary of the terrorist attack on 9/11 and got it all wrong and then everybody thought those poor guys were terrorists? I mean—if I make a big stink about this jogger and insist they find him, and it turns out to be a huge mistake but the cops have already arrested him like Julius and he hasn't done anything but he ends up all full of hate and it's all because of me . . . " I run out of words.

Todd considers this. "Well, I guess you have to trust your instincts."

I shake my head. "That sounds way too much like the

cops being so sure somebody's guilty that they tamper with the evidence and rearrange the facts to prove their hunch—their instincts!"

"That's not the same," Todd says quietly. "I think you know that."

"Why isn't it? Because it's my hunch?"

"That's part of it." Todd smiles. "It all comes down to what sort of person the guy making the hunch is."

I can't help smiling back, a little sheepishly. "You mean, whether you're a good guesser or not?"

Todd laughs. Then he shakes his head and loses the smile. "No. It comes down to whether or not you're the kind of guy who's willing to take responsibility for guessing—whether or not you're a guy who understands the consequences of acting on a bad hunch. If he knows he'll have to pay for guessing wrong, but he's sure enough of his instincts to take that chance, then he should trust himself."

I think of Todd letting guys beat him up and stuff him in his locker because he's different, and not fighting them because he doesn't believe in fighting back with fists. Then I think of his parents throwing him out because he wouldn't change himself. I guess Todd understands about trusting himself and accepting the consequences. I can't meet his eyes. "Maybe I don't know for sure what kind of guy I am yet."

"I'm betting you're the kind of guy who can trust his hunches," he says quietly. After a pause he adds, "Which means you should call the defense attorney—unless your instincts tell you that the jogger was really just a neighbor and Mr. Daine is guilty."

I shake my head. "I don't know what my instincts are

telling me. For a while I couldn't imagine a guy killing his family. But then I started to wonder about some of the family fights—Amanda would come over to my house to try to get away from them. And I thought maybe he could have done it. But now—I don't think he did, but I don't know. I just know I don't feel right keeping quiet and I don't feel right speaking out. But I have the nagging feeling that there's something important about that gray sweatsuit."

"It sounds as if your instincts are telling you that it's up to the jury to decide," Todd says. "But they can't decide without knowing the whole truth. And it's up to you to tell them."

He's got more confidence in me than I have. "Let's finish the script," I tell him.

He studies me briefly, then begins blending in the sections I've written with the parts he's already got in his computer. We've each got our scripts to practice by the time Elise announces she's ready to leave for the hospital and can drop me off on her way.

"Let me know what you decide to do," Todd says by way of good-bye.

As she drives, I try to imagine Todd's parents really believing that doctors should all be men, and all women should be in the kitchen. Even in my home Mom's the computer whiz for the contracting business and Dad's the family chef. I'm willing to bet Elise is a great doctor.

But the nagging feeling that Todd's right about me trusting my instincts remains when I enter my empty house. I should tell someone and leave it up to them to decide whether or not the jogger's important. I reach for my cell phone, then remember Warren's warning and go for the kitchen phone instead. I call information to get the office number for Mr. Rosen, Mr. Daine's lawyer, but when I call, all I get is some voice mail system. I punch in buttons, hoping I'll get a real person, but finally settle for leaving a message for him.

"This is Brian Hammett—I live across the street from Mr. Daine. Look, I don't know if this is important or not, but I saw a strange jogger in our cul-de-sac the day Amanda and Cory and their mother were shot." Just saying Amanda's name out loud to this impersonal messaging system hurts, like throwing away a precious part of myself I can't ever recapture. I force myself to keep speaking. "See, the jogger was wearing this gray sweatsuit, with the hood up. I couldn't even tell if it was a man or a woman. But you said something about gray fibers and—well, I thought it might be important, even though I guess nobody else noticed anything."

I stare at the receiver. "I did tell the police that night, and they said they'd check it out, and when no one else ever said anything about it I thought maybe they had and the jogger wasn't important. But now I'm not so sure. Anyway, if you don't already know about this and you have any questions, I guess you should call me. And . . ." I swallow. " . . . maybe you should put me on the stand." Part of me hopes he already knows about the jogger and it's not important—a big part. But I leave my phone number and hang up, wondering whether I've done the right thing at last, or done something really stupid.

"Come on, kid. Don't give up on me."

CHAPTER

28

I keep waiting to hear something from the attorney, but no call comes. Julius and Coach manage to maintain a careful truce as we sweep to an easy victory over the Wildcats, and the work the team did on the presentations for Fortner's class pays off big. Ray and Phil's trial is a hit, since the class likes the power of being jurors. Then Glenn and Ashley present their "incriminating" database. The students are spooked at finding themselves all listed on it for something, so they get the point.

Mr. Fortner sits in the back, watching the presentations, smiling as he makes notes. Even Julius and Leslie pull their project off, with the awards and "Wanted" posters drawing cheers and jeers from the class, although it's clear that she did the background research and he crunched the numbers for the statistics. I figure Mr. Fortner's going to take points off the partnership part of the grade, but they'll pass. Then it's Wednesday—our showtime.

Todd dims the lights, and I push the play button on the DVD player. The tinny piano-and-guitar music track comes up, and Todd flashes me a grin before starting to read his script. We ran the tape through the DJ system to make the music sound kind of jangly instead of smooth. Todd even added effects that sound like an old projector whirring around—just a bike wheel spinning, with a piece of paper softly slapping the spokes to make a faint clicking in the background.

The title flashes across the screen in old-fashioned billboard-style script on an aged sepia background: "The Murder of—" Then the next frame: "Mary Phagan—" And finally: "Or Leo Frank?" I hear a soft "Ahh," from Mr. Fortner. He sounds pleased.

As the film shows Darla strolling along with her parasol, Todd begins to read. "On a bright Saturday morning in 1913, thirteen-year-old Mary Phagan was looking forward to enjoying the holiday." We sped up the film just enough to give it a dated, jerky quality, and I'm impressed with the way Todd managed to make Darla look younger and smaller.

Todd goes on, "It was Confederate Memorial Day, complete with a parade of Civil War veterans." The clip dissolves into a text box reading, "I cannot wait to honor our Heroes who fought for the Glorious Cause!" and the music switches to "When Johnny Comes Marching Home" as the screen shows pictures of the Confederate parade. I hear some whispers as the other kids who weren't in on the filming figure out it's a silent movie, and I look up to see Mr. Fortner nodding approval.

The scene cuts back to Mary Phagan, stopping with one finger upraised as an idea strikes her, and the text box reads, "But wait! I must collect my Pay, or I will not have any Money for Lemonade or Treats!" Then Todd reads, "With other teenage girls, Mary worked at a pencil factory in Atlanta. She counted pencils and packaged them for shipment. For this work she was paid 5 cents an hour. She had missed some work that week, but she still had $1.20 coming to her, so she went to the factory to pick it up."

The screen shows Mary heading purposefully toward a brick wall (the side of the Francis house) that represents the factory, swinging her parasol. Then it cuts to Matt, sitting outside. A text box flashes "Alonzo Mann, an office boy at the Pencil Factory."

Todd reads, "Everyone was looking forward to the parade. Alonzo Mann, the office boy, had gone in early that morning to finish his work for the manager, Mr. Leo Frank. On his way, he ran into Jim Conley, an ex-convict who cleaned the floors and did odd jobs around the place."

Julius emerges, looking big and hulking in his padded costume. Some of the kids chuckle. He stops where Matt is sitting and the text box reads, "Hey, Alonzo—loan me a Dime so I can get a Drink." The clip shows Matt shaking his head virtuously, then cuts to, "No! You never paid me back those other Loans!" Julius raises his fist menacingly, then strides off.

The murder and the court case unfold on the screen, and I was right: the class is riveted. Even after the novelty wears off, this is something different, and they love it. After the lynching scene, when the text box reads, "Now the good People of Atlanta believed that Leo Frank had at last been brought to Justice!" Brittney mutters, "Served him right, too!" Then the class realizes the film isn't finished yet.

Todd asks, "But had justice truly been served?"

There's a pause, and suddenly the DVD turns into full

color and loses the tinny music as I appear. Even I'm surprised to see how old the makeup makes me look. Superimposed across the bottom of the screen, like an ID on the news, the text reads, "Alonzo Mann in 1982."

I go inside, and the house actually looks like an office the way Todd filmed it. Now the video has regular sound effects, including voices. On the screen I begin Alonzo's confession, and the scene dissolves to Matt running away, his mom telling him not to get involved—Matt kneeling by a cardboard gravestone that reads "Leo Frank," crying. We close with my voice-over, reading what the adult Alonzo Mann said in his statement: "At last I am able to get this off my heart. I believe it will help people to understand that courts and juries make mistakes."

When the movie ends, Todd pauses dramatically, then reads, "Two murders occurred in Atlanta. Jim Conley murdered Mary Phagan, but who murdered Leo Frank? The prosecutor? The lynch mob? Alonzo Mann? Or the justice system itself, warped by politicians and by law enforcement and by citizens who believed they had the right to manipulate it to prove what they wanted it to prove?"

I wait a few seconds, then pick up my script. "And have we learned from the Leo Frank case, or is history doomed to repeat itself?" For some reason, the printed text of the script looks blurry. I blink hard and struggle to keep reading about the careful checks and balances in the judicial system, the guarantees that anyone accused of murder will get a fair trial, the careful search for witnesses. "I mean, you could shrug it off and say the system worked. A jury of twelve good people listened to the evidence and decided that Leo Frank was guilty. But did the system really work? They didn't hear all the evidence. The prosecutor rehearsed his witnesses so they'd say what he wanted them to say, and he didn't tell the jury about any of the evidence that pointed to Jim Conley, because he was saving Conley for his star witness—even though he had coached Conley to tell the lies he wanted him to tell! And the system didn't work because Alonzo Mann, the sole eyewitness, didn't come forward and demand to be heard until it was too late."

It occurs to me that Todd's wrong—Alonzo shouldn't have been crying by Leo Frank's grave marker. He should be at Mary Phagan's grave, apologizing to her that she'd had to wait so long for him to get justice for her by identifying her true killer. I see the girl with blonde ringlets. *Help me.* And I think, justice is the real issue here—justice for Mary as well as justice for Leo Frank. Justice for Amanda, as well as justice for her father. My throat feels tight, like there's something getting in the way of the words coming out, and I'm relieved when it's Todd's turn.

"And does the system work today?" he asks. "At a Christmas Eve party in 1970 at the Pioneer Hotel in Tucson, Arizona, a fire killed twenty-eight people. Louis Taylor, a sixteen-year-old black teen who had crashed the party dressed as a busboy, ran down the hallways, knocking on doors and getting people out. He saved as many as he could. The police interrogated Louis Taylor all night without his parents or a lawyer, even though the kid asked for a lawyer. The prosecutor claimed that Taylor set the fire in order to steal the change people left on their dressers, when everybody fled the hotel in a panic."

Todd looks up at the class, and I see he looks at Julius especially. "The police never followed up on reports of previous fires in the hotel. Louis Taylor was convicted by an all-white jury who never heard the evidence that there was a known arsonist in Tucson, near the Pioneer Hotel, at the time of the fire. That jury never heard the witnesses, one of whom was a college professor, who had tried to tell the police that they had seen a suspicious person getting in the way of the firemen the night of the fire. No one other than Louis Taylor was ever investigated, and the jury only heard the evidence the prosecutor wanted them to hear—the evidence that convicted Taylor. To this day, Louis Taylor refuses to apply for parole, because he says he would have to express remorse for a crime he still insists he never committed. In 1963, at a civil rights rally, Dr. Martin Luther King Jr. said, 'Injustice anywhere is a threat to justice everywhere.' Injustices were done to Leo Frank and to Louis Taylor, and each time such injustice occurs, it threatens every other citizen's right to get justice."

"No," I say unsteadily, picking up my cue but not reading my script about the other cases Todd had researched. "We haven't learned one single thing since 1913, when Alonzo Mann kept silent and an innocent man was convicted of Mary Phagan's murder. People still don't want to get involved. They still look in the other direction and don't say anything, and the jails are overflowing with innocent people because nobody seems to care about the truth—not the prosecutors, not the police, not the judges. They just care about statistics. Do we have a murder? Yes. Now let's get a conviction. So what if he didn't do it? If we call it a conviction, if the court rubber-stamps it, then someone goes to jail for the crime and we rack up another success."

I can hear the hysterical edge in my voice, but I can't control it. Because it's true, every word is true. "Are you different? Are you a kid or an outsider or the wrong race or religion? You must be guilty. Are you the obvious suspect? Why bother to look for someone else—you must be guilty! And if we don't have any evidence, we'll find some—make innuendoes, or just convince people to flat-out lie to prove that you're guilty!" I take a shuddering breath. "Nothing has changed unless people decide to get involved and make the courts listen to the truth!"

"Yeah," Shooter growls unexpectedly. "Alonzo Mann should have said something. The prosecutor would have arrested Jim Conley even though he was willing to testify against Leo Frank. I mean—Conley was a black janitor who was right there on the scene, and he was an ex-con! He should have been the first suspect anyway!"

"That's right—always blame the black guy!" snaps Julius. "Hey, boy, you be black in this here nice white neighborhood, this nice white school, right? So it must be you done something wrong, right? Somebody must have seen you, and we gonna arrest you until they come forward and finger you! Right?" His voice gets shrill. "That's what you saying, white boy?"

"That's not what I'm saying and you know it!" Shooter tells him. "And why are you talking like that, man?"

"I be talking like my brothers now," Julius tells him defiantly.

"But we're your brothers—we're your teammates," Ricochet says, looking back and forth from our top scorer to our sixth man, upset. "And all Shooter meant was that Conley was the only eyewitness who nailed Frank, and he was the one carrying the body around because he was the real killer—Shooter's talking about this one particular case."

"You not be listening," Julius practically spits, the jive talk sounding so alien coming from him. "You not my brother, white boy. You don't know nothing about what it's like to be a black man! And Shooter here, and Brainman, they be talking about black boys in nice clean suburbs who scare the poor white boys so they be helpless to stand up for what's right—which means too helpless to stand up against those nasty old nig—!"

"That's enough, Julius!" Mr. Fortner almost shouts, jumping up from his stool in the back of the classroom.

"What do you know about it, white man?" demands Julius. He stands, fists clenched, eyes glaring, considerably taller than Mr. Fortner. "It ain't nearly enough—not by a long shot!"

"Stop it, Julius," I try to croak out, but no one hears me.

"Sit down, Julius," Mr. Fortner says, almost at the same time. But Julius remains on his feet, chin jutting forward, practically daring the teacher to make him. "Sit down," Mr. Fortner repeats, "or get your things and report to the principal's office."

"Come on, man," Highrise practically begs. "Just sit down."

"Yassuh, massa," Julius drawls, whirling on his teammate. "You wants I should just be a good slave and forget about everything."

"Stop it." This time my voice is loud enough that everybody hears me. "This is all my fault—I'm the one who asked Julius to play Jim Conley in the movie, okay?"

I remember what Todd said about kids listening to me, and I think it's working. I think the tension is easing up and I'm about to get the focus back on Alonzo Mann, but then Leslie ruins it. She leans her head to one side, as if contemplating her partner, and interrupts me.

"I never thought Julius was such a good actor—maybe it was better casting than you realized at the time, Brian." Her voice turns nasty instead of thoughtful. "Maybe the police were right to arrest Julius, after all."

Things happen so fast I'm not sure exactly what the order actually is. I'm gaping at Leslie, trying to figure out how she knows Julius was arrested and guessing that the guys must have told the cheerleaders and one of the girls must have said something to Leslie. Ricochet and Highrise are on their feet, shouting at her to shut up. Keesha reaches out, trying to grab Julius's arm as the bell rings. But Julius lunges across the desk between his row and Leslie's. Over the commotion, Mr. Fortner is shouting at the class to sit and be silent.

The only two motionless people in the room are me, holding the crushed remains of my presentation script, and Todd, standing beside the blackboard, his black sweatshirt almost blending into the blank surface, and his dark eyes unreadable.

Then Mr. Fortner cuts through the chaos at last. "Julius—get your things and go to the principal's office! You're suspended for fighting in school."

CHAPTER

29

The second bell rings as I race out of the classroom after Julius, and finally chase him down in the gym. "Why did you bring the Turd that night?" Julius practically screams. "Everyone knows—he told them!"

"He didn't!" I insist. "Chill, Joyous—I had to bring Todd to get his brother to get you out of jail. But he didn't tell anybody—he wouldn't—he promised his brother."

"Oh, yeah, and since everybody knows about it, that boy's promises mean zip!" Julius shouts, his fury sweeping over both of us, as unstoppable as his drive down the court. "I can't believe you be trusting him instead of me!"

I feel sick. "I know he didn't tell because it's my fault." Julius freezes, staring at me incredulously. "I only told the team. I told them so they'd understand what was going down, and be there for you. And they have been!"

"You told the team?" he whispers, his voice full of more hate than I ever imagined he had in his whole body. "So they told everybody else—Coach, and Leslie, and . . ."

He turns away, shaking with rage.

"Haven't you told anybody?" I demand. "Your parents? Keesha?"

There's a moment's silence. Then he says, his voice cold, "Keesha wouldn't tell."

I stand there thinking that maybe I blamed the guys too fast for telling the cheerleaders—maybe Keesha said something to get them to help her convince Leslie. When you care for somebody, sometimes you have to speak out even when they want you to keep silent. I finally say, "Well, maybe it's better it's out in the open, man."

Julius wheels around, gaping at me. "Better? How is it better? How am I supposed to keep sucking all this up?"

"You're not," I try to say, but he rushes on.

"That fancy white lawyer—he told me in the car that night—watch what you do, watch what you say, every word, every action, every breath! Because they be watching you now. Why? I didn't do nothing to begin with!" The way he keeps trying so hard to talk black sounds as stilted and unbelievable as Hamlet's soliloquies would sound coming from his kid brother. "Why am I the one who's got to watch my step now?"

"You shouldn't have to —" But he's still not listening.

"Why isn't it those bigot cops who have to watch their step? They say—come on, boy, you're going for a little drive, and they're sneering at me like they love seeing somebody they've got the upper hand on, like they're thinking, we know you're guilty of something, just give us a while alone with you and we'll prove it. Why you crying for a lawyer, boy? You keep saying you ain't done nothing, so what's the lawyer for? What are you hiding? Didn't anybody make them go to school and learn the law says a guy's innocent unless you've got proof that says he's done something? Or is that only true for white boys the cops pick up?

Why didn't someone tell them: you watch your step around black kids, too!"

Then he drops down on the bleachers and his eyes get this distant look. I can imagine him sitting there in jail, like he sat on the bench after the guard from Milford creamed him last year and nearly broke his collarbone. He wanted to go straight back onto the court, but Coach Ritter insisted he sit the game out.

The only way to see how much pain he was in then, from his collarbone and from not playing, was by the shine in his eyes that was almost tears, but not quite. Now his eyes look glassy again as he relives the night he got arrested. "Man, those cops—they drag me down this hallway, this cop's hand gripping my arm like I'm going to bolt and run. The guy opens a door into this little room, but it don't look like no room that belongs in no jail. It looks like it should be right here, in the gym!" He sweeps an arm over to the corner, where there's a stack of wrestling mats. "They got those mats lining the floor and hanging up on the walls. And then three more cops in their starched blue uniforms crowd into that tiny room. *Now strip, boy.* That cop has this slow, sneering voice, and I can see him smiling—a black cop, can you believe it? That Oreo cookie was thinking he could make himself look white by trashing me!"

His voice is shaking now. "And they don't even give me time! Two of the guys behind me, they bang me up against the mats on the back wall. Another one pulls off my belt and throws it into this open bag on the floor, then practically rips my jeans down to my knees!

"And I'm saying, *Hey—quit it, man—give me a chance!* But they don't care." His voice gets, if possible, even more bitter. "That black cop can't wait. *You had your chance, punk.* The guys holding me throw me forward and the jeans around my knees trip me up so I sprawl on the floor mats. And then they're on me again, jerking my T-shirt over my head. And when I try to sit up I get a knee in the small of my back. They pull off my shoes and my socks, then my jeans and—" He stares hard at the wrestling mats, not at me.

"I see that black officer pulling on some kind of rubber gloves and smiling like he just won the lottery. *Suspects get the complete treatment, full body cavity search. You want to tell some fancy lawyer about this, boy? Well, it's department policy, so there's nothing a lawyer can do about it.* Then he—and I want to scream and kick him and there's nothing I can do except grit my teeth so I don't give him no satisfaction—and you tell me I'm just supposed to suck it up and say I'm so sorry massa and not do nothin' about it at all?"

I see the tears dripping down his cheeks now, helpless tears like Ray's when the Spartans broke his nose, except this is Cory's Joyous, who loves the game, loves life, too much to cry—at least, until the world screws him over.

"No, you're not supposed to take it!" I tell him, wanting to cry, too, except that crying won't solve anything. "You're supposed to fight back and make them sorry they ever messed with you!" I grip one shoulder, hard bone and rigid muscle. "You make them sorry by beating them, not by changing yourself. Stop talking like you just stepped out of some hood—if you do, they've won, because they treated you like a punk and you've turned into one!"

He shakes my hand off. "Why should I talk like a squeaky clean white boy when I get treated like trash? You don't know what it was like, and you never will! The only guys who know what I'm feeling like are my black brothers. It's high time I find out who I am and live like I am."

"Sure you're black—but you're as squeaky clean as I am or any of the guys on the team. You can't let the cops bring you down—you've got to take them out! And that's what's going to happen to them, isn't it, after you and your folks sue them for every red cent they've got?"

Julius laughs bitterly and drags one arm across his face. "Suing the cops? You're jiving me! That white lawyer friend of yours, that's what he says—bring my parents to see him and sue those guys. So I'm supposed to tell the Prof and the Scribe that I been picked up by the police like some lowdown scum, and thrown in jail and beat up and—" He cuts the sentence off. I can tell he doesn't want to go there again.

"You mean—you're not suing the cops?"

He jumps to his feet, lopes over to the ball rack, grabs a ball, and pounds it on the court in a hard, echoing dribble. "Can't sue them by my lonesome, can I? Can't sue them without everybody knowing everything about my business, can I?" Then he barks that mean laugh again. "Course, everybody knows all my business now, don't they, thanks to you?" And he spins and fires a pass at me with all his might, so hard that I don't even try to catch it, just sidestep it so it shoots by me and crashes into the bleachers.

"I'm sorry," I tell him, even though I'm not sure whether I'm apologizing for telling the team or apologizing for not letting him know they knew. Then the rest of what he said sinks in, and I say, slowly, "You mean, everybody knows—except your parents?"

"That's right," he says, his voice low and hard. "And I ain't ever telling them nothing about this. Nothing!"

"Julius," I whisper, "you've got to tell them."

"And see them look at me like Coach does? Like the rest of the class does? Even Keesha—you see that look in her eyes, like I'm some sort of stranger now?"

You are, I want to tell him. *You're turning yourself into one.* But I've already said as much as I can, so I keep my mouth shut. The ball has tumbled down the bleachers and landed on the floor, rolling downcourt without any energy. Julius strides over to it and picks it up.

"I'm so sick of everything and everybody," he says bitterly, "everything except this." And the ball springs off his palms, as if it has a life of its own, and swishes smoothly through the net. The perfect shot. Julius owns it. And I know I'm still on the sidelines. Or, at best, passing him the ball, if he'll even let a white boy like me still do that. Unless I decide it's my job to speak up and try to change things.

CHAPTER

30

When I get into the hallway, I find I'm not the only person looking for Julius. Keesha is trying to push past Highrise and Ray, and Ricochet's patting her on the shoulder, looking helpless. Shooter stands behind them, shooting resentful glances at Todd, like it's his fault the whole thing happened.

"Let me go," Keesha's saying. "I've got to see him."

"Hold on, everybody," I say. "Actually, I don't think Julius wants to see anybody right now. He's pretty burned."

"That movie was a stupid idea, Brainman," Shooter mutters.

Highrise shakes his head. "No, it wasn't. That's the problem. It was too good. It hit everyone too hard. But Julius has to know it's his own fault he ticked off Leslie about the project. That's why she blew up like that. I don't know how she found out about the mess with the cops, though."

Ray says, "Maybe Coach told her. He probably thought he was trying to give her some sort of lever to force Julius into doing his share of the assignment."

Highrise groans. "Not smart, man. Not smart at all!"

Keesha ducks her head and doesn't say anything, and I don't raise the question of her or any of the other cheerleaders maybe having something to do with it. I just tell them, "Well, that doesn't matter now. It's going to be all over the school soon enough. What really matters is that Julius's parents don't know about it yet."

Todd, who's been slumped against the far wall, straightens up.

"That's right—he hasn't told his folks and he's not suing the police, like Warren said he should." I look at the others. "Warren is Todd's brother, the one who got Julius out of jail." I pause. "Look, guys, he doesn't want to sue because he doesn't want to have to talk about what happened in the jail. It seems the cops . . . roughed him up pretty bad." It's not my place to tell them what Julius told me in the gym. Some of it may end up coming out in court if Julius ever decides to sue, but how much the guys know about it is up to him.

"So what do we do?" I ask. Everybody looks at me like I'm crazy. "He's our teammate. We've got to help him."

Keesha is the one who answers. "If he won't tell his parents, we tell them."

We all stare at her. She looks back at us defiantly. "He's burning up inside about it, and that's why he keeps exploding. I've been telling him he should talk to his parents, but he acts like that would be even worse than what happened in the first place." She shakes her head. "He won't even tell me too many details. He'll start talking, then jump up like he's got to get moving, or he'll grab a ball and start doing harder and harder slam dunks, or he'll hit something like a cushion or a pillow, even a wall once. It's scary, like he's turning into somebody I don't know at all. Sometimes I wish we weren't together—and that's all I've wanted for years, but this isn't the guy I fell in love with. . . . "

She dissolves into tears. The rest of the guys blush and look like they wish they were a million miles away. Then Todd steps forward and puts an arm around her. "You're right," he says softly. "He's hurting, and he needs his friends to help." His gaze sweeps across the rest of us like an accusation. Keesha just leans against him and cries so hard you can see the wet spot growing on his sweatshirt.

Then he looks at me. "You know his parents, Brian. Can they handle it?"

I nod. Ray adds, "If any adults represent intelligent life forms that can cope, it's the Maliks."

That breaks the tension and the guys laugh. Even Keesha's sobs turn into choked laughter, and Todd releases her immediately. "So who's got a ride?" he asks.

Shooter looks nervous. "Now? We'd have to cut study hall and be late for practice."

Todd rolls his eyes. "Well, we wouldn't want you to be late for practice, especially since you're already one man down on the team if Julius's suspension holds."

Highrise reaches out one hand almost automatically and gives Todd a shove, then looks surprised when he doesn't fall over. I guess it hasn't really clicked in for him how much Todd's grown in the last couple of years.

"Stop it," Keesha says sharply, straightening up. "He's right—there are some things more important than basketball, you know!"

Ray says, "Would Ashley loan you the Bomb, Keesha?"

She nods. The two of them are tight. Shooter still balks

at cutting study hall until I point out, "So go, man—that's fine. But if the rest of the team is all missing you can bet people are going to have questions about it, and they'll expect you to know the answers as the only player there."

After that, Shooter squeezes into the backseat of Ashley's car along with the rest of the crowd. No teachers seem to notice when we head out of the parking lot toward the Maliks' house.

Mrs. Malik opens the door smiling, like she usually does. Then she takes in the group, Todd's unfamiliar face, and maybe the fact that Julius isn't with us. Smile fading, her eyes dart over to the clock, and I figure she realizes school isn't out yet. "What's wrong? Brian? Keesha?"

Keesha can't seem to find any words. I feel Ray nudge me in the back, as if telling me it's my job to explain, so I take a stab at it. "Julius got suspended today, Mrs. Malik." She gasps, her eyes widening as if I'd told her he'd been hit by a car, or something really serious. That part's coming, I guess. "But it really wasn't his fault—and it didn't start today. It started when you and Mr. Malik flew to Germany." And I explain about his calling me from the jail, and how he's been acting since.

Somewhere in the middle of the explanation we all come inside, and before I'm finished she asks me to stop and calls her husband. He gets there while the others are taking turns explaining about Mr. Fortner's class, and listens dumbly as Todd tells them about having a lawyer for a brother. I add, "We all just assumed Julius had told you, and didn't want to talk about it with us, until things got bad in class today."

Both his parents look like they're in shock. Todd says

quietly, "It's up to you, of course. But I know Warren's been wondering why you never called him about filing suit against the police officers. He's ready to do it. And if the coach has been treating Julius differently because of this . . . incident, then Warren can probably go to the school board. I'm guessing he could threaten discrimination unless they make the coach treat Julius just like any other student. He might even get the suspension lifted because of extenuating circumstances."

The guys on the team are staring at Todd, open-mouthed. They never realized the Turd had it in him.

The Prof says, "But of course we want to file suit." He sounds bewildered. He looks at Julius's mother. "I just can't understand why Julius didn't tell us himself."

I try to explain, "He said he couldn't stand to tell you, because he didn't want you to look at him like he'd turned into somebody different, like Coach looks at him now."

Mr. Malik shakes his head. "Didn't he know we'd stand up for him?"

"How could he know what to think?" Mrs. Malik says. I can hear her swallowing tears as she struggles to keep her voice even. "He's never gotten in trouble before, never been falsely accused of anything. We didn't want to think that something like this could happen to him, so we didn't prepare him to deal with it."

"We didn't want him to have to feel different," Mr. Malik says heavily.

But Julius's mother says, "He *is* different. He just didn't know it." She looks at the Prof. "We knew we were different when we were his age."

He laughs a little, a sad laugh. "That's because we knew

we had to fight for our civil rights every day. And we did!" He looks up defiantly. "But we moved here so that Julius and Leon wouldn't have to grow up feeling that everyone was treating them like second-class citizens just because they were black."

"It didn't happen here," I say helplessly. "It happened in the city. Here everybody likes Julius."

"Racial profiling may be a city problem," Mrs. Malik says. "But I think we made a mistake pretending we could escape prejudice by coming here. We should have done more to make Julius proud to be a talented black teenager, instead of letting him think he was the same as the white teens around him."

"But he is the same as us," Highrise argues, "just better than we are on the court, most of the time, anyway."

Professor Malik looks at him, as if only now realizing that we're all sitting there, listening to their discussion. He shakes his head. "I know you believe that," he tells Highrise gently, "but you and Julius are not the same in most people's eyes. You would not be treated the same way by those police."

"Well, the police and 'most people' are wrong," Ray says. "That's not how it should be."

"No, it's not how it should be," Mrs. Malik says. "But this is not a perfect world, and we have to deal with it."

"Hey, guys." I stand up, sensing the Maliks want to work things out on their own. "Let's head back to school and see if we can get to practice before it gets so late Coach really hits the ceiling."

Mrs. Malik tries to smile at me. Then she comes over quickly to hug me. "Thank you, Brian—for getting Julius that night, and for coming here today." She lets go of me and I step back, blushing a little. "Thank you all."

The Prof gets Warren's phone number from Todd before we cram into the Bomb again and Keesha drives us back in near silence. Finally Shooter says, "I never really thought about it—about Julius being black, I mean."

"Really?" Keesha says.

"We think about you being one of the girls, and Julius being an awesome player, okay?" Shooter tells her. "Sure, we know you're black, just like we know Ashley's got dark hair—it's something we see, but it's not what makes you or Julius who you are to us." He frowns. "If that makes sense."

She drops us off at the gym entrance. "Okay, Shooter," she says. "It doesn't matter."

But I can hear in her voice how much it does. And I think about Todd, and how they already think of him as being different. How much more different would they label him if they knew he was gay? That's why he doesn't tell anyone, but Julius and Keesha can't hide their difference the same way.

"Yeah, Shooter, it makes sense," I tell him as she drives off to park. "But maybe we're not seeing the whole picture, like how being black feels on the inside to Julius or Keesha."

Todd tips one finger to me in an "on target" gesture and wanders off in the direction of the public bus stop.

Shooter watches him leave, and then turns back to me. "But we can't ever know that, Brainman."

I sigh. "Yeah. I know."

CHAPTER

31

We're so late for practice that Coach makes us run killer drills from the end line to the foul line and back, then from the end line to the center line and back. He'd keep us running them until school starts tomorrow, except he doesn't want us completely burned out for Friday's game against Jackson. He's probably wishing he could bench us all to show us who's boss, but he knows the town would rise up and get him fired if we couldn't put a team on the court against the Generals. So he paces up and down the sideline, slapping his coaching bible against one leg and muttering complaints about troublemakers who mess up the whole team. Somehow we telepathically agree not to tell him Warren's going to be in touch about lifting the suspension and letting Julius play on Friday.

There's no sign of Julius in class or at practice on Thursday, and I figure Warren is working with him and his parents. I just try to stay focused on the game we've got against Jackson. I've dealt with Julius, and I've dealt with Todd and the project for Mr. Fortner, so now all I have left to deal with is beating the Generals. I don't allow myself to think about the loose ends left over from dealing with

Julius (like his anger exploding on the court, or how Coach clearly wants to punish him and has just been waiting for an excuse like this) or with Todd (like his disapproval of my not speaking up about the jogger) or with Amanda. . . . I try not to think about Amanda at all— nothing matters except the rhythm of the ball.

Keep—your mind
on—the game.
All—the rest—
shut—it out.

But that's easier said than done. As I'm heading out to hook a ride home after practice, I hear a roar and Todd's bike swerves to a stop at the curb beside me. He switches off the engine, pulls off his helmet, and says without pre-amble, "You have to speak out now."

I blink, thinking how easily I checked him off as having been dealt with. "What do you mean?"

"It was just on the news. The jury argued through the night, even told the judge they were hung, but he made them go back—he practically ordered them to reach a verdict! So they did."

I stare at him, feeling sick. "And it was?"

"Guilty," Todd says quietly.

I stand there, disbelieving. Is this how Alonzo Mann felt when the jury convicted Leo Frank? I was so sure the defense attorney would call me back if he needed me. . . .

"But I *did* call the lawyer. At least, I left a message," I whisper, hearing how useless the words sound. I feel like I've let Amanda down again. "Now it's too late."

"It can't be," Todd says. "That's not the way the system's supposed to work."

I feel like throwing something, but there's nothing handy. "Well, I think we proved conclusively for Fortner that the system doesn't work!"

Todd just looks at me evenly. "It doesn't work because people don't speak out. We can change that." He pauses. "You can change that."

"I tried! When I called Mr. Daine's lawyer, all he had was this convoluted voice messaging system. I left a message—I told him about the jogger and the gray fibers, and how to reach me and everything. He didn't call back. What more can I do about it?" But I know I've got to do something. I can't just stand by and let this happen—not to Amanda's father, and not to Amanda, either. They both deserve better justice.

Todd shakes his head. "I'm not sure." After a moment he adds, "But I know who'll have some ideas. How about talking to Warren?"

Something like relief floods over me, and I realize I've been holding my breath, wanting to do something decisive but not knowing how. It was easy to think of Warren when Julius needed help, but I never even thought of asking him about this.

As soon as Todd and I go into his brother's office, the whole story pours out—the not-quite fight with Amanda, the glimpse of the stranger who won't meet my eyes, the what-ifs and the maybes, and through it all, the driving, deafening beat of the basketball, drowning out gunshots, screams, even heartbreak.

When I finally run out of words, I hesitantly raise my eyes to Warren's. The man sits leaning back in his leather desk chair, his hands clasped behind his head. Apart from a few scribbled lines on the top sheet of his legal pad, the yellow paper is unmarked.

Warren takes a deep breath, holds it, then finally lets it out. "Well." His voice creaks a little, as if it's been a long time since he's used it. I glance at the clock, surprised to see that I talked for barely ten minutes, not even a game quarter.

"Well," Warren repeats, his voice more normal. "That's a lot of guilt you've made yourself carry around all this time." His voice doesn't sound sympathetic, or even cool and businesslike, the way it did the night in the police station. It sounds almost paternal—almost condescending. Todd abruptly narrows his eyes and studies his brother.

Warren lowers his arms and moves his pen from the center of the yellow page to the side of the pad. He considers the few lines he wrote. Finally he raises his eyes to meet mine, his black eyes coolly assessing, like Todd's, but with none of the warmth I've come to recognize in Todd's expression. "What exactly did you tell the police officer?" His tone is neutral now, but I feel accused.

My stomach squirms, but I try not to show it. "I told him I couldn't really describe the jogger," I say slowly, wanting to be as accurate as possible. "I said I couldn't tell whether it was a man or a woman because of the baggy sweatsuit. I don't even think I remembered it was gray, or mentioned the sunglasses. I'm pretty sure I said something about the hood."

"The officer didn't ask you for any more details?" Warren's skepticism thuds across the desk like a dropped ball.

"Yes," I admit, hearing the echoes pounding in my ears.

"But I couldn't think of any. Then Dad cut in to try to explain why I was so upset. He told him how well I knew Amanda, but the cop wasn't really interested. Dad told him I'd been playing ball with my friends, then shooting hoops on my own all afternoon, and that I kind of tune everything out when I'm practicing. And he told the policeman that there were lots of neighbors and visitors and people who walk or jog on our street because it's so quiet. I didn't really notice anything except Mrs. Daine's SUV leaving and coming back—not even any other cars in the cul-de-sac—nothing except the ball."

Warren drums his fingers on the yellow pad. "What else did the officer ask you?"

I shrug. "He asked me about seeing Amanda's mother drive home. Mostly, though, he wanted to know what time I'd seen Amanda's father come home. His questions about that were really specific—he barely paid attention when Dad tried to tell him anything about Amanda being special to me." I know I'm trying to excuse myself, but it's true.

Warren sighs. "The officer had probably already made up his mind that Daine was guilty and was manipulating the questioning so he'd get the evidence he needed to confirm his assumption. Still, you should have tried to give him more information."

"I wasn't sure it was all that important," I say. "It didn't even start to bug me until the defense lawyer said something on TV a few weeks ago about gray fibers and I realized no one had ever said anything about the jogger. Dad said maybe they'd checked him out and he didn't have anything to do with the case after all. But then, we were working on the Leo Frank case and I read about Alonzo Mann not saying anything about seeing the killer, and I wondered if the jogger might be important after all."

"So you read about some eyewitness who kept silent and saw yourself in the story." Warren sounds just like Dad. Todd straightens in his chair and glares at his brother. "Are you sure you're not exaggerating what you saw?" Warren asks.

"I'm not sure of anything, except that I saw a jogger wearing a gray sweatsuit, and I've never seen him before or since, and I think it's important enough that somebody should check it out before it's too late!"

Warren rolls his gold pen between his hands, then asks, "Which explains why you immediately came forward when you realized how important it must be?" I look down. "Or why you contacted his defense attorney as soon as your friend's father was charged?"

"I tried to call the defense lawyer," I burst out, "but all I got was some machine, and I left a message about the jogger, and the gray fibers, and asked him to call me. I never expected Mr. Daine to be convicted—no one did! The jury was supposed to find him not guilty!" I don't dare look at Todd just then. I know I sound ridiculous, just like Alonzo Mann.

"Supposed to?" Warren repeats softly. "And how were they supposed to do that without all the pertinent evidence, such as, for example, this jogger you saw?"

I open my mouth, then close it. Finally I say, softly, "But I told the police. I called the defense attorney."

The silence stretches until Todd says sharply, "And he's come forward now." He adds in a more normal voice, "So stop torturing him—you sound just like Dad! Why don't you start figuring out where we go from here, instead?"

Warren glares at his brother. "Don't you think I've been trying to figure that out since Brian dropped this bombshell? This isn't like helping your friend after that arrest, you know—"

"Why not?" Todd interrupts, skipping over the fact that Julius isn't his friend at all. "It's still standing up for what's right, isn't it? It's still trying to get justice."

"Are we discussing justice and right and wrong here," asks Warren, "or the law?"

"They're the same thing," I say.

Todd adds, almost as if completing the sentence intentionally, "Or they should be."

Warren sighs and leans back in his chair, looking tired. "The law grants Mr. Daine the right to appeal the conviction, but only on certain very specific grounds. And those grounds do not include the introduction of new evidence such as a mysterious stranger that a witness only mentions eight months later and no one else saw at all."

"But that's not fair," I say.

After a moment Todd asks, "What new evidence does the law allow?"

Warren rocks his chair back and forth. "Pertinent evidence such as a confession from the murderer, production of the murder weapon in someone else's hands—"

"But isn't the jogger pertinent evidence?" Todd demands. "That's what Brian's trying to give you."

"There are strict rules in the law about production of evidence, and if the defense doesn't produce the evidence at the right time it's inadmissible in court!" Warren snaps, as if I'm not even there. "Even if you try to get Daine's lawyer to appeal the verdict because of pertinent new evidence, there's a requirement that this piece of evidence, alone and of itself, would likely have resulted in a different outcome. The last-minute appearance of a mysterious jogger doesn't meet that requirement."

"But I tried to call. . . ." I begin, then stop because I see Warren looking thoughtful.

"Actually," he says slowly, "the fact that you tried to contact the defense attorney with this information could be grounds for a different sort of appeal—incompetence of counsel. And the fact that you did tell the investigating officer is important, also. If the prosecutor failed to disclose that information to the defense, then an appeal could be made on prosecutorial misconduct."

Todd nods eagerly, but when Warren's eyes meet his I see a sad expression in them, like somebody about to tell a little kid there's no Santa Claus. "But even those considerations aren't going to change the verdict now. And with all the motions and countermotions, an appeal takes years. You'll both be out of college before an appeal could be heard and decided."

"But that means Mr. Daine has to stay in jail all that time," I say, disbelieving. "That's not fair. There's got to be something else you can do."

Warren looks at me. "Unfortunately, I think you have unrealistic expectations when it comes to exactly what I can do as a lawyer, Brian. And you both have a terribly idealistic view of the law. A jury of his peers has found him guilty on the basis of the evidence they had at the time. Short of an appeal, there's no way to introduce new evidence that will make the court reconsider right now."

Warren sounds tired and discouraged. "I wish the law were different. I wish Rosen had called you back and gotten an investigator to follow your lead, and then put you and the investigator on the stand. But he didn't, and now it's too late. That's the way the Rules of Criminal Procedure are written. There's nothing you can do for Mr. Daine until an appeal."

"But—" I begin. Then I stop, dumbfounded. I hear the echoing thuds of the basketball:

> Good—but not
> good—enough.
> Now—was not
> soon—enough.

"But he hasn't even been sentenced yet," Todd objects.

"That's right," Warren says flatly.

"But that's wrong." Todd's voice is quiet but insistent.

"Well, that's the Rules of Criminal Procedure," Warren tells him. "You know I don't make the law. I only practice it."

> That's—the law.
> But—it's wrong.

The words thud into my head like the ball pounding up and down the court—pounding but never scoring.

Todd pushes himself up out of his chair slowly. It looks as if the effort of rising costs him a great deal. When he reaches his full height, he looks down at his brother. "You always said that a lawyer's responsibility is to interpret the law in the best interests of his client," he says, his voice hard, every word a blow from the basketball, as if it's now pounding in his head as hard as it keeps pounding in mine. "A lawyer's job is to find precedents that support his case, or to use the case to set precedent. You said that laws were designed to protect innocent people. If they didn't work that way, then your job was to make the jury see it your way, so *they* would protect your client."

"I don't need you lecturing me on how to practice law!" Warren almost shouts, and I cringe inside. Todd and his brother shouldn't be so angry at each other. It's all my fault that they are.

"Well, you sure need someone lecturing you, because you need a lot more 'practice' before you're ready to act like a real lawyer!" Todd takes a deep breath. "I'm grateful to you for listening to Brian and for not charging us anything, but I've got to tell you that right now I'm ashamed you're my brother."

Warren shoves his chair backward so hard it hits the file drawers in the credenza, and I wish I'd never come. I want to say something to stop them, but the basketball is pounding so hard in my head I can't shape words.

Keep—*yourself*
un—*involved*
or—*you hurt*
all—*of them*.

Warren's voice is hard, unforgiving. "This absolute sense that you're always right, you're the only one who's right, no matter what the law says, no matter what anyone else thinks, and your insistence that everybody does it your way or you walk out on them—it's going to get you into big trouble one day, brother mine. At worst, it's going to turn you into some radical law-breaking renegade on the run. At the very least, it's going to leave you pretty lonely."

"I'd rather be alone than know that I let the law run

over some innocent man's life!"

The lock clicks on the door between Warren's office and the house, and then Elise pushes it open.

"What?" demands Warren, rounding on her.

I swallow. Trying to speak out seems to have done nothing except ruin Todd's life.

"I heard voices," Elise says mildly. She's holding a medical journal, one finger marking her place. Her gaze takes in Warren's flushed face and Todd's closed expression before settling on the one silent figure in the room. "All except Brian's." After a moment she adds, "And I thought he was the one who wanted the legal consultation."

In the silence that follows her words, both Warren and Todd turn to me.

I take a deep breath. "I'm sorry, Warren. Todd." I can't say any more to Todd. I just stand up. "I'm sorry, Elise," I mutter as I leave the room, stumbling a little on the edge of the carpet.

"Brian."

Todd's followed me outside. I look at the stars. Time warps briefly and I see the fireworks and feel Amanda's lips again. She wanted me to help her. . . . *But when you try to help you hurt people. Look what happened with Julius, and with Warren and Todd.* But this is different. I can't hurt Amanda, now. And it looks as if I'm the only one who really can help her, and her father. It's time I start concentrating on getting justice for both of them.

"The sentencing hearing is tomorrow," I say, as if I couldn't care less.

"That's right," Todd says.

I turn away from the stars. "So—are you up for cutting

classes and going to the hearing?"

Todd's eyes widen.

"Your bike should get us to the county courthouse," I tell him. "And, after all, the worst they can do is arrest me for saying something they don't want to hear. Whatever Warren says about the law—I've got to believe the judge wants to get to the truth."

Todd smiles. "You're on."

I look back to the stars. *I won't let you down*, I promise Amanda. Despite the silence that answers, I feel good— right—about the idea of going straight to the judge.

"I've got pressure.
Only 40 over 25, but it's there."

CHAPTER

32

There's a huge crowd, like a playoff game, jostling to get inside the courthouse. Todd sees a uniformed man at a door and weaves through the crowd to reach him. A moment later the black-sleeved arm waves me over and the guard passes the two of us through the metal detectors into the courtroom, smiling benignly at us.

"He knows Warren," Todd says briefly. "He thinks I'm taking after my brother, getting interested in the law."

I want to thank him, but my mouth is too dry. I don't think I can choke any words out.

The morning blinks past in brief news-clip flashes of character witnesses, the defense trying to convince the judge and jury to be lenient in their sentencing, and objections from the prosecution that the maximum sentence should be imposed for such a heinous crime. I keep waiting for the right moment to stand up and say something, but the court recesses for a quick lunch and that moment still hasn't come. Apparently judges don't ask the audience if anyone wants to speak now or forever hold their peace. I turn to Todd. "I guess Warren was right. It's too late to speak out in court."

He's frowning, not willing to admit that his brother was right. Finally the lawyers start coming back in.

"But maybe I can at least talk to the lawyer."

"Brian!" he calls. But I'm on my feet and squeezing my way to the front of the courtroom through the other people. I push open the little gateway, over the gasps of a couple of people seated in the first row, and hurry over to the table where Mr. Daine's lawyer has just set down his briefcase. "Mr. Rosen?"

My voice is dry and shaky, but loud enough to be heard. I swallow. "Mr. Rosen, I'm Brian Hammett. I tried to call you, but you never called back. You've got to listen to me about that jogger, before it's too late!"

The thin man who looks like a college professor stares at me, eyebrows drawn together in some expression midway between surprise and disapproval. My words speed up, like a drive down the court that starts out slow and then breaks free from the defenders and moves into high speed. "The day Amanda and Cory and their mom were shot—I saw a jogger. He was wearing a gray sweatsuit with the hood up, and super dark sunglasses, so I couldn't even tell if it was a man or a woman. But I know I've never seen that jogger in the cul-de-sac before. And the police said they found gray fibers at the scene, but nobody found any clothing that matched them. Maybe the fibers came from that sweatsuit, Mr. Rosen!"

The bailiff comes over. "What's going on, Mr. Rosen? Son, you're going to have to get back behind the bar."

But I keep talking, because suddenly what's really been bothering me about the jogger all along comes into focus. "It was just this plain gray sweatsuit—no school name on it

or anything! Don't you see, Mr. Rosen? The jogger was trying too hard to look completely ordinary, so nobody would
notice him! But he was there when the murder happened—and I've never seen him in our cul-de-sac before or
since! He was trying so hard to be unremarkable that it
made him stand out. Don't you get it?"

The prosecutor comes over from his table. He's much
bigger in real life than he looks on the camera. He almost
growls, "Mr. Rosen! Are you trying to use this kid to support that crazy revenge killing theory? Is this your idea of a
last-ditch effort to save your client or try for a mistrial?"

"No, I've never seen that boy in my life!" The college-
professor type glares at me. "You can't speak to me that way,
young man. I'll have the bailiff throw you out of court!"

Behind us, the rest of the crowd, the press—they're all
craning their necks to see what's going on.

"I'm Brian Hammett," I repeat desperately. "I left a message about the jogger on your voice mail! What if this jogger was the killer, not Mr. Daine? The police never found
the gun—what if the gun was hidden inside the sweatsuit?
You've got to let the judge hear my evidence now, before
it's too late!"

I can see people turning to each other in their seats in
the packed courtroom, whispering and pointing at me,
shaking their heads. The bailiff pushes my shoulder, propelling me back to the gate. "Get back behind the bar,
young man!" He looks at the prosecutor. "I'm going to
bring in the defendant now. Do you want me to hold this
kid for future charges?"

My mouth drops open. Is this the way the cops acted
when they hauled Julius in to the police station? How can

standing up for yourself get you in trouble so fast?

Then the prosecutor shakes his head. "Just get the little punk out of here before he causes any more disruption." And he turns back to his table.

Todd has pushed his way through the melee, although he's staying behind the gate. "Brian! Get back! If the defendant's coming in, that means the judge will be back any moment—if he catches you here he's going to hold you in contempt of court and send you to jail so fast you won't know what hit you!"

I let the bailiff push me back through the swinging gate, but I can't just let it go. "But the jogger wouldn't look at me!" I practically yell over the noise in the courtroom. "My basketball almost hit him and he wouldn't meet my eyes or answer me—he didn't want me to hear his voice or see his face! Don't you understand? He didn't want me to be able to identify him! But he could be important—he could be the real killer Mr. Daine's been talking about!"

The bailiff glares at me. "You'd better be out of here by the time I get back with Mr. Daine."

Reporters stand up to see me more clearly as I look frantically from the bailiff to Todd to Mr. Rosen. Todd is eying Mr. Rosen with disgust. Then he turns and shoves me ahead of him, steering me toward the exit.

"We're not going to get anywhere in court," Todd mutters to me, "so it's time to try the court of public opinion." When I shoot him a baffled look he explains, "The press wants to hear you, even if the lawyers don't. I'll get them after the sentencing's over. But right now you'd better get out of here and lay low in the men's room or something, in case Rosen or the prosecutor try to cook up some charges against you to cover their own mistakes."

The center lane opens up like I'm on the court, and I'm past the neat rows of seats, out of the courtroom, into the crowd waiting in the hallway, dodging my way through them in helpless fury because I'm sure now that I'm right about the jogger—whoever it was had to be the murderer, not Mr. Daine. But it's too late to change the verdict.

CHAPTER

33

I run blindly down the courthouse hallway into the men's room and barricade myself into a stall, wanting to hide from the bailiff, the judge, the attorneys—everyone. Dad was right. None of them really wants to listen. Why bother trying?

I hear the outer door open and swing shut again, and brace myself to stay silent in the stall with its warped metal door, the painted-out graffiti making its gray sidewalls look mottled and smeary. But no one pounds on the doors, looking for me. I hear footsteps cross the cracked linoleum floor, someone using one of the urinals, then the casual tread of solid leather soles walking to the sinks. The footsteps stop and the taps screech a little before water splashes into the sink.

"Good idea."

It's a man's voice. I can barely hear it above the sound of the water. My eyes fly up, but I can't see through the metal door, and I tell myself he can't see me either. He must be talking to someone else.

"Just hide out from the whole mess," the voice advises. I hear the faintest trace of humor in it. "It's quite easy when it comes right down to it. That's what everyone wants you to do—the defense attorney, the prosecutor, the judge, even the police—just shut up and disappear. Pretend you never came into court today, never said anything at all."

He's talking to me all right. But I've gone too far to take it back and pretend I never said anything, any more than I can hide out from him. "I can't do that," I hear myself say.

The man's answering sigh is clearly audible. "Look, you're poking your pure little schoolboy nose in where it doesn't belong and isn't wanted. This is a business matter. It has nothing to do with you."

"Business?" I burst out. "How could killing Amanda and Cory—"

"Keep your voice down or I'll take care of you right here." My stomach clenches, and I feel trapped like a helpless animal in a tiny cage.

Finally the man continues. "The business involved their father. There was nothing personal." There's something familiar about his voice. I've heard it before. But where? "If he'd come home sooner he'd have gotten the message directly, but this way worked out just fine. He got the message when he walked into his garage, and he can think about it in a jail cell for the rest of his life."

My knuckles whiten as I fight the urge to tear the door open and face the speaker. Amanda is personal!

Apparently the voice takes my silence for understanding. The taps creak off, but water still drips irregularly into the sink, punctuating his words. "Go home, forget anything you think you saw, forget this conversation. Just think about playing ball." My head jerks up, my neck tendons so tight they creak. Does this guy know me? "You have an important game tonight, Brian. Keep your focus on beating Jackson."

The game. How am I supposed to forget about this man and think what to do on the court tonight? What kind of machine does this man think I've become?

"You make a hundred decisions a day," he goes on. "Do you go out early to shoot free throws before the school bus comes, or do you stay inside until it stops at your driveway? You face a hundred crossroads, and you have to choose which way to turn. Sometimes you choose wrong. Maybe you can get back on track, but some detours lead you so far off course that you can't ever recover. Do you understand what I'm telling you?"

I remember Dad talking about detours. But this isn't what he meant, is it? "Michael Daine could have gone west on the interstate one day," the voice explains. "Instead he went east. He took a wrong turn and angered an associate of mine, who asked me to deliver a message. That detour led Daine to court today, and to jail for the rest of his life. Do you want to make a similar mistake?"

The silence lengthens, broken only by the sound of dripping water. I find myself praying for someone to come in—anyone. No, not Todd, for fear of what the man might do to someone I know, but a stranger—the bailiff tracking me down, a lawyer, the judge, even a policeman. But no one comes.

"All right, then, let me be blunt." Now the man's tone is flat, dead, the sound equivalent of the way I imagine a shark's eyes would look. Would I have seen the dull, flat, lifeless eyes of a shark if the jogger had taken his sunglasses off last summer?

"If you don't stay silent," the flat voice goes on, "if you persist in speaking to the court, or if you go to the press, I will come after you, the way I came after your little friend. I'll come in the shadows, in the dark, and I'll shoot you in your bed, or in your garage, or . . ." An expression that almost sounds like enjoyment comes into his voice, like a bully's taunting. " . . . or in your little sweethearts' hideaway in that workroom your father built but never uses."

I try to swallow, but my throat is too dry. How much does the man know about me? Everything, it seems.

As if reading my thoughts he says, "That's right, boy. I know everything about you. You've made it my business to know all about you. So be smart. Keep your mouth shut."

I can't answer. I focus on the dripping water as if its random splashing is what's driving me crazy, not this man's threats.

"If you make the right decision and choose to keep quiet, I'll toss that knowledge in the circular file as no longer needed. If you stay silent, then you—and your family, I feel I must add —" Now the man's tone turns mocking, triumphant. "You're all safe. Be smart. Live. Be stupid, and you die."

His words hang in the emptiness. Then I hear a last screech of metal as he gives the faucet taps a good, hard twist and the dripping stops. Time stretches to the breaking point while I wait to hear whether those solid leather soles will walk out into the hallway or toward the stall where I'm trapped. Finally I hear soft footsteps and a faint creak that could be the outer door swinging open and shut, but I'm not sure I haven't imagined the sounds because I can't stand the waiting. If I open the door and he's still there—I make myself finish the thought—if I open the door and he's still there, I'll see him and know who he is for sure, but then he'll kill me.

Then the outer door swings open again, and I hear men's voices, strangers.

"Hey, kid, you in here?"

"He must have taken off already."

"You think it was some kind of a stunt, or what?"

"After what's been going on in this case, nothing would surprise me."

The door swings shut on its spring, cutting off their voices, and the sound finally breaks my paralysis. He has to be gone—if he'd been there, he would have said something to them, or they'd have asked him if he'd seen me or something. I fumble with the little catch on the stall door, shove it open, then race outside and down the hallway.

I figure I'll find Todd waiting for me somewhere, but I forget what he said about the press. I'm not expecting the group of reporters surrounding him.

"There he is," Todd says, and they all turn to face me.

I don't know whether to explode like Julius or turn and run. For a second I actually consider telling them about the man's threats, but before the wild idea coalesces into words I squelch it. He meant what he said. Before anybody could identify him, he'd kill me. And Mom and Dad. I can't let that happen.

"I don't have anything to say," I manage, barely recognizing the choked voice as my own.

"Tell us more about the stranger you say you saw," a man over to one side calls out. I jerk around to look at him, almost but not quite recognizing the voice, but then I realize it only sounds familiar because it belongs to one of the guys who came into the men's room looking for me. It's nothing like the cold, dead tone of the killer. I force myself to take a deep breath and say nothing.

"Why didn't you come forward sooner?" another voice demands.

I have plenty of experience keeping silent when opposing players taunt me on the court. It usually unnerves them and keeps my mind clear so I can see the lanes open up. Now I keep my eyes down and my mouth shut as I head down the hallway toward the elevators, even though most of the reporters push their way closer to me, blocking my lane and jostling me along the way. I just elbow my way through—there aren't any refs on this court to blow the whistle and call foul. An elevator door opens in front of me and I can see the car is already full. But I muscle my way forward, figuring the reporters won't be able to squeeze in, even though Todd slips in just behind me.

When the doors close, however, I see one of them made it—Natalie Hart from the news, minus her cameraman. "Okay, let's have it," she says. "You wouldn't shut your mouth in court until the bailiff threatened to hold you for charging. Now you won't say a word. So what happened? Your friend here said you headed for the men's room—I know women go into the ladies' room to gossip, but what happened in the restroom to shut you up?"

I stare at her. "If you persist in speaking to the court, or if you go to the press, I'll come after you," the voice warned. I can't talk to this woman. But she meets my gaze evenly, and I see a glimmer of Amanda's "I can change the world" expression in her eyes before I look away.

"Brian—" Todd's voice is low but incredulous. When I don't answer, he says, "Wrong gets its power from silence. You have to speak out."

But speaking out will bring the man—the murderer.

Should—you speak?

Or—stay hushed?

Dumb—or brave?

Dumb—or dead?

The throbbing echo of the ball in my head makes me remember the game tonight. I can concentrate on the ball, on my teammates, on the game, and not think about Amanda or her father or the stranger who is ready to kill me. Haven't I been doing that all season?

Hero—

Coward—

Fear—

Courage—

The ball's usual steady rhythm crumbles into dissonance.

I feel a hand on my arm. "Brian?" Todd sounds hurt.

I believe the murderer's threat. I believe the man will kill me and my family if I say anything. But will the murderer stop there? Will he remember Todd from the courtroom, and go after him as well? Will he kill Todd and Warren and Elise to punish me?

The elevator chimes, announcing the ground floor. Natalie Hart pushes her business card into my free hand. "My numbers are on there," she informs me. "Cell, office, e-mail—just in case you decide you want to talk to me later."

The doors slide open and I shove the card into my jeans

pocket and jerk my arm away from Todd's hand. "Enough!" I snap at both of them, and I start down the hall, hoping I don't look as unsteady as I feel. I've barely negotiated three steps before the woman's voice halts me.

"I'm sorry you don't want to talk to me now," Natalie Hart says. "But after your outburst in court, I'm going to have to air the story, even without your comments."

"No!" I whirl back to her in shock. "You can't."

"But it's news," she says, and I see another elevator door open. Her cameraman hurries out, then sees us and swings his equipment up to his shoulder. "Officer Daine's sentencing is news," she continues, "so your outburst in court is news."

I stare at the dull, blank eye of the camera lens—the shark's eye, coming to kill me. "All I saw was a jogger," I tell the death's eye, speaking to the murderer, who'll be watching the news, I'm sure. "It could have been anyone in the neighborhood. I was playing ball. I wasn't paying attention."

After a moment, Natalie Hart says, "But you told Mr. Rosen you thought—"

"I was wrong," I cut her off, hating myself, hating Todd for making me think I could do this, hating Mr. Fortner for giving us the stupid project in the first place, most of all hating the murderer—and already looking over my shoulder, not knowing if he's there, somewhere, watching me, listening. "I don't know what I was thinking." I add, "I shouldn't have come here today."

I turn my back on Natalie Hart, on the camera, on Todd, and leave the building.

CHAPTER

34

I stand on the sidewalk, moments or hours later, looking blankly at the traffic passing me by.

"How were you planning on getting back home?"

The question takes me by surprise. Why should Todd want anything to do with me after the fiasco with Natalie Hart?

"There's got to be a bus," I say, even though I have no idea if there's one that will take me all the way to Willisford. Once I could just speed-dial Julius on his cell phone without thinking twice, but it's unlikely that my old friend would come get me now. And no way can I call my parents—how am I ever going to explain to my father what I was doing in court? I try not to think about Dad's reaction when he sees the evening news. Maybe I can get him to postpone watching until after the game.

Todd shakes my shoulder, interrupting my thoughts. Why can't he take the hint and just leave me alone? "I said—if you're planning on playing tonight, you'd better not wait for a bus unless you have some idea of when they run." The impersonal voice doesn't seem to care one way or the other. Hadn't it once sounded more friendly, or is that just my imagination? "Anyway, you're probably going to get into enough trouble for cutting classes today. You don't want to be late for warm-ups."

It occurs to me that Todd must be offering me a ride. "You'll take me back to school?"

Todd studies me for a minute, his expression closed, then shrugs. "Sure. I can't very well leave you stranded here, can I?"

"Well—thanks." I hate how awkward the words sound. It's as if time is running backward now, and we're the enemies we were when we started the project. I rub my eyes. If Todd and I are enemies again, does that mean Julius and I are back to being friends again? What does that make me and Amanda now? I feel as if I'm going crazy—I can't make sense out of the tangle of relationships anymore.

But I can't let myself go crazy. I have a game to play tonight. I have the rest of my life to figure out how to live tomorrow. Julius and I aren't the same sort of friends anymore. And Todd and I aren't the sort of enemies we used to be. Everything has changed. I follow the black-sheathed figure to the bike and take the helmet he hands me.

"One question," Todd says, watching me pull it on. I tighten the strap silently.

"Why? You had a chance to do something in there, something important." He shakes his head impatiently. "A chance to change things! Why did you clam up?"

I stare at the cracked concrete underfoot. I want to say: Because I have to keep my parents safe, because I have to keep *you* safe, because I want to live, and not end up dead, like Amanda.

But some kind of shame keeps me silent. We all end up

dead in the end. What matters is how you live, more than when you die. But I can't bring myself to say, as much to myself as to Todd: Because I'm a coward.

"Because I don't care about changing the world," I say flatly. I climb on the back of the bike. "I only care about playing ball."

After a few moments, Todd straps on his own helmet and mounts the bike. He kicks the starter and roars into the street without answering.

"I think I've got the blood loss stopped. I'm coming out. Get me a drain tube."

CHAPTER

35

I thought they might suspend me for cutting class a second time. (There's justice for you: cut class voluntarily and they make you cut class deliberately.) But a suspension would bench me, and the principal doesn't want that. He assigns me Saturday detention instead—after the playoffs are over. I can't see that far into the future to care. I go through the motions in the afternoon, call home and leave a message that the team's hanging together for supper before facing Jackson, and eat without thinking about it, packing carbs for energy automatically, like a robot. Somebody tells me that the Maliks got the suspension lifted and Warren made Coach agree to let Julius play, but I don't know whether or not that's good news. Everybody's on edge, and I'm drifting.

The locker room comes into focus, all of us pulling on the familiar, freshly washed uniforms. I picture the Generals suiting up and high-fiving in the locker room next door, building their confidence with every breath as they get their minds ready for the game. I look around our locker room, silent except for the squeak of rubber soles. Every man's keeping to himself, not looking at his team-mates at all. Everybody thinking separate thoughts, probably no one with his mind on the game any more than mine is.

"Listen up," Coach says, trying to energize us, "It's time to focus! Remember, we're a team. Keep your eyes on the ball, be there for each other, and listen to Brian! He's the point guard for every play."

Everybody's nodding, but nobody's listening. We jog out onto the court, shoes thudding flatly on the wood as if we're wondering what we're doing here. The gym is packed, with uniformed officers on the sidelines making sure nobody runs out onto the court—added protection for the big rivalry with Jackson. We certainly don't get that sort of special attention in ordinary games. The crowd roars at our appearance, and even some of the cops turn and clap, grinning. The cheerleaders erupt into action, in contrast to our unaccustomed apathy, leaping into their routine:

"We play hot,
We play cold,
On the court
We explode!
We drive,
We spin—
Warriors
Are here to win!"

Only we don't feel like winners. And we don't act like warriors.

Highrise loses the opening tip-off. The Jackson point guard grabs the ball and swings it cross-court to their forward. He pivots and fakes a pass, sending Take-away Ray back on his heels. Then, with his feet just behind the arc, the guy soars up to sink a quick three-pointer before Ricochet can even raise his arms or rush him. There's no doubt, we're off to a bad start.

It doesn't get better as we struggle through the first half. We start racking up points, but they're never as a team— each guy playing one-on-one, trying to beat his guard to the basket, trying to prove he can do it on his own—each guy losing sight of his teammates and ignoring my calls to swing the ball. We can't win this way, especially against a team like Jackson. They're perfectly coordinated, passing to each other as if the ball is on a string and knows how to flow from hand to hand. They're like the Harlem Globetrotters, and we fall and flail around them like clowns in a circus, not a team on the court.

Soon it's 24–10. Julius charges coast to coast for a layup. He's already in the air when a Jackson guard gets in his face. I see Ray is open. "Dish it off, Julius!"

He doesn't even consider passing. On the way down, he simply scoops the ball underhand and flicks it with his wrist so it pops up and over the rim for a score.

The crowd cheers, and Julius jogs backward, glaring contemptuously at Coach—and in my direction, too—as if to say "Watch me teach you." Ray jogs by Julius and brushes him bluntly with his shoulder in frustration, but Julius ignores him. I know we're in trouble.

It gets worse, speeding us into a darker and deeper hole. We're playing as if we don't even know each other—like a pick-up game after the best players leave. Finally, Take-away Ray slaps the ball away from Jackson, but instead of hitting me to start the break, he dribbles toward the basket, looks surprised at the center planted like a tree in front of him, and stutter-steps as he tries to decide what to do. The whistle echoes as he's called for traveling. Meanwhile Ricochet keeps missing rebounds, ones we've relied on him to handle all season. When Wrestler comes in, he's too scared of being fouled to successfully throw the Generals off their rhythm, and even Shooter misses the outside shots that usually take our opponents by surprise. Highrise's timing is off, and for every acrobatic shot Julius makes, he misses two gimmes when he's wide open.

When Ray does remember to get me the ball I can't read the court. No one's ready. No one's making clean cuts or flashing open. No one's talking. Worst of all, I don't believe we can find the zone. So my passes float and my eyes keep telegraphing my thoughts to the defenders. While they rack up the steals and scramble for loose balls, my guys stand around. All I can think about is the warning I heard in the courthouse, pummeling my ears louder than the basketball's pounding.

Black—and white.

Ab—solutes.

Is it ever right to kill someone? Absolutely not. It's black and white, and no room for sitting on the bench claiming you didn't see anything. Is it right to put people you love in danger? Absolutely not. Certain things are absolutely right. Other things are absolutely wrong.

Black—and white.

Sports—manship

on—the court.

Off—the court?

Shades—of gray.

The grays confuse the issue. If the absolutely right

choice to help one person hurts someone else, wasn't it the wrong choice?

Shades—of gray.

Right—or wrong?

Wrong—is right.

Julius pounds the ball as he rushes down the court again, that black chip so heavy on his shoulder that he can't see gray anymore. That's thanks to those black-and-white-thinking cops. If he's black, he's a criminal. If he's white, he's just a kid who needs directions.

Black—and white.

I see Todd slumped in the bleachers, that righteous chip so heavy on his shoulder that he can't imagine anyone not immediately seeing the choice he thinks is right. That's thanks to those black-and-white-thinking parents of his. If he's straight, he's okay. If he's gay, he's not their son anymore.

Black—and white.

When I stand up for Julius to my father, to Warren, to the cops, to Coach, I'm absolutely right. Then he acts like a ball hog on the court, ruining the game, shattering the team—so I must be wrong. When I stand up to Warren, to the lawyers, and say I saw someone, I'm absolutely right. If I stand up to the killer and he kills my family, I must be wrong.

Shades—of gray.

What—to do?

Not always black or white at all. You've got to find the shade of gray that fits you best. Prison gray? Coward gray? Kinda-sorta wishy-washy gray? Corpse gray that made the wrong choice and ended up on a detour he can't change?

It's not a hundred decisions I make in the course of a day—it's a thousand decisions I make on the court.

Ricochet fires an unbalanced pass in my direction that the Jackson point guard dives for. But he misses the interception and only succeeds in bumping the ball out of bounds for us to bring back into play. I chase the ball across the sideline before it runs into the row of scattered cameramen with their blinding flashes and uniformed policemen keeping their eyes more on the game than the crowd. The ball almost hits one of the cops, and I scoop it up, apologizing in winded gasps, but he barely waves an arm indicating he's okay before he turns back to scanning the crowd, never answering me, leaving me to give the ball to the ref. The zebra tosses it back to me to put into play and I'm at another crossroad.

Do I pass to Julius? If I do, will he put the ball in the hole, or will he make another off-balance, wild shot with no hope of finding the net? Do I dribble down court to get inside for a shot myself? Do I bounce-pass to Ricochet or Highrise for a quick layup? Which of them would follow my lead to find an open space? Or should I just toss it back to Ray and buy some time to read the defense? Where are we going to find some points?

I used to be able to see all the passing lanes radiating out from me like shining paths. I always know which move to make. But now I'm lost. Flying hands and shouts from the other team swirl my mind into a foggy, misty gray detour until I can't see anything. Brainman? That's a laugh. I'm brain-dead with limp arms pumping the ball helplessly up and down with no path to take.

Last year, my biggest gray areas were making the perfect

shot and getting up the nerve to tell Amanda I loved her. Now I can't even make a decent pass and it's too late to ever have a chance at the second. As I chase the Generals down the court on defense, wishing it were last year still, I almost stagger with the weird dizziness that comes with déjà vu. The ball, rolling away, almost hitting—a jogger, and then, tonight, a cop. And both men turning away, barely waving an arm to show they're okay, never saying anything. . . . My stomach turns to ice, despite the sweat running down my chest. Then Jackson scores, Ricochet takes the ball out and passes it back in play to me, and I grip it in numb fingers, struggling to shut out the past and decide what to do here and now, all over again.

At halftime we're down 48–22 as we stumble over to the sidelines to recover our warm-up jackets. Dad reaches out from the bleachers and grabs me, like he wants to shake some sense into my head. "What were you thinking?" he practically shouts, and I see mingled fear and confusion on his face. "Everybody's telling me how you were on the news tonight—you went into the courtroom and made this big deal that you saw something the day the Daines were killed and you had to speak out —"

"Mr. Hammett." That's Fortner. What's he doing here? He comes to the home games, like most of the teachers, but I don't think I've ever seen him speak to anybody on the team or their families. "I think I can shed some light on this—"

But Dad cuts him off, having no clue he's snubbing a teacher. "Leave me alone—I'm talking to my son." He looks at Mr. Fortner like he's some alien. "Who are you, anyway?"

"I'm Brian's history teacher, Mr. Hammett. He just finished an excellent project on American justice. He showed the whole class that citizens have to come forward with evidence if the system is going to work."

Dad turns back to me. "You think you can fix the American justice system?" he demands. His tone, incredulous, completely runs over Mr. Fortner's interjected, "Yes, he can make a difference!"

"What difference can one person make in something big like government?" Dad demands, shooting Mr. Fortner a quick glare before focusing on me. "Zero—zip! I told you not to get involved. You get involved, you get your priorities turned upside down, your head's not in your game anymore! Stick to where you can make a difference, Brian—here, on this court—in your game!"

"But Mr.—"

Now Dad's totally ignoring Mr. Fortner, like he doesn't exist, like Mr. Daine doesn't exist, like Amanda never existed. He's just staring at me, like he can drill some sense into me, like he can somehow keep me safe on the basketball court forever. I hear the band and realize the halftime show is starting, and I pull away from him and jog toward the locker room.

Do I know for sure what I'm doing in the game, on this court, like Dad says? Sometimes I think my best moves are by instinct, not knowing what I'm doing for sure until I'm in the middle of the play. I hear the echo of Todd's voice, telling me, "It comes down to whether or not you're the kind of guy who's willing to take responsibility for guessing—whether or not a guy understands the consequences of acting on a bad hunch. If he knows he'll have to pay for guessing wrong, but he's sure enough of his instincts to take that chance, then he should trust himself."

Black—or white
does—n't count.
Shades—of gray.
Trust—yourself.

I trust myself on the court, or I always have until tonight.

CHAPTER

36

It's quiet in the locker room. None of the guys knows why we're playing so badly, and it scares them too much to even bang lockers or yell at each other. But I know. I know I'm letting them down because I'm scared of making a mistake. And Julius—maybe he knows, deep inside, that he's burning up with too much anger and hate and shame to just play the game for its own sake.

Coach comes in, and we all look to him for answers. But the moment I meet his eyes, I see he's scared, too. He doesn't know what to tell us. And I remind myself he's not really a coach. He's a guidance counselor who loves the game. That's not the same thing at all.

Finally he says, "I don't know what's going on out there." After his encounter with Warren and the Maliks, he carefully avoids looking at Julius or me. "But you've got to come together—you've got to look at each other and really see each other. You've got to play together as a team, the way you've played all year. Not a bunch of talented prima donnas sharing the same court, but a team!" He shakes his head. "It's like I don't know you—who you are, why you're playing. It's like you don't know each other anymore. I want you to take a good look at each other before you go back on that court. See each other. Remember what you can do together. And then play together. That's all I've got to say."

Then he turns his back on us and goes out of the locker room. He's telling us to look at each other, but he can't bear what he sees when he looks at us. I can feel the other guys' eyes glaring after him, angry, skittering around the room and sliding off each other's faces, defensive and ticked off at the same time.

Ricochet catches sight of the *High School Coaching Bible* half hidden under a bench and kicks it across the room. "If he'd get his head out of that stupid book and act like a coach, maybe we'd have a chance!" Then he rounds on Wrestler. "And if you'd work on those free throws maybe we could get some use out of you on the court!"

"Yeah!" Highrise almost snarls, before Wrestler can say anything. But then he glares at Ricochet, eyes narrowed. "Even if Coach used some brains and Wrestler had more experience, we're the starters—we're the ones who have to make the plays. If you'd just make some of those rebounds you're so famous for, maybe we'd start getting some points!"

"So it's all my fault?" Ricochet shoots back. "Well, if you'd gone higher on the tip-off, Highrise, we'd have gotten off on the right foot!"

"I'm not the ball hog taking all those wild shots," Highrise retorts. "And I'm not the take-away artist who keeps fumbling interceptions, either, so don't lay it all on me!"

"Yeah—you guys start playing ball, 'cause I'm the only one putting any points on the board," Julius shouts.

I want to slap my hands over my ears and scream to drown them all out, but I'm the team captain. I'm the one who's supposed to be the leader. I've got to do something. Not sure what it's going to be until I do it, I spin, slam the heel of my hand into the locker door so hard it leaves a dent in the sheet metal, and roar, "If we suck so bad, why don't we all shut ourselves inside our separate lockers and just quit?"

Shocked, they all shut up. I see Ray's startled eyes and Highrise's mouth hanging open. Only Julius still looks more angry than surprised.

"Jackson is bigger than we are," I tell them. "Jackson's headed to the Class 2 Championships. Right now they're thinking we'll never be in their class—we don't stand a chance against them and we'll never even come close to beating them. And if I listened to you, I'd believe that, too. But I don't buy it—because when we play like a team, when we're there for each other, we're unstoppable."

As I say the words, I know what I'm going to do. I'm not living scared of that flat, dead voice forever, thinking I don't stand a chance against him. I'm going to be there for Amanda, not keep her from getting justice by keeping my mouth shut for the next seventy years like Alonzo Mann. I'm going to talk to Natalie Hart and make so much noise that the killer has no chance of silencing me, and get both Amanda and her father the justice they deserve. Knowing the decision is made, and it's right, I know I'm going to lead the Warriors back onto that court looking like a different team.

Julius snorts. "The way you and the rest of these clods are playing, what's the point in this team BS? I'm better off playing my own game."

"No, you're not," I tell him flatly, before the other guys turn on him. "I was lost in my own game, just like you, bringing things onto the court that have nothing to do with hoops." I get right in Julius's face. "You should understand this, man—I wasn't feeling good about myself. I was thinking about taking the safe way out instead of doing the right thing. I forgot what you do on the court, you do in life. But I made up my mind I've got to make the hard choices, not the safe ones, off the court as well as on."

He has no idea what I'm talking about, any more than the other guys do, and there's no time to tell them. I just say, "You've got to make the hard choices, too, Joyous, the way you used to. We've all got to! I'm going to play right the rest of the game—you've just got to trust me."

But it's the wrong thing to say. Julius shakes his head slowly. "I don't trust nobody no more, not Coach, not cops, not that smart white lawyer—"

"Not your teammates?" Ray interrupts. "Because we're white? You used to be color-blind, man!"

"Guess I learned better," he snaps.

"Guess you learned wrong," I retort. "Guess you let the cops win after all! Because you've lost it—remember Cory, Joyous? He never would have believed any cop, even his dad, who said you did something bad, any more than I do or any one of your teammates here do. But Cory wouldn't recognize you now!"

Julius shrugs, but he looks like that chip has slipped a little. I press on, forcing the ball down the court. "You called me," I remind him, "and I came. I know you didn't do anything—we all know that." I look around, including the rest of the guys. "I know we've got to be here for each other. We *need* each other. I know Coach is scared of what he doesn't understand and dumb about some things. He's only human, like us—which means it's not too late for him to learn better, if we teach him. But we've got to get our own heads on straight again, and trust each other."

Each guy looks around at his teammates, maybe remembering the way they were ripping into each other just a couple of minutes ago.

"I love this game," I say. "I love the noise and the pressure and the excitement, but what I love best is the way we trust each other—we trust each other to play clean and do what's right on the court."

"Oh yes," Ray says, his voice low, but his face smiling.

"Trust me," I tell them. "I'll be there for you the rest of the game. I trust you guys to be there for me."

In the silence that follows, Coach calls from the doorway, "Come on, guys."

They crowd around me, hands stretching into the center of our circle, gripping hard. Julius's hand comes down last, crowning the clasp.

"Team!"

Julius holds onto us for a long moment. Then he whispers, "Team, Brainman."

CHAPTER

37

As the second half begins, we're firing on all cylinders. No one is looking at the scoreboard or thinking about the challenge for points—we just charge onto the court like the team we used to be. Like winners. Highrise leaps up, his arm stretching just an inch higher, a second faster, and wins the tip-off, tapping the ball to Ricochet, who races down the court in front of the defense for a sweet layup. Keesha signals the girls and they leap into formation, hope on their faces again, cheering:

"Tip-off,
fast break,
Warriors drive,
Warriors score,
Warriors
Warriors
Win some more!"

I see the Jackson players dart quick looks at each other as their center takes the ball out. They realize something has changed since the first half. The center loops a lazy pass to the guard who looks open—until Take-away Ray appears in an instant, snatching the pass and flipping it over to me.

I pass it to Julius who shoots for three, his wrist perfectly flexed as he watches it with no doubt that it's a score. The girls chant:

"Defense, feel it,
Bad pass, steal it,
Shoot it, pass it,
Warriors' basket!"

A Jackson guard pushes his own center out of the way and takes the ball out. It's clear they're off balance now, trying to avoid another turnover. They get the ball into play and rush down the court, trying to beat us to the paint for a good look at the basket, but Highrise is just too fast for them, leaping two steps ahead and slapping the ball away with a grin. Then they manage to get it in the hole on a lucky rebound. We answer immediately with a basket from Ricochet, another steal by Ray, a behind-the-back pass from me, and an open backboard shot from the side by Highrise for two more.

But Jackson begins to find their defensive focus again, fighting us for every point. It's good, clean, hard playing, not like the Blazers, but we're so hot we could beat the Knicks—if only we'd been playing this way the whole game, not just this half. I begin to call out plays and distribute passes, one eye on the scoreboard with the clock counting down. Do we have enough time to come back?

Even in a game with solid play and good defense you get some fouls, and finally, with 3 minutes to go and Jackson desperately holding on to a 4-point lead, Highrise fouls out. "Sorry, man," he tells me as he heads to the bench.

"Don't sweat it, Highrise," I say. "You played great.

Anyway—it's high time Shooter saw some real action." Shooter and Wrestler have come in a few times to give Julius and Ricochet breathers, but the Generals haven't seen what Shooter can really do. I figure they'll underestimate him now. It might give us the final edge we need to pull out a victory.

The Jackson man Highrise fouled sinks his free throws, and they're up 86–80. But when Ricochet gets the ball from the ref, he inbounds quickly before most of the Generals leave the line and I catch the pass with plenty of room to move. Julius is open, even if he's too near the hoop now to pull back in range for a three. My pass flies to him like a fastball, with just the right spin to hit him in full stride. Joyous soars high enough to slam but just lays it in over the rim and yells his triumph back to me. I smile. Our score rolls to 82. Only two buckets between us and Jackson.

As the 2-minute warning sounds, the Generals spread the floor to slow down the pace. But Take-away Ray chops into one of their passing lanes to steal the ball and we fly back into offense. Shooter's open and I get him the ball. He goes up for three, but the Jackson player guarding him goes up too early and hacks him on the way down, sending the ball backward into the bleachers. Shooter moves to the line for his three free throws as the Jackson fans groan.

This is where all our pick-up games and practices pay off—this is what Wrestler still has to learn about what counts in this game. If you want to win games, you put in those extra hours shooting free throws until your arms burn. Shooter calmly sinks one shot after another, nothing but net. We can hear the band and the cheerleaders and our fans going crazy as we slap him on the back. Above us the score reads 86–85. We're so close! But we keep the celebration short because we've got to get over that last hurdle: one point. We don't want another free throw to tie it—we want to win! We have to find a way to get the deuce.

The Generals get the ball and take their time moving down the court. I wish, more fervently than I've ever wished, that Indiana had a shot clock rule! Without that rule to force a scoring attempt, their strategy is clear: no more shots, run the clock. We press them as hard as we dare, looking for double-team opportunities and slapping at the ball, but we know—no fouls, no mistakes now. We don't want to put them at their line with a chance to put the score out of reach. Suddenly, their point guard fakes a pass and shoots off toward the basket, right out of a double team between me and Shooter.

"Help—Ricochet!" I shout. But he's on the Jackson shooting guard, out of position to cut off the point guard's lane. The guy goes under the rim for an easy reverse layup. Now it's the Jackson side of the gym shrieking with delight as the score rolls to 88–85. I know a three-pointer will only tie the game. Only 24 seconds left and we've got to score twice!

Ricochet takes the ball out. I'm covered. He passes to Ray, who starts up court as I try to shake my man. A second player scrambles toward Ray to make sure he can't pass to me. I signal to Ray to take the shot himself. He pump-fakes as if he's going up for three and sends one player up into the air all alone. Then he cross-dribbles past the other player and heads inside for a sweet layup, rolling the score to 88–87 with 16 ticks left on the clock.

The Generals quickly get the ball back on the court, their two guards passing it back and forth, just hoping to kill the clock. Then one of them remembers the 10-second rule and races for the center line. Ray and Julius meet each other's eyes and know what to do. Ray crouches down to force the dribbler to the right—and swooping in from his blind side comes Julius to slap the ball away. Now it's 7 seconds on the clock and Julius has only one player to beat. It's one on one, but this time every guy on the team wants it this way. All we care about is finding the other four Generals, blocking them out of the play, and watching Julius along with the crowd.

"Joyous, Joyous!" the crowd chants. Then they start the countdown, so he'll know when to let it fly. "5. . . 4. . ."

I can see the last seconds ticking down. Julius's eyes dart my way. If he makes the shot, the game is ours, and he's the man. But the Jackson player crowds him, knowing the refs won't blow the whistle now. The zebras don't want to decide the game by giving us free throws. They're just going to let us play these last 5 seconds on our own—the last seconds of a great game, and only one team will walk off winners.

It's a shot Julius could make, but it's also a block the Jackson player could make, and I see he knows it. Then, out of the corner of my eye, I see Shooter, up in the corner, edging away from his man, who's focused on Julius. I shout, "Joyous—Shooter!"

The Jackson player goes up to block Julius, and I realize he's thinking I yelled "Shoot her!" But Julius gets the message. In the first half he would have forced the shot, but now he flicks the ball behind his head, a blind pass to

Shooter. Shooter takes the pass and, in a single motion, shoots up into the air from just behind the three-point line, his arm muscles flexing as he launches the ball into space. The buzzer sounds as all eyes watch the ball, now falling back toward earth, heading for the target: a small round hole hovering in the space between it and the floor.

Swish—the perfect shot!

For a moment, that's the only sound in the gym. But as the net recovers its balance, the crowd thunders into life. And the score rolls its final time to read 90-88. Victory for the Warriors.

The crowd sweeps onto the court, overrunning the Generals, who fall back, stunned. Our fans are cheering the team, raising us onto shoulders as the band plays triumphantly, the lights impossibly bright, the music impossibly clear, Keesha and Ashley and all the girls leaping impossibly high. It's a perfect feeling I've never experienced before of everything coming together the way it should be.

Somewhere along the way the thrilling volume in the gym diminishes as if someone's turned a stereo down, and the loudspeakers boom out the final score and tell everyone to be quiet for the presentation of the game ball. I get ready to cheer for Julius. Even with the first half he's the high scorer and deserves it. But instead I hear my name echoing off the gym walls as cheers erupt around me. I don't really take it in until hands shove me forward—black hands and white hands, pushing me into center court and clapping behind me.

Coach hands me the game ball and says into the microphone, "For Team Captain Brian Hammett, who pulled the Warriors together and led them to this victory."

And all around me the gym reverberates with cheers and applause—not for the team, for me. Heart pounding, even if I can't palm the ball like Julius, I raise it one-handed over my head, and the noise gets even louder. Across the gym I meet my father's eyes and see his pride. I can't imagine a better moment.

"I think pressure's coming up."

CHAPTER

38

What a comeback!" Todd looks flushed, as if he's been on the court playing with us. "You guys were terrific, all of you! But you, Brian—you brought it home." He gestures to the game ball. "You deserve that. You earned it."

I hold it up like a trophy. "Thanks, man."

Todd's flush fades. He says, more quietly, "I'm sorry about this afternoon, what I said. It was unfair of me to tell you what to do."

I lower the ball. "Yeah. You're right."

His faces closes in its old withdrawal. "Right. So—"

"You're right that it wasn't fair," I run over him. "I'm not you. I've got to make my own decisions. But you're also right that I can't keep quiet about this any longer."

He looks up, surprised.

"I knew it was the right thing to do, and I thought they'd listen to me, in spite of what your brother said."

"But the press," he practically splutters. "They wanted to hear what you had to say, and you blew them off!"

"I know. I blew off the first half of the game tonight, too. I had my reasons, but I was wrong." I take a deep breath and tell him what happened in the men's room. "I was scared—scared for my family, scared for myself." I meet Todd's eyes. "Scared for you, too. He must have seen you with me in the courtroom."

Todd takes this in, frowning but unafraid. He should be frightened. This isn't like bullies shoving you into your locker. "I'll call Warren." His voice sounds a little grudging as he admits, "He'll know what to do. First thing is probably to get out of the house with Elise, unless she's working late at the hospital, in case you're right about the guy identifying me. You and your folks shouldn't go home, either." Then he interrupts himself. "You say his voice sounded familiar? Can you place it yet?"

I shake my head. "I'm just sure I've heard it, but not really paid attention to it. If I hear it again, I'll know. Anyway, after the way I ran from the reporters, I'm guessing he figures I'm too scared to do anything right away, so you probably don't need to overreact tonight. I just wanted you to know."

"Come on, Brainman!" Julius grabs my arm, then lets go as he sees Todd.

"Awesome game," Todd tells him honestly.

Julius studies him a moment. "Thanks, man." He punches Todd's shoulder and grins. "Tell your brother thanks, too, okay?"

Todd smiles. "Will do. And thanks for the win. Tonight," he spreads his arms, taking in the whole gym, "this was magnificent. It's a night no one in this town is ever going to forget."

And the night's only beginning. When the team charges out of the locker room, it's not only families and cheerleaders who are waiting for us. I swear it looks like the whole town's there, car headlights cutting across the parking lot's night shadows, blaring horns punctuating the cheers and whistles. The victory parade sweeps along the streets, and it seems like every door bangs open, and even more people run outside to cheer us as we go by.

They put me in the front car. Dad's truck is second in line so Dad can see them all cheering for me. I keep looking back. There's so much light from the houses and the other cars that I can see his broad smile. Or maybe I'm only imagining it, because I know it must be there. The rest of the team is strung out in cars behind us, so he doesn't have to think about the people cheering for Julius and Ray and Highrise and Ricochet and Shooter and Wrestler, only me. I've never seen him look so happy—anyway, not since the days when he used to smile in his wood shop.

I wish the parade could go on forever. I wish I could hover above this moment of my life for all eternity. The hero who won the game, even if I never sank the perfect shot. But the magic is almost at an end. The car leads the parade into my street, into the cul-de-sac, and we're home. The headlights still blaze as Dad pulls into the driveway and I climb out of the car. Around me, horns blare and cheers erupt. The Francis twins run out, screaming their delight. Every house is alive, celebrating the victory—every house except the empty Daine house.

I stand beside Mom and Dad, waving at my team with one hand, hugging the game ball under my other arm. The cars circle through the cul-de-sac, shadows dancing in their headlights, shadows from waving arms, from swaying tree branches, from neighbors running up to join us.

I turn to show the twins the game ball, even though I

won't let them play with it. It's my trophy, not a toy. In the shifting light pattern, another shadow catches my eye, moving away from my house, dissolving into the darkened trees beyond the cul-de-sac. But the patterns change so fast with the sweeping headlights from the parade that I can't be certain if I actually see anything at all. Then the parade is only glowing taillights. But before they fade, the remaining neighbors are crowding around us. Those who couldn't come to the game want to hear the play-by-play, and I'm replaying the second half all over again, and I know this is a triumph that no one can ever take away from me.

CHAPTER

39

When we finally go inside I drop my book bag in the hall-way and kick it underneath the trophy shelves so we won't trip over it. Then I follow Mom and Dad into the kitchen, still reliving the second half of the game. We sit around the table the way I can remember us doing while Dad was still finishing the house, laughing and all talking at the same time, the way we used to do then, too. I don't mind it, sitting up with them, talking and laughing. In fact, I love it. I can't ever imagine feeling this good again—this good about life, this good about myself.

They don't ask me about the first half, and I don't explain. I figure they just assume one of the other guys was having a problem, and we got it straightened out in the locker room. They're so proud of me, I know the idea that it could have been my fault doesn't even cross their minds. And Dad never gets around to saying anything else about the news story. Maybe he's forgotten it or just doesn't want to deal with it now. Since they don't raise the subject, I don't either. Why spoil this moment for them? There'll be time later on.

After they go upstairs to bed, all I really want to do is

hug the game ball like a much-loved teddy bear and fall asleep replaying the game highs. I can still hear echoes of the action, the squeaks of rubber soles on the court, the shouts of the players, the zebras' whistles and, throughout it all, the pounding of the ball.

Make—the pass.

Take—the shot.

Just—this night

you're—the best.

My face aches from smiling, but I can't stop. I can't imagine ever again having such a perfect game as that second half.

In my bedroom I kick off my shoes and strip off the jeans and sweatshirt I pulled on before the parade—a triumphant lifetime ago, not just a couple of hours. But there's one more thing to do before I can crash, and I don't want to do it out in the hallway or kitchen, where Mom or Dad might hear me. I don't want anything to spoil their night. I fish out Natalie Hart's card and punch her number on my cell phone, then sit on the side of my bed, rolling the game ball on my knees. I get her voice mail since it's so late, but I'm way past feeling self-conscious about trying to tell my story to a machine. I take a deep breath and leave a message.

"This is Brian Hammett. I'm—I'm sorry I didn't give you the full story today at the courthouse, but—well, I'd just had a shock." I pause to swallow, because my mouth feels stuffed with cotton. But I make myself go on. "When I was in the men's room, I was threatened. The guy said that killing Amanda and her brother and mom was just business, it was because her dad had gone the wrong way on the interstate one day and done something that upset an associate of his—I think he meant when her dad arrested that drug mule on the interstate last year, like her dad tried to say on the stand in court. Anyway, this man said he was hired to deliver a message. And he said he'd—he'd kill me and my family if I said anything—to the press, to anybody."

In spite of having made up my mind, I feel kind of sick and loose inside just remembering the flat voice and his threats. "So I was scared—but I can't . . . Well, tonight I made up my mind I had to do what was right anyway. I guess the lawyers aren't going to listen to me, but I'm hoping you'll still let me tell the truth on the news. I didn't see the guy's face, but there was something about his voice—I know I've heard it before. Maybe we can identify him from that."

The phone beeps at me. At first I think it's call waiting, but when I look at the display it says my battery is low. I remember my charger is in my bag out in the front hall, so I finish fast, trying to ignore the way the phone keeps beeping. "Anyway, I know it's late, but please call me as soon as you get—"

Then the battery sputters and the phone cuts off abruptly, before I can leave my cell phone number. I stand up to go for my charger so I can finish the call. I figure I know my front hall well enough to see my way even in the dark, nearly moonless night—there's no point in waking my parents. And then I hear a branch crack.

It could be a deer. We sometimes get them in the backyard, out by Dad's wood shop. But I remember the shadow I thought I saw moving away from the house, and I get a cold feeling inside, like waking up from a nightmare just before the worst happens. Except this time I'm afraid I'm waking into a nightmare. I stand there, motionless, barely breathing, straining to hear, but there's nothing except the pounding of my heart, the creaks and groans of the house as it shifts in the night. Then I hear a faint scuffing sound. This time I'm sure it's a footstep.

He's come for me.

Keeping one arm wrapped around the game ball so it won't thud to the floor, I automatically reach for my cell phone to call 911—then remember the dead battery. The strength goes out of my arm, and it's all I can do to keep it from flopping heavily to the bed. *Do something,* I order myself. *Think!* I take an unsteady step forward, my feet soundless on the carpet in their socks. I wait, hugging the ball, but there's no sound of frightened footsteps running off. *He's not frightened, though,* I tell myself. *He's listening.*

I remember what Warren told me about cell phones. Did the killer listen in on my call to Natalie Hart somehow and find out I was ready to talk? But the shadow that ran from the parade lights had been waiting for me. . . . The image of the policeman turning away from me in the gym leaps into my head with the lurch of déjà vu—a policeman who saw the game and how we changed in the second half as if someone on the team had made up his mind. A policeman who can monitor cell phone frequencies and knows I decided to talk to the press, despite his threats. A policeman who knows tonight is his last chance to silence me.

My mouth goes dry. I force leaden legs to move across the carpet, through my open door into the dark space between stairway and wall, partly shielded by the trophy cabinet. Faint breathing drifts down the stairs, punctuated by an occasional snore or snort. My parents have no idea what's about to happen because of me. They're lost in dreams of the earlier victory.

There's a soft click, so low it almost sounds as if it might only be my imagination, or a bird beak tapping softly on a distant windowpane, if all the birds weren't already asleep. I listen hard and make out a second click, then a third—it's the tumblers falling in the front door lock as he picks it. Then there's a pause, and a fourth click, a little louder this time, and then the soft scraping as the brass doorknob slowly turns.

The front door makes so little noise that the breathing upstairs doesn't alter. The door eases open, the shadow slips inside, then he pushes the door shut. Dark clothes, dark gloves, dark hood, something dark masking his face. He moves toward the stairway, his right hand reaching behind his back. I wish I could have remembered where I'd heard his voice before to tell Natalie Hart. I don't know if I'll get another chance.

I almost bounce the ball first, automatically, the way I do before a free throw. It steadies you as the ball slaps back into your hands. But I don't even let myself take a deep breath. Nothing fancy this time, no complicated plays, nothing but me and the ball—what I do best.

I rise out of the shadowed alcove to my full height, suddenly fearful that my legs will betray me by buckling when I need them steady. They don't let me down. I stand, swinging the basketball up to my chest. Maybe he feels the shift in the air or hears me move. He turns to face me, his right hand coming up.

I launch the game ball in a hard pass so it hurtles across the space between us. It smashes him in the face, breaking his nose the way the Raiders' player broke Ray's. It knocks him off balance, back against the living room doorframe. I hear the basketball thudding on the hardwood floor and his body crashing into the wall, but unbelievably I don't hear any sound of a gun hitting the floor.

I'm running now, socks sliding on the polished wood, grabbing for the cabinet to keep my balance and then reaching into it before he can recover. I fumble for one of the heavy trophies from the bottom shelf. I grab it by the bronze figure and charge at the shape in the doorway, chopping down on his right arm, the one I saw him swing to point at me. I feel the shock run through my arms as the marble base of the trophy connects. I hear a sickening crack and a muffled cry of pain, and finally I hear the metallic thunk I'd been waiting for and know he's dropped the gun.

At the same time I hear sounds upstairs—voices and footsteps, Mom's voice yelling at a 911 operator on their bedroom phone, then the sudden click of a light switch. I shut my eyes as dazzling light streams down the stairway from upstairs. The scene crawls in slow motion as I squint through my eyelashes, seeing the man writhing on the floor, crying, swearing under his breath, his broken right arm flopping as he tries to cover his eyes. Or maybe he's trying to wipe the blood away from the eyeholes in his black mask—I see splatters of blood everywhere, or are those just red spots from the light in front of my eyes?

Then I see two things almost at the same time: the gun, lying at the foot of the stairs just barely out of the man's reach, and the killer himself, twisting awkwardly down to his right ankle with his left hand for some reason. I can't let him get the gun again. If he doesn't have it, he can't hurt us. Then I think—that's got to be the gun that shot Amanda. The court will let Mr. Daine go if they see it. I've got to get it. I dive the way I've saved so many balls from going out of bounds, but this time I'm diving for a gun, not a ball.

As I recover it, fumbling with its unfamiliar shape and balance and stumbling backward toward the dining room, I see the man's left hand come up with a second gun. And I see Dad appear at the top of the stairs, holding the shotgun he keeps in the bedroom. Dad reacts faster than I would have thought, working the pump action and swinging the gun up to his shoulder, but the man is even faster. Still lying on his back, with his right arm flopping as it tries to shade his face, he fires left-handed up at my father, silhouetted perfectly in the light.

"No!" I hear myself scream. I hold the gun in both hands, point it at the man on the floor, and pull the trigger. I feel the gun jump in my hand at the same time I hear Dad's shotgun go off, then watch to see the man collapse.

For a second nothing happens. Out of the corner of my eye I see Dad still standing, somehow not shot by the killer who made those perfect shots to wipe out everyone else I care about. Maybe he's a right-handed shooter who never thought he'd have to shoot with his left hand. A lot of players make that mistake, only to find themselves in a corner where they have to take the shot from their weak side. They usually miss.

I see the killer turning on the floor to face me, and it

sinks in that he's not shot either. Did I miss him? Did Dad miss, too? I wish I'd gone hunting with Dad the way he wanted me to. Then I'd have a better idea of what I'm doing. All I can think is I can't let that man pull the trigger again. I've got to get closer, so I won't miss this time.

I cross the front hallway, the gun held in front of me, still in both hands, barely hearing Dad's voice above me. "Brian—get out of the way!" But this is not a moment to pass to him. This has to be a one-on-one play.

I stand in front of the man who killed Amanda, the man who terrified me and shamed me, the man who broke into my house and tried to kill my family. I point the gun very carefully, hardly even noticing him raising his gun in his unsteady left hand. Dad says the perfect shot either severs the spine or goes straight through the brain. I'm not sure I can find the spine, but I line the sights up with his masked head. I tell myself I can't miss this time, and pull the trigger.

CHAPTER

40

The gunshot is much louder than I expect, and the muzzle flash is brighter. Then, strangely, my chest burns, and I double over, hugging myself. How did the front hallway get so hot? My hand feels wet as it comes away from my side and I look at it, wondering why it's covered with dark blotches. I've got to sit down, and suddenly the wooden floor rushes up beneath me. The gun has grown too heavy to hold. I know I can't lose it, because the court needs it to set Mr. Daine free, but if I'm on the floor I guess it's okay to let it slip out of my hand, as long as it stays right beside me.

My eyes burn in the brilliant light, so bright I can hardly see the scene around me any longer. There are too many people in the room. Why are they shoving at me, banging on my chest? I need to sleep—just let me sleep. I can work out what's going on later, if they'll only let me alone.

There's so much blood, everywhere. Mom's going to kill me. No, maybe not. Maybe she knows there's been too much killing already.

What was that song Amanda sang in *Hamlet* last year? *And will 'a not come again?*

No, no, he is dead,
Go to thy death-bed,
He never will come again.

The killer never will come again. Amanda never will come again, either. She's gone on to heaven, or wherever. Or is she reliving her life, seeing it all pass before her? Has she figured out how to change any of it? I haven't. *Thud*-thud, *thud*-thud, *One*-life, *un*-changed. The light keeps brightening, a white light that bleaches the confusion of people and action.

All the while, the gunshot goes on echoing inside my head, a double *thud*-thud, *thud*-thud, *Bri*-an!

Dad?

I need to tell him I'm okay, I'm not really hurt, and he and Mom are going to be safe now, and Mr. Daine's going to be all right, or as all right as he can be, but free at least.

Then I realize those are only thoughts—not words—lost in the blinding light. Even the thud-thud is growing softer, weaker, fading into silence as the bustle and noise simply stops around me. I feel a sense of absolute peace, like I've never felt on the court, or in Dad's wood shop, or looking up at the fireworks with Amanda—a sense of zero pressure, zero sound, zero pain. I'm falling. Not the kind of falling you do in dreams, sliding down and suddenly waking up safe before you fall too far. I feel impossibly heavy, yet I'm falling up, toward the ceiling. Except I never actually pass through the ceiling—it just seems to rise with me as I fall higher and higher.

"*Bri*-an!"

That voice is clear, and I turn, feeling my eyelids moving in slow motion, the way I remember from the concussion the Wolverines center gave me last spring. But I don't have that sick, headachey feeling I had then. I don't feel anything. I'm just sort of floating. I see a soft white mist around me, which lifts to become clouds—puffy white clouds overhead, above a perfect green park.

"Bri-an!"

Her voice is full of light and I see her—Amanda—running toward me across thick grass, a radiant smile spreading across her face. Now she's in my arms, and I'm hugging her, twirling her around and around, taking in the clean, flower-fresh smell of her hair and loving the way her long crepe skirt swirls around the pair of us. It's just as good as I always dreamed it would be—as I dreamed until the day she was killed.

I stop twirling her, only now realizing that she's as light as air in my arms. "Are you an angel?" I whisper.

Amanda laughs, the sound like a thousand bright Christmas bells jingling all around us.

"Is this heaven?"

Her laughter fades to the smile I remember so well. "I think it's some sort of in-between place," she tells me. "A place you go when you're not finished with your life yet, when you're still thinking about the people you miss."

The sunlit park around us dims as dark clouds scud overhead. Are there storms in heaven, or limbo, or wherever we are?

"Am I dead?" I ask her softly, as darkness engulfs us. "Did he shoot me, too?" I think I want her to tell me yes. I want her to reassure me that I made the perfect shot at last, when it counted, and now I can stay with her always. Is that what I really want, though?

Amanda hugs me fiercely, but now I can barely feel her arms or smell her hair. Her skirt feels like a breeze, not like real fabric.

"I knew you'd help us." Her voice sounds far away, even though she's right here in my arms.

"I think," she says, articulating the words slowly and clearly, as if she realizes she's fading in the dark mist swirling around us. "I think you're here because—because—I wanted so much to see you again." Her voice is so faint now that I have to strain to hear her. "Because I wanted to tell you I'm sorry I was angry with you—because I wanted to tell you I love you, Brian."

"I love you, too," I tell her at last, even though I can't feel her in my arms any longer. I realize she's moving in a different direction, one that I can't see to follow in the darkness that is carrying me away.

"Amanda—good-bye! I miss you so much." I feel my voice break into a shower of heartsharp fragments.

Then, for a moment, her face comes into focus in front of me again, hazy and blinding, lit by an inner radiance. "Don't worry, Brian—it's not good-bye. We'll meet again, when it's time."

Then she disappears into a darkness filled with screaming sirens. The pain is back, burning horribly in the right side of my chest, and the noise is increasing to a din in my ears. I still have the feeling I'm watching my life pass by, instead of living it. I'm floating high in a corner of the ceiling, seeing myself down below, looking indistinct, almost ghostlike, lying there with blood staining my underwear. There are more than a dozen people—and me in my underwear! But I'm beyond embarrassment as I watch them work. One is a woman kneeling by my chest, blood pooling on the floor, spattering her white blouse.

I dimly hear those distant voices again.

"I've got a pulse again—I think we've done it."

"You, tape the incision so air doesn't get in."

At the sound of the woman's voice, I feel my heart ache for Amanda.

"Brian! Brian—can you hear me? Brian, it's Elise Pollian."

And I open my eyes, not to the green park of Amanda's limbo, but to my living room, crowded with people, lights on tripods, strobes of red and blue flashing lights coming through the open front door. I see clear plastic bags swaying above me, the light bending as it passes through them. I see Dad's drawn face, and Mom's face, white and tear-stained beside his, the two of them trying to see over the people crowded around me. Beyond them I see what looks like Todd and his brother Warren, but I can't imagine why they'd be here.

"You and you, hold the bottles. Gurney team, let's get him into the wagon. Full emergency run to the ER!"

They've put me on something and it suddenly raises, and I feel a childlike sense of wonder, like riding an elevator for the first time.

Then, from that new perspective, I see the body no one is working on, slumped in the living room doorway, half in and half out of the hall. Dad's going to have to strip the wood paneling and redo it completely to get out the blood and fix the damage the bullets did to the wall. The man's mask has been pulled off, and at last I recognize the face and realize where I heard that cold, flat voice: Officer Recks. The officer who testified against Amanda's father in court. The officer who questioned me the day Amanda was killed.

Why isn't someone there, helping him?

Maybe Elise already took care of Officer Recks. The mask is pulled off, leaving his face wiped clean in patches except for the smear of blood on his forehead. He's watching the chaos through half-open eyes.

CHAPTER

41

At first, what I notice most is the silence. There's a steady background of hospital noise—the clatter of crutches and bedpans, the banging of carts and trolleys and the squeak of nurses' rubber shoes on the hallway tiles, the voices with undercurrents of hope and fear, the tears. But the constant pounding of the basketball in my head has stopped.

Life isn't just passing by me anymore. I'm living it again. It isn't easy. The police try to question me while I'm still in intensive care, but I can't talk with all the tubes stuck into my chest and up my nose. I just close my eyes, and they finally go away. I tell them what happened later, when I get out of the sterile little ICU cubicle, one of the lucky patients who gets wheeled upstairs to a regular room instead of downstairs to the morgue. I tell Natalie Hart, too, who's already broken the story based on my phone call and an interview with Todd and Warren. Mom and Dad don't want her to bring her cameraman into my room, but I tell them it's all right. I want everybody to know the truth.

One by one, almost furtively, the guys on the team come to see me. They want to complain that I should have told them what was going on—they want to apologize for not being there beside me when I needed teammates. I tell each of them the same thing. What you do on the court is what you do off the court. If you stand up and play right with your team around you, you'll stand up and do right when you're on your own. And all of them were with me, in a sense. I made the perfect shot that broke Recks's nose with the game ball the team gave me.

Julius is the hardest. "You were there for me, man, every minute. Even when I didn't want you getting in my way you were there for me."

I know how he feels, so I tell him the truth. "We were in the same boat, man. You were too ashamed of ending up at that jail to fight back, and I was too ashamed of letting Amanda down last summer to make sure somebody listened to me about the jogger before things got out of control."

He thinks about that, sitting beside me, head bowed. I hope he understands.

Todd must have a sense of their timing, because he waits to visit until after they've all had their turn. I try to find the words to thank him for being there with Warren and Elise. He waves his hand. "No problem," he says. Then he smiles. "If you thought Warren was something getting Julius out of that jail, you should have seen him at the local station after I told him how the guy cornered you. He raised the roof and threatened each officer in his individual capacity and the force as a whole with lawsuits if they didn't give your family and our family protection. And when they finally caved in and charged out of there full steam, he looked at Elise and said that wasn't good enough—we had to go, too." He pauses, and looks at me steadily. "I think you might have died if a doctor hadn't gotten to you so soon."

"You're right," I tell him. Todd might be the one person who'd understand about seeing Amanda in her heaven-limbo park. But that's something I don't think I can ever put into words for anyone. "Tell Elise how much I appreciate it," I finally say. "And tell her I can't wait to say thank you in person."

"I will." He looks out the window. "At your house, Warren wouldn't let the police touch the guns or anything. He told them it was part of an ongoing investigation, and the evidence related to the Daine murders. Then he got on his cell phone and called independent experts he'd used before." He pauses. "Later, he told me he thought the gun might have conveniently disappeared, especially when the cops realized it was a brother police officer who'd sold out to drug dealers. He's already working with the defense attorney, Rosen. They've filed a joint motion to throw out the sentence based on newly discovered evidence. If the prosecutors challenge it, he'll move for a new trial, but he thinks they'll go along."

Relieved, I tell him, "That's great." Then I add, "We might have been a little hard on Warren that night."

Todd looks at me. "I was too hard on him, Brian, not you. I still think I was right to be angry—but I didn't have to ride him so hard. He came through when it mattered."

We sit in silence for a while. Finally I say, "I guess I confirmed your worst fears about violence." By now I know I killed Recks. He and I both shot at the same time, but he couldn't make his perfect shot with his weak hand. He came close—apparently his bullet hit just to the side of my spine, nicking one lung so it started filling up with blood. I swallow, still finding it hard to think how close I'd come to dying. But I turned out to be the killer that night.

By moving closer to Recks, to be sure I got him, I got in the way of Dad's shot. But something—Amanda's spirit, or Dad's will, or my own luck or stubbornness—steadied my hand and I made the perfect shot when it counted, straight through the brain to drop him against that wall.

Todd half shrugs one shoulder, staring down at the linoleum on the hospital floor.

"If I hadn't stopped him, he would have done what he threatened," I say. "I couldn't live under that threat forever, like Alonzo." Todd doesn't answer. "He'd already killed Amanda and Cory and their mother. Sometimes you do have to fight back."

Todd finally raises his eyes and meets mine. "I've been thinking about it a lot. I don't think I could have done what you did. I think I could have stood in front of someone I cared about to save them, but I don't think I could have killed someone else to do it."

I don't point out that the killer would have simply shot him and then shot whoever he was protecting, but Todd says it for me. "Only that wouldn't save them, would it? I could let myself be killed, and he'd just go on to shoot whoever else he wanted. So that's not the solution. But . . ." His voice trails off. "I just can't accept that fighting back and killing someone is the only answer."

I'd shrug, but my chest hurts too much for that. "It shouldn't be the only answer. If I'd said more about the jogger earlier, maybe they would have figured out it was Recks and arrested him. If Mr. Daine's lawyer had listened to me in court, maybe they would have caught him in the courthouse." I pause for breath. "But if the justice system isn't working the way it's supposed to, and murderers can come into your house and threaten you, then somebody has to stand up and stop them.

"I hate Recks!" My voice sounds even more bitter than I intend. "I hate him for killing Amanda—for putting me in a position where I had to pull that trigger—I wish it hadn't come down to killing him, but. . ."

"But it did," Todd says uncomfortably. Then he sighs.

I remember him admitting to me that he's gay, and fearing it would make me see him differently. "So," I ask awkwardly, "does knowing that I killed someone change the way you look at me? The project's over now—the school year's almost over. We don't have to know each other anymore."

Todd half smiles at me. "I stand by what I said. You're the kind of guy who understands the consequences of acting on a bad hunch and is willing to put himself on the line for what he believes is right. That's the kind of person I'll always want to know."

I hadn't expected him to say that. "I'm still not arrogant enough to be sure I'm always right. What if I'd made a mistake about the jogger?"

Todd shakes his head. "That became an irrelevant issue the minute that man broke into your house to kill you." He grins. "And your lack of arrogance is one of the things I like most about you."

I can't help trying to laugh, but it hurts so much I have to stop. We've come a long way since Mr. Fortner stuck us together, and a lot farther from the locker days. Amanda would be pleased. I'm pleased to have him for a friend.

Time slows as I lie in the hospital bed, staring up at the tiled ceiling while sports news plays in the background. I decide that if I'm living my life for real now, that means I can make changes.

Of course, life's already making changes for me. I'm missing the final game of the regular season. If I'm lucky, I'll be able to ride the bench for the playoffs, but I won't be playing this year. It's going to mean a lot of physical therapy before I can play again. I discover I don't mind this too much. The whole team comes to see me the day before the game, bringing after-practice pizza with them—extra pepperoni because they know it's my favorite. Shooter looks scared, thinking about starting in the last regular season game.

Highrise tries to joke, "What are we going to do without you, Brainman? Now we've got nothing but muscles and skill—how're we going to win without a brain?"

"You'll win, Highrise," I reassure them. "Let Take-away Ray loose to grab those balls, and Ray—you distribute the passes. Remember that Shooter's in, and he can make those outside shots as well as Joyous, so surprise them if they double up on Julius. That'll open up the court for all of you. Just get those steals and rebounds—the Hornets are a good team, but I'll bet they're scared of us, and counting too much on my not being there to spoil your rhythm." The guys are nodding, and looking more cheerful.

"And Shooter—" He looks up, a little spooked again. "Remember they won't have been able to study you as much. When they see you're a serious threat, they'll probably try to guard you too close, so let them foul you. You're a whiz on the free-throw line."

He grins and nods. "Just remember you're a team," I say. "Julius, you make those long shots, but don't hog the ball. Everybody, drag Wrestler out in the time you've got left, and make him put in some heavy work on the free-throw line—he can do it if he practices, and then he'll be ready to fight for those balls without being scared of getting fouled. Keep the Hornets off balance so they don't know where our attack's coming from. You'll win as a team—all of you together."

"All of *us* together," Julius says. "Whether you're on the court or not, Brian, you're still our Brainman."

They leave me with the rest of the pizza, and I end up sharing it with the nurses. It's hard to eat lying down.

Dad comes in after work, like he's been doing every day. The first time I really woke up, he was crying, telling me he'd said I shouldn't get involved. Look what I'd gotten for it—shot, almost killed. Then he said he should have gotten downstairs faster, he should have taken that shot for me. I still seemed to be watching life go by when Dad said that, and even when I told him he was wrong. If you don't get involved, if you don't try to do the right thing, no matter what it costs, you're not really here at all—just passing by. And it was my job, not his, to face Amanda's killer.

"I hear the team came in for another visit," he says, trying to sound upbeat.

"Yeah. They even brought pizza." We smile at each other. "Dad, I want you to do something for me."

"Sure—anything."

"I want you to go to the game tomorrow and cheer on

the team, even though I'm not playing. It'll mean a lot to them, seeing you there." When he doesn't say anything right away, I add, "You know how you like basketball."

He smiles, almost sadly this time. "I like watching you play, Brian. I can't say I care much about the game otherwise." He sighs. "But I'll go, if you want me to."

For me. He'll go for me. "Dad," I say slowly, "will you do one other thing for me? A really big thing?"

He cocks his head to one side, his expression faintly worried.

"Come on—you said you'd do anything," I tease him a little.

"Okay, I'll try."

"Will you go back to carving? Making guitars and furniture and things? Doing what you love?"

"Oh, Brian . . ." He's already shaking his head. "I tried that—but I can't make a real living at it, not to take care of you and your mother."

"I'll get a scholarship to college, or I'll go to a state school. You don't have to worry about taking care of me. And Mom . . ." I try to choose my words carefully. Almost dying makes you think about how important life is, every moment, every decision. "Remember how happy she was when you guys went to craft fairs with the guitars and carvings? Remember how she even liked living in the house while it was only half built, because you two were having so much fun planning it out and making the plans happen? That's making a real living, Dad—that's making a life."

He looks unconvinced. "It's my job to make a life for you, son. You deserve your chance to shine—you're the best."

"You warned me not to get lost on a detour," I remind him. "The construction company, that's your detour. I think you got burned by those shoplifters and by the cops, and you decided you had to make a better living for us as a family, but it took you away from everything you loved doing. The thing about a detour, though, is that you can find your way back to the right road, if you want to enough." Julius did, even if it was really hard. And I did, even if it almost killed me.

"Talk to Mom," I beg him. "At least do that for me. Talk to her about selling the business and doing what you really like. I want you guys to laugh again and be happy." *I want you to come back to life, like me. . . .*

Dad finally nods reluctantly. "I'll talk to your mother," he says, "but I can't promise more than that."

"Sure. It's up to you two." *It's your lives—just don't waste them thinking it's better that way for your family. Live them.* "But I really want you to think about it." Just like it's time for me to think about it. Is basketball my track or my detour?

I remember when it used to be part of my track, but not my whole life. My life was so much bigger, with Amanda and Cory and school. Basketball was just part of it. When Amanda died, my life died down to nothing except basketball, until Mr. Fortner's assignment.

Friday is game day, and it feels so weird to lie here in the hospital bed, not lost in the game. But it makes me think about all the game days yet to come. Is the court really where I want to be?

Mom comes in earlier than usual. At first I think she's just come to shake me out of the game-day fog, but then I see she looks different—younger, somehow. It's the smile, brighter than I've seen in a long time. She gives me a hug, a bigger, warmer hug than I've felt in years.

"Thank you," she whispers in my ear as she holds me.

She doesn't have to say more. I know Dad kept his promise and talked to her. And I can guess what she told him, even if it's too soon to be sure what they'll do.

But her smile is even better than the team crashing into the ward Saturday morning to give me the play-by-play news of how they crushed the Hornets 87–65 in a packed gym to start us on the road to the playoffs—all of us, because I'll be with them every game, helping them outthink the other team, going all the way to State Championship with my team.

MAY
AFTER

Rehab turns out to be tougher than basketball practice. I think something inside me—my lung, or maybe my heart—is always going to ache. It's nearly two months before I'm strong enough to get to the cemetery to see Amanda. I'd avoided visiting her grave after the funeral. But I have something for her, and I decide it's time.

As I make my way slowly down the path, however, I see I'm not the only visitor. Amanda's father is already there.

Mr. Daine hears my footsteps and looks up from the tombstones. He's so different from the way I remember him—stooped, thinner, a lot more lines carved into his face. "Brian?" He swallows, as if talking to people is hard. "Thank you. For getting justice for them at last." He gestures toward the graves.

"I'm sorry I didn't do more sooner," I tell him. "I'm sorry you got arrested and had to go through all that."

He shakes his head and turns back to the graves. "No, I'm the one who's sorry—sorry for getting you shot, for ever putting you in the position of having to—to shoot Recks that night."

Ever having to kill that killer is what he really means,

not just shoot Recks. Kill him. When I don't say anything, he gives me a sidelong look. "Are you all right—about that?"

I shrug and he sighs. "You're so young . . ." Young? I feel ancient as crumbling parchment. ". . . to have learned what price you pay to kill a man."

I've been paying a price for a long time—for not shooting hoops with Amanda and Cory that day, for listening to my parents when I should have made them listen to me, for picking on Todd when I should have seen what he was really like. The price has been not liking myself very much. I don't see that the price for pulling the trigger and setting Amanda's father free can be much higher. I ask, "Have you ever killed anybody in the line of duty? What price did you pay?"

He doesn't answer for so long that I'm afraid I shouldn't have asked. Finally he says, very softly, "No, Brian, I've never killed anyone."

I'm shocked. He's a policeman—he's supposed to stand on the front line, to protect us! I realize I'm thinking he's supposed to pull the trigger so someone like me doesn't have to.

But is that what I really want?

He's a policeman, like the cops who "arrested" Julius and the jailers who worked him over. Sure—Amanda's father would never have done that because he knew Julius. But could he have done it to a nameless black kid? Do I want to rely on someone like that to protect me?

Or am I making unfair assumptions about the way Amanda's father would have behaved in uniform, based on the way the city cops treated Julius? Amanda's father was a good cop. That's why the drug dealers went after him. It's another one of those gray areas where I have to trust my own instincts and decide for myself.

I didn't like pulling that trigger. I'm glad that Recks is dead and can't hurt anybody else, but I don't like being the one who had to kill him. And yet I don't know that I'll trust anybody else to protect me ever again. Even on the best team, each player has his special strengths. No one else can substitute and make the same contribution. Pulling that trigger was my responsibility.

I hope I never have such a responsibility again.

If I do, I hope I'm strong enough to pull the trigger again.

"Will you be okay?" I ask him.

He stands motionless, head bowed. "No. I don't suppose I'll ever be okay again." We stand side by side for a while. "How about you? Will you be okay?"

"I don't know yet," I tell him honestly.

After he leaves, when it's just me and Amanda, I sit down on the spring grass beside her grave and gaze at the redbud trees blooming around us. Then I pull her conch shell from my backpack and prop it securely against her tombstone.

"I guess you're far away from Indiana now," I tell her. "I'm betting you're making music with the angels, even if it's not exactly the sort of music you planned on making to change the world." I pause, looking down at the soft green grass. "I'm thinking about not doing what I planned, either. I don't think I'm going to leave Willisford, like we talked about. Julius is—he says his parents are moving to Atlanta. They think things are better there, so what happened to him won't ever happen to his kid brother. Todd's leaving, too."

I look at the carved gravestone. "But I don't think you can just leave behind the black-and-white mindset people have here. I think you'll find it anywhere. I can't run away from it by leaving town and trying to make it as a big NBA player. I'm good, but not really good enough, and I'm okay with that. And no, I'm not going to be a guitarist, either." I smile a little. "So don't cringe at the thought of people listening to my terrible playing."

I'm buying time. I thought a lot while I lay there in the hospital and while I rode the bench and cheered my teammates, but this is the first time I speak the thoughts out loud. "I've been thinking about trying to teach high school—history, like Mr. Fortner. I want to get guys to ask the right questions and come up with the hard answers themselves."

I add quickly, "That doesn't mean I'm quitting basketball! But I'm thinking about coaching instead. I really believe how you act on the court is how you'll act off the court. If I can teach guys sportsmanship as well as plays, if I can show them how to play right on the court with their team, then I'll be giving them the perfect shot at life."

It feels right to say the words. I know Amanda understands, but now I can believe Mom and Dad might understand, too.

"Yes," I tell Amanda, answering her question from long ago, "if we really do see our whole life pass before us, and if we go on living after, I think we do get a chance to change things." Amanda's not going to get that chance, and it's not fair. But I will. And I intend to make the most of it before I see her again.

AUTHOR'S NOTE

While Brian's story is a work of fiction, the project he researches for Mr. Fortner's class is based on a real murder that happened in Atlanta, Georgia, in 1913, and the facts of the case are as Brian discovers in his research. Thirteen-year-old Mary Phagan stopped to collect her pay from the pencil factory on the morning of Confederate Memorial Day. Her body was found in the basement by the night watchman late that night. The two suspects the police focused their investigation on were the watchman and Leo Frank, Mary's boss, a Yankee who had moved to the South and married into a prominent Jewish family. They quickly focused their sole attention on Frank, despite his insistence that he was innocent.

The prosecutor, Hugh Dorsey, built a case of innuendo against Frank, claiming that he had made improper advances to many of the teenage girls who worked for him. By telling each girl in turn that other girls claimed that Frank had come on to them, the prosecutor used peer pressure to convince many of the girls to testify against their boss at the inquest—few girls wanted it to look as if they were so unappealing that Frank wouldn't have made advances to them also. Dorsey even claimed that Frank had raped Mary (although physical evidence proved she was still a virgin). He also made it seem sinister that Frank had come down to the South from New York, hired innocent girls who should be home with their families, and corrupted them. This came at a time when the South was making a difficult transition from an agricultural way of life to an industrial way of life. Eager for someone to blame for the changes, the people of Atlanta turned against Frank in something approaching mob frenzy.

The prosecution's star witness was Jim Conley, a black ex-convict who had run away from a chain gang and was working as an odd-jobs man at the pencil factory. His clothes were bloody and his alibi was questionable for the day when Mary was killed, but Dorsey wasn't interested in charging him with the murder, even though one witness told the prosecutor that Conley had bragged about killing a little girl at the factory. Instead, Dorsey used a combination of payment and threat (sending Conley back to the chain gang) to convince him to testify that Frank often took women into his office, and that Frank had told Conley he killed Mary and ordered the odd-jobs man to dispose of the body.

The jury unanimously convicted Frank and sentenced him to hang. It was the first time in Georgia that a white man had ever been convicted on the testimony of a black man. But the case was less about race, or even justice, than it was about an angry city closing ranks against an outsider who had become a symbol of the forces that were changing their way of life.

Lucille Frank had stood by her husband throughout the

trial and became his staunchest ally afterward, fighting tirelessly for an appeal. When the Georgia Supreme Court ruled that the conviction should not be overturned even though witnesses had lied under oath, Mrs. Frank turned to Governor John Slaton and appealed to him to commute her husband's sentence to life imprisonment instead of hanging. Appalled at the way the trial had been conducted, Governor Slaton examined the witnesses and the evidence himself and commuted Frank's sentence. His decision abruptly ended his promising political career and caused Atlanta to erupt in anti-Jewish riots.

And it failed to save Leo Frank. After Frank went to the prison farm, he was seized in the middle of the night by a lynch mob made up of "good citizens" who insisted they were only carrying out the jury's sentence. These men hanged Leo Frank from a tree near Marietta, the town where Mary Phagan had been born, just outside Atlanta. You can see a list of the lynchers (who included a judge, two mayors, a sheriff, and several attorneys) online at http://www.leofranklynchers.com>.

Alonzo Mann was also a real person. Fourteen at the time Mary was killed, Alonzo worked in the pencil factory as an office boy. He saw Jim Conley carrying Mary's body down to the basement. Conley threatened Alonzo, telling him to keep silent or he would kill him. Frightened, Alonzo ran home and asked his mother what to do. She told him to say nothing, and his father agreed. Throughout the trial and the appeals, Alonzo kept silent, only coming forward with his testimony in 1982, almost seventy years too late to save Leo Frank or to get real justice for Mary Phagan.

The frenzy that overtook the people of Atlanta in 1913 carried some members of the press along with it. The *Atlanta Constitution* seemed to accept that Frank was guilty from the beginning, relying more on rumors and the prosecutor's speculations and claims than on the facts of the case. Other reporters were concerned that truth and justice had been casualties of the trial. The *Atlanta Georgian* and the *Atlanta Journal* tried to be fair in their reporting—the *Atlanta Journal* even called for a new trial after Frank's conviction. C.P. Connolly, a writer for *Collier's Weekly*, was so shocked by what he saw that he published an enhanced collection of his articles in 1914 in a small book, *The Truth about the Frank Case*. Connolly's articles attack the prosecution and legal system that condemned Leo Frank. You can read many of these stories online at Georgia Stories: History Online.

While it may be easy to understand how justice can miscarry so disastrously in an earlier century, it's harder to accept that such miscarriages of justice continue to happen today. The Louis Taylor case that Todd mentions in his presentation is only one instance of law enforcement officers making up their minds early in an investigation and only considering evidence that points toward one person. In this case, that person was an African American teenager—one of many instances of racial profiling in the history of American law enforcement.

What happens to Julius is entirely fictional in the context of this story, but it is inspired by the problem of racial profiling that is still commonplace today. Nearly every American city newspaper reports incidents in which African Americans have been targeted by law enforcement agents. These African Americans have been pulled off the road for minor traffic violations, stopped on the sidewalks for looking suspicious, arrested on the circumstantial evidence of being in the wrong place at the wrong time. Several of my husband's friends who are professional NFL players have been stopped by police for "DWB"—the crime of "driving while black." In New York City in 1999, four white police officers fired forty-one shots at a black man, Amadou Diallo, killing him as he tried to take his wallet out to show them identification. The officers claimed they felt in danger of their lives, assuming that he was pulling out a weapon. However, they kept shooting long after Diallo's hand appeared with the wallet.

Since 2000, there have been multiple race riots in Cincinnati, Ohio, inspired by white police officers killing black youths—twice shooting them in the back as they were running away. The situation in many cities has become so serious that federal courts and agencies have mandated extra training for law-enforcement officers in an attempt to prevent racial profiling. Following a police shooting of a young black man in Louisville, Kentucky, after which the officers involved were awarded medals by their chief, the mayor brought in a black chief and ordered racial sensitivity training. However, the Louisville Fraternal Order of Police held a vote of no confidence, demanding that the mayor replace the chief. No American citizen should have to fight for equal treatment from the police or in front of the courts because of race or appearance, and it is the responsibility of every citizen, regardless of age, to speak against and stand against such treatment, whether it happens to you or to someone you know.

The other projects that Brian's fellow students work on for Mr. Fortner's class are also based on real historical events. George Washington's farewell to his troops was a decisive moment in American history when a fledgling democracy could have toppled over into military dictatorship. The army that had fought so doggedly under Washington to win American independence wanted to make Washington the military leader of the new country, but General Washington ordered his army to disband and allow the citizens to choose their own leader. In the Battle of Niihau at the start of World War II, nonmilitary citizens used privately owned firearms to fight off and kill a Japanese pilot who had crashed on their island. Someone who isn't in the police or the army who fights back can be seen as a dangerous vigilante—or as a citizen exercising the constitutional right to bear arms. The interpretation is still argued today by many. *Gideon v. Wainwright* was the Supreme Court's decision that gave every citizen the right to an attorney if he or she is accused of a crime. Before this ruling, if you were accused of a crime like theft and couldn't afford a lawyer, you were on your own in court. But with overworked and underpaid public defenders, many citizens still go into court with unprepared attorneys.

The Posse Comitatus Act of 1878 limits the use of American military troops in domestic law-enforcement problems. In light of the military assault on the Branch Davidian compound in Waco in 1993, this act begs the question of how far the federal government can go in order to call in the military over the heads of the local police. The eighteen-year-long secret FBI investigation and reports filed on Dr. Martin Luther King Jr. during the civil-rights movement represent one of the earliest database compilations intended for use by only a select few law enforcement officials. Now, with the Patriot Act, these databases have grown so broad that law-enforcement officers in one state can look up a citizen and find investigative speculation about him or her and records of activity (including credit card purchases) that an official in a distant state has entered secretly.

A book that blends so many historical events and contemporary issues is a challenge to write, and I would like to thank some of the many people who have helped me along the way. I particularly value the input of the members of my critique group in Indiana, where Brian's story takes place: Marilyn D. Anderson, Keiko Kasza, and Elsa Marston. And I also value the input from the members of my critique group in Kentucky: Virginia Dulworth, Amanda Forsting, Elaine Hansen, Barbara Larkin, and Lynn Slaughter. I would also like to thank early readers Karen Grove and Pamela F. Service. All of these colleagues have raised important issues and challenged me to write the best book I had in me, this time and as they do so often. I am so grateful to all of you.

Three members of my critique groups brought a particular expertise to bear on this book. It's been far too many years since I used to play basketball in school, and I relied greatly on Judy Carney, Michael Ginsberg, and especially Stuart Lowry for their knowledge of the game as it is played in Indiana high schools today. Thanks so much, guys!

I would also like to thank my editor, Shannon Barefield, who offered wise insights and asked probing questions that helped me bring Brian's story fully to life.

The more I revise, the more I realize that asking the right questions is at the heart of what transforms an effective editor into a brilliant editor. I've been blessed with many fine editors so far—Shannon, you are one of the brilliant ones.

Finally, I would like to thank my husband, Arthur B. Alphin. A retired U.S. Army officer, Art now testifies as a firearms expert witness in a number of murder trials. He generously shared procedural and technical information with me, even inviting me to attend one of the trials in which he testified so I could witness the process firsthand. I could not have written this book without him from a technical aspect, but even more from a personal aspect. I have been suffering from a serious wrist injury that has made the physical task of writing this book a painful ordeal, and I don't know if I could have completed the novel, or done justice to Brian's story, without my husband constantly encouraging me; supporting me through doctor's visits, surgery and physical therapy; and reminding me how very deeply I cared about this book. Thanks to him, you now hold *The Perfect Shot* in your hands.

ABOUT THE AUTHOR

Elaine Marie Alphin's award-winning mysteries include *Picture Perfect*, a VOYA Top Shelf Fiction selection, and *Counterfeit Son*, winner of the 2001 Edgar Allan Poe Award for Best Young Adult Mystery. Ms. Alphin lives in Bozeman, Montana. Readers can learn more about her work at www.elainemariealphin.com.